To Dream Again

Jeanne Whitmee

ROBERT HALE · LONDON

© Jeanne Whitmee 2013
First published in Great Britain 2013

ISBN 978 0 7198 1036 7

Robert Hale Limited
Clerkenwell House
Clerkenwell Green
London EC1R 0HT

www.halebooks.com

2 4 6 8 10 9 7 5 3 1

Typeset in Palatino
Printed by TJ International, UK

CHAPTER ONE

Platform one at Liverpool Street Station was packed to overflowing and the noise was deafening: a mixture of howling children; crying babies and frantic-looking officials shouting in a vain attempt to get people to cooperate with their carefully organized plan. To Judy it seemed like a scene from hell.

Some of the older children were clearly excited by the prospect of a new adventure while others were silent and clinging to their mothers, frightened eyes looking up in bewilderment, silently asking the questions no one seemed able to answer. *Where are we going? When will we come home again? Why do we have to go away?*

Judy had never seen such an assortment of people and children all together in one place before. So many kids, all with their identity labels tied or pinned securely to their collars; gas masks in cardboard boxes hanging round their necks and a few pathetic belongings packed in an assortment of containers, tiny suitcases, canvas shopping bags, brown-paper parcels, Judy even spotted one or two dragging grubby pillow cases.

She looked down at her own two. They too wore labels bearing their names. She had protested at first, thinking it would not be necessary as she was going with them but the WVS lady had insisted. *Just in case you get separated*, she'd said. Judy held tightly to Suzie's little hand now, terrified at the thought. Her other hand held the suitcase she had packed with basic clothing for the three of them and she urged five-year-old Charlotte not to let go of her coat sleeve. Looking round her at the chaotic mass of children and adults on the platform she could see that the lady had been right. In a crush like this there was a very real danger of being separated and when a train steamed into the station and drew to halt with a ear-splitting hiss of steam and a scream of metal the danger became even greater as everyone surged towards it in a disorganized scramble.

Four-year-old Suzanne began to cry and Judy hoisted her up into her arms with her free hand. 'Don't cry, luvvie. We're going for a lovely ride. Mum's here and Charlie's going too.' She nudged Charlotte's shoulder with the suitcase. 'Keep tight hold of my sleeve, Charlie,' she urged. 'Don't you dare leave go.'

'Ow! You're hurting me,' Charlie complained as they were borne inexorably towards the train by the tide of humanity. 'Let's go home, Mum. I don't *wanna* go on a train.'

Judy looked down at her. 'Never mind that now. Just hold on tight to me. You don't want to get lost, do you?'

Charlotte turned round to a big boy behind her, her little face screwed up with indignant fury. 'Stop *shovin'* me,' she shouted. 'Mum, tell 'im to leave off pushin'.'

At last somehow they were on the train. Judy spotted a vacant seat and pushed the two little girls onto it while she hoisted the suitcase and three gas masks onto the luggage rack. She sat down, pulling Suzie onto her lap and clasping Charlie tightly to her. 'There, we'll be all right now,' she said, trying to sound confident. 'I've got some sandwiches in my bag. We'll eat them when the train gets going.'

After a while, pacified by the jam sandwiches Judy had hastily packed, Suzie and Charlie began to look sleepy. They'd been up since half past five and it wasn't surprising. Judy tucked both little girls into her seat and made them as comfortable as she could. When they'd both nodded off she stepped out into the corridor to get a breath of air. The atmosphere in the packed carriage had become oppressive. The mingled odours of cigarette smoke, stale sweat and the variety of food that some had brought for the journey were making her feel sick. She wasn't a good traveller at the best of times.

After a few minutes a figure wearing a volunteer's armband came lurching along the swaying corridor. As the woman drew level with her she cleared her throat and ventured, 'Excuse me. Can you tell me where we're going?'

'Norfolk, dear,' came the reply.

Judy frowned. 'Where's that?'

'East coast.'

'Will it take long to get there?'

The woman shrugged. 'Can't tell. There could be hold ups, what with the troop trains and everything.'

'Is it safe there?' Judy asked.

The woman shrugged. 'Reckoned to be – if anywhere's going to be safe.'

The woman staggered on down the corridor and Judy sighed. Where would they all end up, she wondered. Would Hitler really invade? Would the planes really come and bomb London to smithereens as some folk said? There had been such stories: rumours of everyone in the city being killed within days of war being declared. It was enough to worry the life out of you, especially when you'd got kids. With Mum and Dad going off to join ENSA and Sid volunteering for the army, she was left alone in London; sole responsibility for the girls lay on her shoulders. It had been down to her alone to decide what to do. She only hoped that she'd made the right decision.

Feeling in her pocket Judy found a mint and popped it in her mouth gratefully, hoping it would stave off the feeling of nausea. She missed her mum and dad. If she was honest she couldn't really say she missed Sid all that much though, and oddly enough the girls hadn't asked about him at all. In a way she was grateful. There was enough upheaval for them to cope with at the moment.

Standing looking out of the train window as the crowded suburbs gave way to green fields her thoughts went back to her childhood. Some would say it hadn't been an ideal childhood and in some ways she supposed it hadn't but she'd been happy enough. Her parents, Harry and Christine Mitchell both worked in the evenings, Harry as a pit musician at the Hackney Empire and Christine as a dancer in the resident chorus troupe. The plus side

7

was that they were there for her in the daytime so she had more of their company than most kids. And they loved her. There was never any doubt about that. There was always someone to take her to school and be there when she came home. In the holidays there were always trips to the park and jaunts 'up West' to look at the shops and visit the zoo.

In the evenings and on matinée days she was 'minded' by 'Auntie Lily' who lived next door. Auntie Lily had cried this morning when they left. She was in her seventies now and she loved Charlie and Suzie as if they were her own grandchildren. Judy only hoped she would be all right, left all on her own in Hackney.

Judy left school when she was fourteen and got a job in the sweet kiosk at the Empire, which meant she was at work at the same time as Mum and Dad. It was there that she met Sid, who was a commercial traveller. He worked for a well-known confectionery firm and often called in to take the theatre's order for sweets and ice creams. He was a lot older than Judy and had a line of patter that could sell ice to Eskimos. Right from the first she'd secretly admired his strong handsome features and his dark, slicked-back hair, shiny with Brylcreem. He wore a pinstriped suit and his trilby hat was set at a jaunty angle. He soon had her swept off her feet with his flattering chat-up line and his saucy winks and it wasn't long before she had agreed to go out with him. Sunday afternoons with Sid soon became a regular feature in Judy's life. Although Christine thought her daughter a bit young to be courting she told her to bring him home for his Sunday tea so that she and Harry could get a look at him. But when Judy asked him he made excuses.

'They'll think I'm not good enough for you,' he said. 'They'll say I'm too old and put you off me.'

'No they won't,' Judy had assured him. 'Anyway, no one could put me off you, Sid Truman,' she added shyly.

'Oh, and why is that?' he'd asked with a twinkle in his eye.

'Wouldn't you like to know,' she replied teasingly.

When Harry and Christine did eventually meet Sid they said exactly what he'd foreseen.

'He's much too old for you, love,' Christine said gently. 'He must be twenty-six if he's a day.'

'Too smart for his own good too, if you ask me,' Harry put in. His wife had given him a reproving look. She knew only too well that her daughter was smitten and that the more they tried to put her off, the keener she'd be. With a bit of luck, if they said nothing the whole thing might just fizzle out.

Judy would have preferred her parents to like Sid as much as she did but she was determined not to let anything spoil their relationship whatever her parents said.

Sid was wonderful company. He was an exciting lover too, sweeping her off her feet with his passionate kisses and close embraces and it wasn't long before he was urging her to take their relationship a stage further. Although Judy was too young and naive to recognize it, Sid had used the age-old tactic of emotional blackmail to get what he wanted.

'Aw, come on, Jude,' he'd wheedle. 'If you loved me as much as I love you, you'd want to. You're drivin' me barmy, don't you know that, girl?'

She stuck out persistently, although it was beginning to put a blight on their time together. Sid seemed obsessed. He could think of little else and eventually he played his trump card, suggesting that they part company.

'I can't take it no more,' he told her. 'I want you 'cause I love you so much, that's only natural. But I can tell that it's not the same for you. Maybe it's best we go our separate ways.' He turned to walk away but Judy couldn't bear the despairing look in his eyes or the thought of losing him.

'No, Sid, *no*! Don't go. I do love you and – and if that's what you want....'

That first time had been a hurried affair in the park behind some bushes. Judy had wondered what all the fuss had been about. She hadn't enjoyed it at all and felt guilty and slightly ashamed afterwards. The trouble was that after that he expected it every time they met and if she refused he would sulk and sometimes say nasty, hurtful things.

Eventually they quarrelled and split up. Judy told him he wanted his own way too much and he told her that she was frigid. She had to look that word up in the dictionary and when she discovered what it meant she was more certain than ever that she had done the right thing.

It was three weeks after that that she discovered she was pregnant.

At first she'd been at her wits' end. She kept hoping it would all come right – go away, but when another month passed and she began to be sick in the mornings her worst fears were confirmed and she knew she would have to tell her mother.

Christine had been saddened rather than angry by her daughter's revelation. 'Oh, love, you're so young,' she'd said, making Judy more upset than if she'd been angry. 'I've been hoping and praying that this wouldn't happen. But don't you dare think of doing nothing to try and stop it.' She took a weeping Judy into her arms. 'Listen, love, I was only sixteen when I had you. Your dad and me met while we were in a concert party on Southend pier. It was love at first sight.'

She sighed reminiscently. 'When the season ended we came back home and both got jobs at the Empire, but then I found I was expecting and I had to leave off dancing till after you was born.' She looked into Judy's eyes. 'But your dad stuck by me. We got married straight away and we've never looked back. So you see it can work out all right. Your dad is one of the best and I love him now just as much as I did then.'

'But Sid doesn't know,' Judy had pointed out. 'And I don't think I love him anyway.'

Christine hugged her. 'In that case you mustn't marry him,' she said. 'Don't worry, love. We'll manage somehow.'

But unfortunately Harry didn't see it that way. When he heard about his daughter's pregnancy he was furious – not with Judy but with Sid.

'Taking advantage of an innocent young girl!' he shouted. 'A man of his age – near enough old enough to be her father. I'll find the bastard and when I do I'll make him pay.'

'Don't, Harry,' Christine begged. 'Let it be. We'll stand by Judy and everything'll be all right.'

'Let that bugger get away with it?' Harry roared. 'Not bloody likely! He's gonna be made to pay for what he's done.'

He was as good as his word. Harry tracked Sid down and threatened to get in touch with the firm he worked for. 'I wonder what they'll think of a salesman who takes advantage of the young girls he meets in the line of duty,' he said menacingly. 'Apart from anything else she wasn't even sixteen when you got her in this mess. I could go to the police and have you charged with rape.'

Sid knew full well that it would mean the sack if Harry kept his word and he was left in no doubt that he meant business. He also knew that his instinctive reaction, which was to put the blame on Judy, would only make matters worse, so he capitulated.

'I was always going to ask her to marry me,' he said with an appeasing smile. 'Only I wasn't sure if she'd have me and I love her so much I couldn't bear to have her let me down.'

'Oh, she'll have you all right. I'll see to that,' Harry assured him grimly. 'I'm having no grandchild of mine born out of wedlock. You come round next Sunday afternoon and we'll fix the date. And don't even *think* of scarpering or I'll go to your boss like I said. *And* I'll have your guts for garters too when I catch up with you!'

'Mum – *Mum!*'

A frantic tapping on the glass in the compartment door behind her snapped Judy out of her reverie. Charlotte was fumbling with the door catch. At last she managed to slide the door open. 'Mum – Suzie wants to wee.'

It was an hour later when the train stopped. Judy looked for the sign on the platform that would tell them the name of the place but it had been painted over in black.

'That's so the Germans won't know where they are,' she heard someone behind her say.

They were all ushered onto the platform and out of the station, where a line of buses awaited them. Judy and the girls waited their turn and were eventually allotted to one of the buses. As they got on Judy asked the driver where they were.

'This is King's Lynn, my sugar,' the man said in a strange accent. 'You're going to Summerton-on-Sea.' He took in Judy's bewildered expression. 'That's near Cromer.'

None the wiser, Judy asked, 'Is it far?'

He winked. 'Not as the crow flies, my luvvie.'

Judy nodded. Did everyone talk in riddles round here? Was that something to do with muddling up the Germans as well? She gratefully claimed a seat for herself and the girls. When they'd returned from the train toilet someone had taken their seat and they'd had to stand the rest of the way. Charlotte looked up at her expectantly.

'Did that man say we're going to the seaside?'

'Looks like it, love.'

'We've never been to the seaside before, have we?'

'No.'

Charlie nudged her sister. 'Here, Suzie, we're going to the seaside.'

But an exhausted Suzie was having trouble keeping awake.

Judy rummaged in her bag for a colouring-book for Charlie and a bag of crayons. 'Here, why don't you do some colouring?' she suggested. She pulled the drowsy Suzie onto her lap and cuddled her close, stroking the fine fair curls back from her brow. Suzie's eyes closed and her thumb found its way into her mouth.

Judy looked down at Charlie's glossy dark head as she concentrated on her colouring book, the tip of her tongue protruding from the corner of her mouth.

Looking out of the bus window at the gently undulating countryside she wondered how they'd adjust to this different life they were coming to. There were cows and sheep in the fields and not a single shop or house in sight. What was ahead of them, she wondered? Had she done the right thing? Would she be able to find a job so that she could support the three of them? Sid had been in the army for weeks now and so far she hadn't received a penny. It was very worrying.

The wedding had been a brief affair, conducted in the local register office. Christine had been a bit weepy. She'd always imagined her only daughter getting married in a big church, a vision in white satin and lace, followed by half a dozen bridesmaids. Flowers, music, cake and champagne would be the order of the day. She'd promised herself that Judy would have the best: everything that she and Harry had missed out on. It was so disappointing that it had come down to this.

Sid had managed to rent a couple of furnished rooms for himself and Judy. They were above a fish-and-chip shop and he joked that if Judy's cooking wasn't up to much they could always slip downstairs for a 'piece and a penn'orth twice'.

Judy continued working at the Empire in the sweet kiosk until the manager pointed out tactfully that maybe it was time she took the weight off her feet. That was only a fortnight before Charlotte was born. Auntie Lily offered to mind the baby while Judy went back to work again but barely two months had gone by before she realized that she was expecting again.

Being a commercial traveller, Sid was away from home a lot of the time but when he did come home he insisted on what he called 'his rights' at every possible opportunity. He spent most of his evenings at the pub and often came home late, the worse for wear. If Judy upbraided him he would shout and swear at her and it wasn't long before the verbal aggression developed into physical violence. More than once Judy got in the way of his flying fists.

Christine was very supportive. Living nearby, she visited every day and took a lot of the strain of young motherhood from Judy. Her dislike of her new son-in-law only increased as the months went by, especially when she saw for herself the telltale marks of his violence on her daughter. She knew that Harry regretted insisting on Sid's marrying Judy. More than once she asked about her bruises, but the girl always made excuses and refused to discuss the matter. Christine hated keeping her suspicions to herself, but she knew better than to mention her suspicions to Harry for fear of making matters even worse.

Judy herself was half-asleep when the bus stopped. It was now early evening and for most of the journey it had been raining, but now it looked as though it was clearing up. The driver announced that they had arrived and everyone got up to leave the bus. Judy roused the girls and they alighted to find themselves outside a wooden building. Once they were all assembled they were ushered inside by two of the volunteers. Inside the little church hall the billeting officer awaited them. A lot of the local people were waiting to choose their new charges. One after another the children were taken away by new foster parents, looking lost and often tearful. Judy and her daughters seemed to be the only three-some there, and it soon became obvious that no one had room for three evacuees together. In the end they were the only ones left and Charlotte and Suzanne were beginning to whimper from hunger and exhaustion. At last the billeting officer came over to them. He was an elderly man with a kindly face.

'I do know of a couple who might take you in, m'dear,' he said. 'They run a guesthouse on the cliffs so it might only be temporary, but at least you and the little girls will have a roof over your heads for tonight. If you wait here a moment I'll just slip out to the phone box and give them a ring.'

Charlotte tugged Judy's sleeve when he'd gone. 'Mum, I want to go home,' she said in a small voice.

Judy slipped an arm round her small daughter's shoulders. 'We can't go home, sweetheart,' she said. 'We have to stay here now and make the best of it.'

Presently the man came back with a smile on his face. 'Come with me,' he said. 'Mr and Mrs Hurst will be happy to put you up. I'll run you round there now in the car. I can see that the little'uns are just about dead on their feet.'

When they got out of the car outside a large house on the cliffs Charlie stared, her eyes like saucers. 'Mum, look! Is all that water the sea?'

Judy nodded, intrigued in spite of her weariness. She herself had only seen the sea once before. It was on a day trip to Southend with Mum and Dad and it had rained all day. 'Yes, it is,' she said. 'Isn't it lovely?'

'And look at the sky.' Charlie pointed. 'What's that lovely thing, all colours?'

'It's called a rainbow,' Judy told her.

'What's a rainbow, Mum? What's it for?' Charlie persisted.

'It comes after the rain,' Judy said, searching her memory for a half-forgotten description. 'It's a promise – the promise of – of a new beginning.'

CHAPTER TWO

Bill and Maggie Hurst stood at the open front door of Sea View guesthouse with welcoming smiles on their faces as the billeting officer introduced them.

'This is Mrs Truman and her two little girls.'

'Oh, just look at these two poor little lambs,' Maggie said, holding out her arms to the children. 'You look done in, my luvvies. Come on in and have a cup of cocoa and something to eat, then we'll find you a nice bed.' She held out a hand to Judy. 'I'm Maggie Hurst, dear and this is my hubby, Bill.'

Judy held out her hand. 'And I'm Judy. These two are Charlotte and Suzanne.'

'Oh, what lovely names.'

'Yes, but we like being called Charlie and Suzie best,' Charlie piped up.

Maggie laughed. 'Right then, my sugar, Charlie and Suzie it shall be. Just come you in and we'll have you settled in no time.'

The woman's kindness brought a lump to Judy's throat. All the way here she had been wondering what they were coming to and it was such a relief to find warmth and kindness.

In the Hursts' big kitchen a fire burned in the range, throwing out a warm glow, and the big table in the centre of the room was set for a meal.

'Now, sit you all down,' Maggie said. 'I hope you like egg and chips. It was all I could rustle up at short notice, and there's some fruitcake for afters.'

Charlie looked delighted and sat up to the table eagerly but Suzie was half-asleep on her feet and could only manage a drink and a few chips from her mother's plate. Judy quickly outlined their background and apologized for descending on them without warning.

'Don't you worry your head about that,' Maggie said. 'There's a war on now and we're all in the same boat. If we can't help one another it's a poor lookout.'

'They'll probably find us somewhere else tomorrow,' Judy said. 'So we won't inconvenience you for long.'

'Ah, you're thinking about the business,' Bill said. He looked at his wife. 'The season's over now, anyway, and Lord knows when folks'll feel like going on holidays again. They'll be wanting to stay close to home, I reckon, in the foreseeable future.'

Judy frowned. 'But it's your livelihood.'

Bill smiled. 'We were about to retire,' he said. 'We had our sights set on selling up and finding a nice little cottage in the country, but those plans'll have to wait, thanks to Mr Hitler.'

'That's a shame,' Judy commiserated.

Maggie shook her head. 'We're a lot luckier than most, 'she said. She looked at her husband. 'Bill did his bit in the last war so he won't have to go this time, thank God.' She sighed. 'It doesn't seem five minutes ago. The war to end all wars, they said it was. And yet here we are again.'

There were five bedrooms at Sea View and Maggie told Judy that she had prepared one for her and another for the girls. Judy followed her up the stairs where Maggie pointed out the bathroom before ushering them all into a spacious room at the back of the house. There was a big double bed into which she had placed two hot water bottles. Quickly Judy unpacked their nightdresses, undressed her daughters and helped them climb into the big bed, where they snuggled up together in the warmth. Before she could close the door they were both asleep.

Outside on the landing Maggie sighed. 'Poor little lambs,' she said. 'What a good job they've got their mummy with them, not all alone like a lot of the poor little mites.' She looked at Judy. 'Will you come downstairs with Bill and me for a nightcap?'

Judy would have preferred to go to bed herself. It had been a long, tiring and traumatic day, but it seemed rude to refuse so she nodded. Down in the kitchen Bill had made cocoa for the three of them.

'I've put a nip of brandy in yours,' he told Judy. 'I reckon you can do with a bit of something warming.' As they sipped Maggie filled Judy in on the local scene.

'Summerton's not a bad little town,' she said. 'We've got plenty of nice shops and the market on Wednesdays and Saturdays. Then there's a couple of cinemas, the Roxy and the Savoy and then there The Little of course.'

'What's The Little?' Judy asked.

'The Little Theatre,' Maggie explained. 'We locals call it "the rep". They have a company of actors and actresses and they put on a new play every week. They're very good.' She shook her head. 'They're all closed at the moment, of course, but I daresay they'll have to open again before long. Folks is going to want cheering up, aren't they?'

'I used to work at the Hackney Empire,' Judy told them. 'My mum and dad too. I worked in the sweet kiosk and I used to take the tray of chocolate and ice creams round in the interval. Maybe when the theatre opens again they'll have a job going there for me.'

Maggie nodded. 'Maybe. You never know. You say your mum and dad worked at the theatre, too?'

'Yes. Dad's a musician. He was in the orchestra. He plays the piano and the saxophone. Mum's a dancer,' Judy told them proudly. 'But the Empire's closed so they've gone off to entertain the troops. I don't know when I'll see them again.'

'Aah, you must miss them.' Maggie eyed Judy speculatively. 'So - hubby in the services, is he?'

Judy nodded. 'In the army. He didn't wait to be called up. He volunteered as soon as war broke out.'

'Good for him,' Bill said. 'I like a man who knows his duty.'

Judy didn't add that Sid had only volunteered because he'd had the sack from his job and couldn't find another. The war had come at just the right time for him. So much for duty. She stifled a yawn and Maggie reached out a hand to her.

'You're tired out, aren't you, love? Don't mind us if you want to turn in. We'll have a good old chinwag tomorrow.'

Judy found a hot-water bottle in her bed too and curled up with it gratefully in the cosy feather mattress. But although she was tired sleep didn't come immediately. She couldn't quite get over their luck at finding such a nice billet. She only hoped they could stay on. At home the girls had to share a single bed and the one she shared with Sid had been lumpy and sagging. They'd never been able to afford furniture of their own or to move out of the rooms above the fish-and-chip shop where the smell of frying fish permeated everything, including their clothes. Maggie and Bill were so kind. Her thoughts went to her mother-in-law and the first time Sid had taken her down to Gravesend to meet her. Annie Truman had brought up four sons, Sid being the oldest. She was a big woman with pale, glittering eyes which swept over Judy suspiciously as she met them on the doorstep.

'So this is the little tart you've got yourself saddled with,' she said bluntly. Although it did not augur well for their first meeting Judy held out a tentative hand.

'Pleased to meet you, Mrs Truman,'

The older woman tossed her head, ignoring the proffered hand. 'Well, since you're 'ere I s'pose you'd better come in.' She turned back into the little terraced house, leaving Judy and Sid to trail after her down the narrow hall.

'Don't take no notice of Ma,' Sid whispered. 'She's well known for callin' a spade a spade.'

And a tart a tart, Judy thought to herself, though she said nothing.

Annie Truman made no attempt at hospitality and when Sid had gone out into the back yard to help one of his brothers with his motorbike she looked Judy up and down with disapproval. 'I s'pose you think you're clever, trappin' my Sid into marryin' you!'

Judy shook her head. 'No! I mean, I didn't trap him.'

'Bit of a kid like you an' all. I don't know what the world's comin' to. What d'you think he sees in you, gel, apart from the fact that you can't keep your knickers on? He had a lovely gel a while ago. She'd a'made him a *good* wife. Same age as 'im she was. Not some tarty little schoolkid like you, daughter of some loose livin' chorus gel! You needn't think he loves *you*, 'cause he don't! I knows my boy! He's just doin' what's right by you 'cause you got yerself up the stick.'

Red in the face, Judy stood up. 'I'm not a tart, Mrs Truman and

I don't like being called one. And my mother is not a loose-living chorus girl.'

Annie folded her arms across her grimy pinny and threw her head back. 'Oh! It *speaks*, does it? Hoity-toity!' The pale eyes narrowed. 'Don't you use that tone to me, miss.'

'Tell Sid I'll wait for him at the end of the road,' Judy said and walked out of the house.

She stood on the corner for several minutes, a lump in her throat and tears stinging her eyes. She was just about to find her own way back to the station when she saw Sid running towards her down the street. 'Jude! Wait. What's up? Why did you walk out on Ma like that?'

'I didn't come here to be insulted,' Judy told him. 'She doesn't even know me and yet she accused me of trapping you and of – of being a tart.' The tears that filled her eyes brimmed over and she fumbled in her pocket for a hanky. 'She said a horrible thing about Mum too and she doesn't even know us.'

'Aw, I told you. You don't want to take any notice of Ma. She's always like that. Her bark's worse than 'er bite.'

'I want to go home,' Judy said with a sniff.

'No, come on back,' Sid wheedled. 'You ain't had no tea yet.'

'I don't want any. I want to go home.'

It hadn't been the best of starts. Annie hadn't attended the wedding and after that first visit Judy could feel nothing but relief. She'd quite expected Sid to insist on taking the baby to show her when Charlotte was born, but to her surprise he hadn't and mercifully he hadn't insisted on visiting Annie again.

It had been at the beginning of July this year that Sid had come home to tell her he had lost his job. He insisted that there had been some kind of deeply unfair misunderstanding over money but Judy didn't quite believe him. He was very fond of a flutter on the dogs but he'd never been what you could call lucky. It wasn't unusual for him to come home on a payday without any money. Very often all she had for housekeeping was what she earned at The Empire, but if she asked Sid where all his money had gone he would fly into a rage, so she usually gritted her teeth and bought what she could for the girls, often going without herself. It wasn't unknown for her to go to the pawnshop with the few bits of jewellery her parents had given her for birthdays and Christmas. When Sid made up feeble reasons for his dismissal she suspected that he'd been involved in some kind of fiddle, or as Dad had wryly put it, 'got the firm's money mixed up with his own.'

Sid applied for several jobs but didn't get any of them. Although he hotly denied it she suspected that his old firm had sacked him without a reference. While he was hanging around at home life was difficult. He was bad tempered with her and snappy with the girls, especially at mealtimes, when he was constantly shouting at them to sit up straight and take their elbows off the table. At every meal he insisted that they finish every scrap of food on their plates, telling them they were lucky to have food to eat at all. He would persist until he reduced them to tears. Sometimes causing them to be physically sick. The atmosphere stretched Judy's nerves to the limit and the girls became silent and edgy. When the threat of war caused conscription to be put into place and Sid decided to volunteer she could feel nothing but relief.

'If I go now I'll probably get a nice cushy number in the Catering Corps,' he said, misguidedly. 'At my age I reckon I won't get called up till they're getting desperate. Then who knows where they'll send me?'

As it happened Sid was assigned to the Royal Artillery and there was every chance that he'd be sent abroad at the earliest opportunity. When Judy's mother Christine heard, she heaved a sigh of relief.

'Time Judy and the kids had a bit of peace and quiet,' she remarked to her husband.

The Empire, along with all the other theatres and places of entertainment closed as soon as war was declared. Harry and Christine were immediately out of work and had to think hard about their future. They gave the matter a lot of thought and when they had eventually decided what to do they came round to tell Judy their news.

'We've decided to join ENSA,' Harry told her.

'ENSA? What's that?' Judy asked, slightly alarmed.

'Entertainments National Service Association,' Harry explained.

'It's been created to entertain the troops.'

'Your dad and I are going as a double act,' Christine told her. 'I'm getting a bit long in the tooth for the high-kicking routines now, but I've got a fairly decent singing voice. So I'm going to be a soubrette with Dad accompanying me on the piano. We've worked out a routine and we've been rehearsing. I reckon we're not half bad. We're going to call ourselves the Musical Mitchells. Glamour and songs at the piano. How about that? Look good on the playbills, eh?'

They both seemed quite excited so Judy smiled her encouragement, but she couldn't help wondering what would become of her and the girls, left all alone in London.

'We've been up the Lane and auditioned,' Harry told her. 'Drury Lane Theatre, that's the headquarters. We went the day before yesterday and we heard this morning that we're in. We have to go and get our uniforms and a rehearsal schedule tomorrow. We're going to be in one of the first shows to go out.'

'Go out where?' Judy asked, even more alarmed.

'It'll be camps up and down the country to begin with,' Harry explained. 'Though it's on the cards that we might get sent abroad later.'

'I've always wanted to travel,' Christine said with a smile. 'I've never been further than Southend.'

'But won't it be dangerous?'

'No,' Harry assured her jovially. 'Your mum and I are far too valuable for them to put us in any danger!'

A week later they were off down to some place in Wales to begin rehearsing. They weren't allowed to disclose the actual destination but Judy had received a postcard to say they had arrived safely, were looking forward to their new work and might get the chance to pop home between tours. That was when Judy decided to go along with the evacuation scheme that was being organized by the local school. Charlotte had started at the school at the beginning of term, so Judy went along and put their names down to join the scheme. One wave had already been dispatched and they were to be on the next. She gave notice that they were leaving the flat, packed the few belongings they were allowed to take and said a reluctant goodbye to Auntie Lily.

And here they were.

'Mum – *Mum*. Wake up! Come and look.'

Judy rubbed her eyes, unsure just for a moment of where she was. Charlie was shaking her shoulder vigorously. 'Come and look, Mum. The sea's all gone. Why's it gone, Mum – where is it?'

She sat up, blinking and trying to get her bearings. 'What are you talking about?'

But Charlotte seized her mother's hand and tugged hard until she stumbled out of bed to follow her across the landing and into the room she shared with Suzie.

'Look, Mum, look!' She pulled her mother across to the window where she had drawn one curtain back. 'The sea was there last night and now it's *gone*!' She looked up at Judy, her blue eyes wide with bewilderment.

Judy laughed. 'The tide's gone out,' she explained. 'It'll come back again later today. You'll see.'

Charlie pointed. 'But that thing in the sky's gone too.'

'What thing?'

'That thing with all the colours.' Charlie looked up at her mother, her little face completely baffled.

'Oh, the rainbow.' Judy bent down to give her daughter a hug. 'They only last a few minutes, love. They come when it's been raining.'

'But you said it was a promise. And now it's gone and the sea's gone as well.' Charlie's lip trembled. 'Has the promise gone too?'

'No. The promise is still there. I told you, the sea will come back and when it rains again the rainbow will come too.' Judy looked at the disappointment on her little girl's face. 'Tell you what, later on you can get out your paints and paint your own rainbow – one you can keep.'

A bathroom and indoor lavvy was a luxury to Judy. She'd always had to bath the girls in the kitchen sink and as for her own toilet arrangements, she had to make do with an all over wash. The bathroom at Sea View seemed enormous with a big bath tub, a wash basin *and* a lavvy – no having to go outside to the yard in the cold. When Charlie and Suzie saw it their eyes grew round and when Judy filled the bath and began to take off their nightdresses Charlie protested.

'It's too big. We'll drown. Do we have to get in there?' she asked fearfully.

'Of course you do. You must be filthy after all that travelling yesterday. Come on, both of you.' She lifted a protesting Charlie into the warm water and Suzie after her and after a few minutes their fear vanished and they were laughing and splashing each other joyously.

'Aren't you coming in too?' Charlie asked.

Judy hesitated then stripped off her own nightdress and climbed in with the girls to their shrieks of delight. 'Might as well make good use of the hot water,' she said with a giggle.

When they arrived downstairs in the kitchen Maggie was frying bacon and eggs for breakfast. She turned with a smile when they walked in.

'I reckon the three of you had a rare old time in the bathroom,' she said. 'I heard you all laughing.'

Judy bit her lip. 'I'm sorry, I should have asked if we could have a bath. We did all share it, though, so we didn't use all your hot water.'

'Don't you worry about that,' Maggie said. 'This old range keeps us in hot water all day.' She lifted sizzling bacon onto three plates, following it with eggs. 'It did my heart good to hear you all laughing. You looked so done-in last night. Come on, sit you down and tuck in. They reckon we'll be rationed before long, so might as well make the most of it while we can.'

The girls tucked into their breakfast enthusiastically, joining Bill at the kitchen table. He had already finished his meal and was smoking his pipe and reading the paper. He eyed the girls over the tops of his glasses, amused by their healthy appetites.

'Your little'un don't have much to say for herself,' he remarked, nodding his head towards Suzie.

Judy smiled. 'She's shy, but once she's used to you you'll have a job to stop her.'

'The sea's all gone,' Charlie said, looking up. 'Why has it?'

'That's what we call low tide,' Bill explained. 'It'll be back this afternoon, don't you worry.' He looked at Judy. 'We're lucky here. Water's too shallow for an invasion force, even at high tide, so we don't have to have beach defences.'

'That's good.' She glanced at him. 'The billeting officer said this might only be temporary. He might be back today to move us somewhere else.'

Maggie laid a hand on her shoulder. 'Not if you like it here, m'dear. S'far as we're concerned you're more than welcome to stay. We'd have to take someone and you and the girls seem to us like just the right people, don't they, Bill?'

Bill nodded, taking a long slurp of his giant cup of tea. 'Couldn't have put it better myself. I reckon we'll all get along fine.'

'You'll be needing to go to the school this morning,' Maggie said. 'With little Charlie here.'

Dismayed, Charlie looked up from her plate. 'Oh, have I *got* to, Mum?'

'I'm afraid so,' Judy told her firmly.

'If you like I could come with you and show you the way,' Maggie said. 'Then afterwards I'll show you round the town – help you get your bearings.'

'That would be lovely,' Judy said. 'It's very kind of you.'

The school was only a short walk away. When they arrived the playground was in chaos, with children, teachers and volunteers trying to put some kind of organization into play. But Charlie, along with a group of children of similar age, was soon assigned a classroom where a harassed teacher was desperately trying to fit everyone in.

'I'm afraid they'll have to sit three to a desk,' she told Judy. 'It's not ideal. There are far more children than we'd allowed for and it looks as though we'll have to find extra classroom accommodation elsewhere; either that or teach half in the mornings and the other half in the afternoons!'

Anxious not to be in the way, Judy kissed an anxious-looking Charlie goodbye and promised to be back to collect her at lunch-time, then she joined Maggie in the playground. Suzie looked relieved to see her and clung desperately to her hand.

'Don't leave me here, Mum,' she begged, looking up with huge tear-filled eyes.

'No, of course I won't.'

'Why do we have to leave Charlie?'

'Because she's a big girl and has to go to school. We'll come and get her later, don't worry.'

Maggie smiled. 'Come you on, my sugar. I know a nice café where we can get some lemonade and a nice bun for you.'

Fortified by cups of coffee and, in Suzie's case, lemonade, Maggie took them on a tour of the little town. The Little Theatre was down a side street close to the town hall. There was a canopy outside the front entrance, made of wrought iron with stained-glass panels, and on either side of the swing doors were glass cases with photographs of the company of actors and actresses. Judy thought they all looked very glamorous.

'It's lovely inside,' Maggie told her. 'Red velvet seats and lots of little gilt cherubs. And they put lovely plays on. Bill and I never missed a single week. Always went of a Wednesday night, regular as clockwork.' They stood gazing sadly at the padlocks that secured the doors. 'I'm sure they'll open up again soon,' Maggie added optimistically. 'I can't believe there'll be no entertainment for the whole duration.'

Judy had written two postcards after breakfast: one to Auntie Lily to give her their address, asking her to pass it on to her parents when and if she saw them. The other was to Sid. So far she'd had no money from him since he joined up. Other army wives seemed to have pay-books through the government scheme and be paid directly but somehow hers must have been delayed. She'd managed to save a little from her own wages but the money was rapidly running out and Judy was beginning to feel anxious.

She posted her cards at the post office and went with Maggie to Woolworths where she bought Charlie and Suzie a little teddy bear each. Apart from Charlie's beloved paints and crayons they'd had to leave their toys at home and she knew they'd miss them. She counted the coins left in her purse and bit her lip, hoping that she'd be able to find work of some kind soon.

When they returned to the school Charlie ran out, pleased to see them, all her earlier anxieties forgotten. She was full of the morning's adventure and bubbling over with news.

'Our teacher is called Miss Black and I sat next to a little girl called Dinah Jones,' she said, grasping Judy's hand. 'She's from London too – a place called Poplar. Her dad's a sailor but she ain't got no sisters.'

'She *hasn't got any* sisters,' Judy corrected.

Charlie looked puzzled. 'That's what I said.' She tugged at her mother's hand. 'When we get home can I paint the rainbow like you said?'

Maggie smiled at Judy. 'She's calling Sea View home already,' she said. 'That's a good sign, isn't it?'

'Red, orange, yellow, green, blue, indigo, violet. Those are the colours.' Judy laid the crayons out on the table in the right order and handed the red one to Charlie. 'There you are. Now you can do it.'

'What's indigo?'

'A sort of dark purple.'

Charlie picked up a red crayon and carefully drew an arc with it, her little face frowning in concentration. 'Is the rainbow always the same colours?' she asked.

'Yes, always.'

'Why?'

'Because it is.'

'How do you know?'

'I remember learning about it at school,' Judy told her. 'I've never forgotten.'

'And what's the promise the rainbow makes?' Charlie asked.

For a moment Judy was stuck for an answer. 'Let's say it's whatever you want it to be,' she said at last. 'What would you like the rainbow to promise?'

Charlie considered carefully for a moment, then she said. 'I'd like it to promise we could stay here for ever and ever,' she said. 'And for Dad not to shout at us any more.' She looked up into Judy's eyes. 'And for him to stop making you cry, Mum. That's what I'd like the rainbow to promise me.'

Judy slipped an arm round her little daughter's shoulders and hugged her, her throat tight. She was shaken. She had no idea that the child was so perceptive.

CHAPTER THREE

As the autumn progressed the upheaval seemed to settle down. Charlie loved her new school and soon made friends. Suzie, hearing about all the fun, couldn't wait to join her sister and grew bored with staying at home. Judy had already taught her her numbers and letters and she watched sadly every morning as they left Charlie at the school gates to run off and join the playground fun without her.

To Judy's delight regular letters began to arrive from her parents. They were quite short and did not disclose exactly where they were but they wrote of how much they were enjoying their new work and said that their act was going down well with the servicemen.

Auntie Lily sent postcards. The bombing everyone had dreaded had come to nothing and she declared stoutly that Hitler must have thought better than to arouse the fury of the British people. It seemed that life went on as normal in Hackney.

A lot of the children who had been evacuated at the same time as Judy and her daughters had returned to London. But Maggie and Bill expressed their opinion that it was far too early to be sure nothing would happen and that it was asking for trouble to return too soon.

Not that Judy needed any persuasion to stay. She loved their new life in Summerton-on-Sea. Maggie and Bill were so kind. Never in her life had she known such wonderful cooking. She worked happily alongside Maggie in the kitchen and learned so much that soon she was taking her turn at making meals and baking cakes.

So far the threatened food rationing hadn't taken place. The Hursts had friends who had a farm in the Norfolk countryside and

29

they were promised a roasting bird for Christmas plus a joint of pork and all the fresh vegetables they could eat.

Charlie and Suzie flourished, blossoming under Judy's delighted gaze. Fresh sea air and good food brought the colour to their cheeks and Charlie stayed free of the chesty colds she had suffered every winter since babyhood and which Judy always dreaded.

'They look like different kiddies,' Maggie proclaimed proudly. 'Mind you, so do a lot of the other little evacuees.' She looked at Judy. 'And if you don't mind me saying so, luvvie, so do you.'

Judy smiled. 'I'm going to have to watch my weight. It's your good cooking, Maggie.'

Maggie chuckled. 'Never you mind about that. In my experience hubbies like a bit of something to get hold of.' She nudged Judy playfully. 'Just wait till that Sid of your comes on leave and sees how pretty you are.'

Bill watched the news avidly, studying the newspapers and listening to all the radio bulletins. And when in mid December the *Graf Spee* was sunk he was thrilled.

'Now we can have a proper Christmas,' he said delightedly. 'It looks like things are going our way!'

Sid wrote shortly before Christmas to say he was due for a forty-eight-hour leave. He'd pop down to Kent to see his mum first, then he'd be with them on the nineteenth for a day and a half. To Judy's relief he had been sending her postal orders. They weren't regular but at least they had gone some way to help her to keep on top of her finances – just.

As the nineteenth drew closer she became nervous. She hadn't set eyes on Sid for four months and she wondered whether the army had changed him.

He arrived at teatime, looking handsome in his uniform. Judy introduced him to Maggie and Bill who discreetly left them alone after the meal was over. The girls had been shy and silent, seeming uneasy at the sight of their father in these unfamiliar clothes. The fact that they didn't rush to make a fuss of him seemed to irritate him.

'What's up with them?' he demanded of Judy. 'Anyone'd think I was a bleedin' stranger.'

'They're just shy,' Judy said. 'They've been through so many changes since the war began.'

'Don't you talk to them about me – show them snaps with me on them?'

'Of course.' Judy glanced at the girls who were playing quietly in the corner. She wished Sid wouldn't swear and talk about them as though they weren't in the room. She could see it was making them nervous.

Sid leaned forward towards her. 'What time do they go to bed?'

'Usually about half past seven.'

He looked at his watch. 'That's another hour. Can't you get them off early for once?'

'I'd have thought you'd want to spend some time with them,' Judy said.

He winked. 'There's something else I want more.' He reached out a hand to squeeze her knee. 'Come on, Jude. We've only got one night. It's been months.'

The girls seemed quite glad to go to bed early and after an interval Judy took Sid up to her room. What followed could hardly be called lovemaking. He was rough to the point of brutality, leaving her bruised and tearful. Taking her distress for dread at their impending parting, Sid pulled her roughly into his arms.

'Don't get upset. I reckon I'll get regular leave now that I've finished square-bashing. I'll be back again before you know it.' He raised his head to look down at her tearstained face. 'What's up?'

Judy shook her head. 'I – I don't want to fall for another baby,' she muttered.

He chuckled. 'We'd better keep our fingers crossed then, hadn't we?'

Next day was a school day and at breakfast Maggie volunteered to take Charlie to school and have Suzie for the rest of the day so that Sid and Judy could spend some time together. Sid made no attempt to thank Maggie for the offer and Judy nudged him.

'Isn't that kind of Maggie?' she urged but he merely raised an eyebrow as though it was only to be expected. Later when she upbraided him he objected.

'Looks to me as if she's got a free skivvy in you. Why shouldn't she give you a bit of time off?'

'That's not fair,' Judy protested. 'Maggie and Bill have been kindness itself to us so it's only fair that I give her a hand with the housework. It's a pleasure, anyway. We've never lived in such a lovely house or had such smashing food. We're really lucky to be here.'

'Oh, I see!' he returned with a scowl. 'Better than what I've ever given you, is that what you're saying? You're chucking it in my face that I've never been able to provide a whole house for us!'

'No! I'm just saying…'

'Then don't! Shut up.'

She glanced at him. 'Sid – I'm finding it really hard to manage. I'm grateful for what you send us but why don't I get my money through the government like other army wives?'

'Because I chose to send you it by postal order,' he snapped. 'Lots of the fellers do it that way. Like that you get more.' He glared at her. 'Why – is there something wrong with that an' all?'

'No. It's just that it isn't regular. I can never rely on it.'

He gave an impatient snort. '*Well*! I don't bloody know! I get a day and a half's leave and all you can do is moan, moan, *moan*! A fine leave this is turning out to be.'

He was in a bad mood for the rest of the day. Judy took him into town to show him round but he sneered at everything she showed him. 'Can't hold a candle to the Smoke,' he said. 'Can't see what you're going on about. If you ask me it's a lousy, dead-an'-alive dump.'

After they'd had a cup of tea in the bus-station café Sid looked at his watch. 'It's another hour before I have to catch the train,' he said. 'Time for a bit of how's-yer-father. Shall we go back to your billet?'

Judy's heart sank. 'Maggie and Bill and the kids will be there.'

He laughed. 'So what? What do they think I want to do on my leave – sit drinking tea with the vicar?'

'Don't you want to spend some time playing with the girls?'

He shrugged. 'They didn't exactly seem overjoyed to see their old man, did they?' He nudged her. 'I'd rather play with you.'

Although she wouldn't admit it, even to herself, Judy was glad when Sid had gone. Maggie noticed that she was quiet and withdrawn but put it down to Sid's absence, though, as she remarked to Bill, Sid wasn't the kind of husband she had expected Judy to have. He seemed very rough and coarse to her. The children's nervousness around him bothered her too, though she made no comment on it.

With Christmas round the corner there was a lot to do and Judy was eager to help. The days seemed extra short now that the blackout had to be erected before teatime. Bill had made frames for each window, covered in dense black material so that every chink of light was obliterated. The ARP warden's cry of 'Put that light out!' was never directed at Sea View. Bill had bought them all a torch each in case they needed to be out after blackout. With all the streetlights turned off moonless nights were pitch dark and stories abounded of people bumping into lampposts or missing their footing on the kerbs.

The Broughtons, Maggie and Bill's farmer friends, provided them with a fine fat cockerel and a joint of pork and on Christmas Eve Mr Broughton brought round a basket of fresh vegetables: potatoes, cabbage and sprouts; onions – which were in short supply – and beautiful aromatic celery, crisp and white; all of it a far cry from the limp vegetables Judy was used to buying from the street barrows and markets back home.

The Little Theatre had reopened soon after the outbreak of war, as Maggie had predicted, though they now only gave one performance a night instead of two. Judy had seen the posters around the town advertising the pantomime and wondered if she could afford to take the girls, but before she could think any more about it, Bill announced that he and Maggie were taking all three of them as a Christmas treat.

The pantomime was Cinderella and the five of them went to the Boxing Day matinee in the best seats. Charlie and Suzie were entranced, loving the colour and the pretty costumes, the music and the atmosphere, not to mention the ice creams Bill bought them in the interval.

Judy hadn't seen the interior of the Little Theatre before and she loved its cosy, intimate ambience. The red velvet seats and curtains and the gilded plasterwork reminded her of the Empire and made her feel quite homesick. She wondered again if they were likely to have any vacancies. She needed a job and she'd rather work in a theatre than anywhere else, even if it was only cleaning.

On the morning that Charlie returned to school after the holidays Suzie had a slight cold, and as it was a frosty morning Maggie had suggested leaving her at home in her care while Judy did the daily shopping. When Judy had bought the things on Maggie's list she took a walk down Guildhall Road where the theatre was and stood for a moment outside, looking at the photographs and the bills advertising forthcoming attractions. The box office opened at ten and as she stood there someone came and unlocked the doors.

She hovered indecisively for a moment, then she told herself that she had nothing to lose. If you don't ask you don't get, she told herself firmly, and if they didn't have any vacancies there would be no harm done. Taking a deep breath she pushed open the door and walked into the foyer. At once the 'theatre aroma' met her nostrils. The familiar scent that she had tried hard so many times to analyse: it was a mixture of coffee, cigar smoke, greasepaint and dust. To Judy it was better than the most exotic perfume and she breathed it in appreciatively.

'Good morning. Can I help you?'

The voice made her turn guiltily to see a middle-aged man looking at her curiously. 'Oh! I – er – I was just passing and I wondered – do you have any vacancies – for – well, anything really: usherettes, sweet salesgirls – anything.'

'Vacancies eh?' The man held out his hand. 'First things first, eh? I'm Bob Gresham, front-of-house manager, and you are?' He raised an enquiring eyebrow at her.

'Oh, yes.' She took the proffered hand. 'Judy Truman. Me and my children are evacuees – from London – Hackney. I used to work at the Hackney Empire.' She opened her handbag and fumbled inside until she found the envelope containing the reference the Empire's manager had given her when she left. She handed it to Mr Gresham. 'This is my reference,' she said.

He took the envelope from her with a smile. 'Thank you, though I haven't said yet whether I have a job to offer you.'

She blushed. 'No – no, you haven't. Sorry.'

'But I like your enthusiasm,' he added kindly. 'I take it you like working in a theatre.'

'Oh yes, I do,' she told him. 'My parents both work in the theatre too. On the other side of the curtain though. Dad's a musician and Mum is a dancer. They're with ENSA now.'

'I see.' He took the folded sheet of paper out of the envelope and scanned it. 'Well, your last employer certainly seems to have valued your work.' He slid the paper back into its envelope and handed it back to her. 'It so happens that we're about to lose two of our usherettes to the ATS in a couple of weeks' time. I haven't had time to insert an advert in the local paper yet. Maybe I won't have to.'

Judy felt her colour deepen. 'You mean – you think I'm...'

'Suitable?' He smiled. 'I wouldn't be at all surprised. Suppose you start next Monday and have a week with one of the girls who's leaving so as to get you into our ways? We can have a month's trial on either side - to see if we like one another. How would that suit you?' He named a weekly wage which sounded like riches to hard-up Judy. To be earning money again and able to buy things for the girls was like a dream come true.

'Thank you, Mr Gresham,' she said. 'Thank you so much.'

'We only do the one show per night now of course, matinees on Wednesdays and Saturdays. Be here at half past five next Monday and we'll sort you out a uniform. And thank you for dropping in, Mrs Truman.'

'Judy, please. Thanks again. And don't worry, I'll be there.'

She rushed home and poured out her news breathlessly to Maggie. 'I've been thinking about it on the way home,' she said. 'If you and Bill don't mind baby-sitting for me in the evenings I'll take on more of the housework – even some of the cooking if you can trust me with it,' she added. 'Then there's the matinees.'

'I can pick Charlie up from school on Wednesdays,' Maggie cut in, almost as excited as Judy herself. 'And on Saturdays we can all do things together. Don't you worry yourself about it, luvvie. Bill and I are going to enjoy it.'

Judy presented herself at the theatre dead on the dot of half past five the following Monday and was introduced to Molly, the pretty, dark-haired girl who was about to leave to join the ATS. A uniform was found in Judy's size. She tried it on and it fitted her quite well apart from one or two adjustments which she assured Molly she could do herself at home. Standing in front of the mirror in the staff changing room she thought that the uniform suited her very well. In dark-red velour to match the theatre's décor it had a plain skirt and a tunic with gold braid frogging across the front. It was finished off with a little pillbox hat that sat jauntily on her blonde curls.

'You look a treat,' Molly declared, standing behind her. 'Now I'll take you into the auditorium so you can get a feel for the layout.'

That evening Judy worked in the dress circle. She soon got the hang of the seat numbering and a bonus was that she got to see the play. Standing in the shadows at the back of the circle when the curtain went up, she was enthralled. The actors she had seen so recently in the pantomime now performed a straight play with just as much skill and realism as before. By the time she returned to Sea View she felt happy and fulfilled, looking forward immensely to the weeks to come in her new job.

As Maggie had predicted, food rationing came into force in January. 'I daresay we'll manage,' she said stoically. 'We managed in the last lot so we'll do it again. Anyway I'd rather have rationing than shortages.'

But shortages there were. Fresh fruit like bananas and citrus fruits were scarce and so were eggs, but the Broughtons came up trumps, often arriving at the door with eggs and maybe a rabbit or a boiling fowl. Maggie was nothing if not resourceful. Bill once said proudly that she could make a good dinner out of a bundle of sticks and a bucket of water.

'Well, I hope it never comes to *that*!' Maggie said stoutly.

At last winter gave up its hold and spring came, daffodils bloomed as usual and the days lengthened. In April Charlie celebrated her sixth birthday and three weeks later, Suzie became five. Maggie invited Charlie to ask some of her school friends along for a little party. They decided to have it on a Sunday and she and Judy worked hard all morning, baking cakes and making sandwiches. Bill organized games for them and Judy reflected later that Maggie and Bill seemed to enjoy it as much as the children. That night, when she was putting the girls to bed Charlie said,

'Mum, can we live here always with Auntie Maggie and Uncle Bill?'

Suzie clapped her hands in agreement. 'Ooh yes – can we, Mum?'

'Well, we'll have to stay here until the war's over,' Judy told them.

Charlie sat up and studied her mother's face. 'When will that be?'

'I don't know, probably quite a long time.'

'Hooray!' Charlie cheered and Suzie echoed her.

'Hooray!'

'Mum…' Suzie tugged at her mother's sleeve. 'Dad's not coming again, is he?'

Disturbed, Judy looked down at her younger child. Suzie had always been the quieter of the two girls. They were so different. Charlie had glossy dark hair like her father and an outgoing, assertive nature, while Suzie had inherited her mother's soft blond curls and diffident personality. 'Dad will come and see us as often as he can,' she said gently. 'When the army lets him have leave.'

'I don't want him to come,' Suzie whispered. 'I don't want him to shout at us.'

'I told her,' Charlie cut in. 'He's just a bossyboots.'

'No he's not. You mustn't say that,' Judy chided. 'It's very hard, being in the army. Dad has people shouting at him all the time. I'm sure he'd rather be at home with us.'

'He used to shout at us before he was in the army,' Charlie pointed out punching her pillow. 'Night, Mum.'

As Judy kissed them goodnight and went downstairs she pondered over what Charlie had said. She said nothing to Maggie. She had already sensed that the older woman hadn't taken to Sid and she had no wish to make matters worse. But it wasn't right that the girls should feel so afraid of their father that they wished him out of their lives. Of course they were too young to realize what they were saying, she told herself. Next time Sid came on leave she would have to talk to him about his attitude towards his daughters.

CHAPTER FOUR

In May came the evacuation of the stranded Allied Forces at Dunkirk. Bill was horrified, but so proud of the way ordinary people had responded, taking their boats, large and small across the channel in a valiant rescue operation.

'We'll show Herr Hitler that the British people ain't done yet,' he said, patriotic tears glinting in his eyes. 'God! I wish I was twenty years younger and could join up meself!'

Maggie raised her eyes to the ceiling. 'Thank heaven you're not then,' she said. Out of his sight she grinned at Judy. 'God help them Nazis if his nibs got hold of them,' she joked. 'Tear 'em apart with his bare hands, he would.' She winked. 'England's last hope, that's him.'

A beautiful spring blossomed into a hot summer and Charlie and Suzie were introduced to the beach. They were used now to the tides and the way the sea would 'disappear' for a while each day, but they soon learned that the rock pools that were left behind were great fun to splash around and play in. Bill taught them to look for tiny sea creatures, little crabs and minute darting shrimps, so camouflaged that they were almost invisible against the sand. He even found a couple of shrimping nets, left behind at Sea View by holidaymakers, and the girls would spend hours, frocks tucked into their knickers, playing on the sands and paddling in the pools. The sun soon tanned them nut-brown and rosy-cheeked and their limbs became plump and rounded.

'They're different kiddies from what turned up on our doorstep a year ago,' Maggie declared proudly. And Judy had to agree. Despite the war and all the upheaval generated by it, coming to live in Summerton-on-Sea was the best thing that had happened to them.

More and more of the children who had been evacuated at the outbreak of war had returned home to their families. As the months went by and the dreaded bombing of London and England's major cities failed to materialize people grew relaxed and complacent. But Bill, who never missed a BBC bulletin, was not so confident. He was especially upset by the news that Italy had joined forces with Germany and a couple of days later even more distressed to learn that Germany had invaded France. That was when he decided to join the Local Defence Volunteers, soon to be named the Home Guard. Maggie made her usual affectionately teasing jokes.

'Oh well, we'll be all right now *he's* joined,' she said with a wink. 'He'll put them on the right track.'

Judy settled happily into her working routine at the theatre. She loved her job and made several friends, in particular Sally, whose husband was in the RAF. Sally was about the same age and they found that they shared a lot in common. She was a local girl and had moved back in with her parents when her husband was called up so there was always someone to look after her two-year-old son, Michael. Judy often talked about her time at the Hackney Empire, reminiscing about the loaded tray of chocolates and ice creams she used to take round in the intervals. Now there was a shortage of sweets so the theatre kiosk in the foyer had been forced to close.

In early September, when the school holidays were over, Judy took Suzie along to join her big sister. The little girl who had longed so much to go was nervous when the big day arrived and clung to her mother's hand as they waited in the playground for the new intake to be registered. Things were quieter now that so many evacuees had returned to London, although the teachers still complained that the classes were much larger than normal.

Charlie took her sister's hand and announced that she would look after her. 'You needn't worry, Mum,' she said in a very grown-up voice. 'I won't let nothing happen to her.'

'You mean you won't let *anything* happen to her,' Judy corrected. Charlie gave her a pitying look.

'Ain't that what I said?'

'*Isn't*...' Judy sighed and gave up.

When Suzie realized that her sister would be in a different

class her face puckered up. 'I wanted to sit next to Charlie,' she whimpered.

'But I'll see you at playtime,' Charlie promised. 'I'll be waiting for you.'

She was as good as her word and before the week was out Suzie had settled and made friends of her own.

It was late on Saturday afternoon, the end of the first week of the new term, when news of the London bombing shocked them all. Bill was glued to the wireless for most of the evening.

'Well, it's come just like they said,' he announced, his face grave. 'I always knew it was foolhardy, all them kids going home. It's the docks they're after, o'course. The East End has really copped it. And now that Hitler's started it he won't give up, you mark my words,' he added gloomily.

Seeing Judy's worried expression Maggie chided him. 'Oh, leave off being so gloomy, Bill. You're frightening poor Judy.'

'It's just Auntie Lily,' Judy said. 'I must write to her straight away. I know what she's like. I doubt if they'll get her to leave her house to go to the shelters.'

She was right. Auntie Lily wrote of the blitz in defiant terms. *'They're opening up the underground stations as shelters but you won't catch me going down there to sleep,'* she wrote stoically. *'If I've got to die I'll die in my own home. I believe that if my name's on a bomb it'll find me where ever I am.'*

Seeing Judy's distress Maggie suggested that she should write and invite Auntie Lily to come to stay with them in Norfolk until the bombing eased. Judy wrote off immediately, but Auntie Lily would have none of it. Her reply came back by return.

'I never left my home in the last war and I'm not going to give in now,' she wrote. *'Though it's very good and kind of Mrs Hurst to invite me. Please thank her very much for me.'*

Sid had not been on leave to Norfolk for almost a year. Judy knew that he'd had short leaves but as he was stationed in Yorkshire he wrote that there wasn't time to make the journey. When she had a letter from him in November announcing that he would be coming on leave for seven days she wasn't surprised.

'Do you think it might be embarkation leave?' Bill asked.

Maggie shook her head at him. 'Don't frighten the girl,' she said. 'It's probably nothing of the kind.'

But as soon as Sid arrived he announced that he and his unit were to be shipped off in a few weeks' time. He wasn't allowed to say where but Bill had his own ideas, as he told Maggie when they were on their own.

'The Western Desert if you ask me,' he said in a dramatic under-tone. 'Wavel's been dyin' to have a go at them Ities for weeks. Bet your bottom dollar that's where they're off to.'

At the end of his first day's leave Sid was waiting at the staff entrance for Judy at the end of the evening performance. At once she could see that he'd been drinking and also that he wasn't in the best of moods.

'I'd have thought you'd have taken time off for my leave,' he said petulantly.

'I couldn't,' she told him. 'So many people have gone off to join the forces or been called up that we're really short-staffed. Nobody asks for time off.'

As they stood there Jim Granger, the stage manager, came out.

'G'night, Judy love,' he said cheerily. He looked at Sid. 'This your hubby then?'

Judy quickly introduced them and Jim held his hand out to Sid. 'Nice to meet you. You're a lucky chap to have a lovely girl like Judy waiting at home for you.'

Sid ignored the hand and his eyes narrowed as he stared at the man, his head jutting forward. 'Oh yeah, and why's that?'

Jim looked taken aback. 'She's a little gem. We all love Judy – and those little girls of yours. Have a good leave, then.' He tipped his hat and walked away.

'What did he mean by that?' Sid demanded, his fists clenching at his sides.

'Nothing,' Judy told him. 'They're a great bunch. We all get along really well.'

'Oh? *How* well?'

She knew the look only too well. Trying to jolly him out of it she took his arm. 'Everyone's in the same boat, Sid. There's a war on and we're friends. Everyone helps out, that's all.'

'Anyway, what's he doing out of uniform. Is he a conchie?'

She shook her head. 'No. Jim's fifty. He was badly wounded in the last war – gassed. He's suffered from asthma ever since.'

'Oh yeah, that's the tale he puts about, is it? I've heard that one before.'

Judy's heart sank. 'Come on, it's cold,' she said. 'Maggie said she'd have some hot soup waiting for us when we got home.'

Back at Sea View Sid ate his supper in a menacing silence and when they were upstairs in their room he brought the subject up again.

'Listen to me, Jude, if you're carrying on behind my back...'

'I'm *not!*' she said indignantly.

'Here's me fighting for King and country and you playing around behind my back. It's not bloody good enough.'

'But I'm *not!*'

'So you say, but I saw the way that feller looked at you. I reckon he was having a good laugh at me. *Lucky chap to have a girl like you waiting for me.* Just what did he mean by that? Is he getting something I should be getting?' He crossed the room to stand menacingly over her.

'Sid, you've got it all wrong. Jim is just a nice man. He's old enough to be my father.'

He snorted. 'Huh! When did that ever stop blokes like him? Tell me that!'

'He's got a nice wife and three daughters.'

He grasped her shoulders. 'Seems to me like you're putting up a hell of a defence.'

'Whatever I say it's going to be wrong, isn't it?' she protested. 'You're on leave, so why are you behaving like this?'

'I'll behave any way I like. And you – you stop your nonsense, do you hear me?'

'I haven't looked at another man since you and I were married,' Judy said bravely. 'What you're saying is very insulting.'

'*Insulting!*' he roared. 'I expect you to be faithful and you call it insulting!'

She backed away from him, afraid of the menace in his eyes, but suddenly he lashed out, the back of his hand catching her on the side of her head. Staggering backwards across the room she fell heavily against the wardrobe with a crash. A moment later the door flew open and Charlie stood there in her nightie, her little face white with fear.

'What are you doing to Mum?' she shouted at Sid. 'Leave her alone!'

Scrambling to her feet Judy went to her. 'It's all right,' she said gathering her daughter close. 'I slipped and fell, that's all. You know how clumsy I am sometimes.'

But Charlie would have none of it. 'I heard him shouting,' she said, pointing accusingly. 'Like he always used to at home.'

'No, no. You must have been dreaming. Come on, love. Let Mum put you back to bed. Everything's all right.'

Charlie submitted reluctantly to being put back to bed, only partly reassured by her mother's explanations. When Judy returned to the bedroom Sid looked slightly shamefaced.

'I never meant to hurt you, but you drove me to it.'

'I won't have the children upset,' she told him. 'They're good kids and they've been through enough upheaval.'

'Seems to me they're on to a good thing, never mind cheeking their own father,' he protested. 'Do they know what kind of woman their mum is?'

'I haven't done anything wrong, Sid,' she said quietly. 'Why accuse me? I've never done anything to make you suspicious of me, have I?'

He shook his head. 'You don't know what it's like, being hundreds of miles away from your wife and kids.'

'We're all away from home and family,' she reminded him. 'So why do you have to make us miserable when you are with us?'

He shrugged. 'Let's just forget about it, eh?'

It soon became clear that Sid intended to spend every evening at the pub while Judy was working. Bill tried once or twice to encourage him to spend the evening with him and Maggie.

'We like listening to the wireless once the kiddies are in bed,' he said. 'There's lots of good programmes as well as the news. We like that ITMA. Tommy Handley is a real card. Then there's some lovely concerts on.'

Sid refused, none too politely, complaining to Judy afterwards that he hadn't come home on leave to sit listening to rubbish with a couple of old biddies. 'I'd rather go for a drink,' he said.

Which is what he did every night, except that he didn't stop at one. By the time he met Judy she could see that he'd had far more than was good for him. His words were slurred and his eyes slightly unfocused; worse, he was ready to fight with his own shadow.

On the last night of his leave he was more drunk than usual. To make matters worse Judy was late leaving the theatre. One of the girls was leaving. Her husband was about to be stationed in Scotland and she was moving there to be nearer him. After the final curtain they had a little celebration to see her off and present her with a small memento. Foreseeing Sid's displeasure, Judy stayed behind for only a few minutes but by the time she emerged he had worked himself up into a fine fury. He insisted that he had been waiting half an hour and demanded an explanation. When she told him the reason for the delay he refused to believe her.

'You do it just to show me, don't you?' he accused. 'You reckon you're the boss and you'll do as you like just because I'm away. Well, I'm here to tell you, girl, that you're not! And another thing – you get them kids into line. They should have more respect for their father, and you'd better behave yourself proper or you'll feel....'

'The back of your hand? Judy countered. 'You get a kick out of hitting me, don't you? Does it make you feel like a real man?'

'You little bitch! I'll...' He clenched his fist but Judy stood her ground.

'You'll *what*? Hit me again – for nothing, as usual.'

'Don't you think I won't!' He took a step nearer.

'You're a coward and a bully, Sid Truman!'

The next moment he hit her full in the face, knocking her backwards so that her head hit the wall behind her. Her knees buckled and she sank to the pavement, blood streaming from her nose.

The door opened as some of the staff came out, including Judy's friend, Sally, who gasped and rushed over to her.

'*Judy*! My God, you're bleeding! What happened, love?'

Someone produced a handkerchief to staunch the blood from her nose; another person suggested sending for an ambulance. By the time they had managed to help Judy to her feet Sid had vanished into the blackout and was nowhere to be seen. They escorted her inside and found her a chair. Sally knelt beside her.

'What happened, Judy? Shall I ring for the police?'

Judy shook her head. 'No, please don't fuss. I'll be OK in a minute when the bleeding stops. Someone hit me as I came out of the door. It was dark. I didn't see who. The police wouldn't find him anyway and I don't need an ambulance.' She looked up at their concerned faces. 'Did he rob you?' someone asked.

'No – no, he didn't get anything,' she muttered, ashamed that she was forced to lie about it. 'My handbag is safe.'

Mr Gresham, the manager was summoned and insisted on taking her home in his car. At the gate of Sea View she assured him that she was completely recovered, thanked him and got out of the car. As she let herself in at the front door she wondered where Sid was. She dreaded seeing him. He'd been bad enough before the war but being in the army seemed to have made him ten times worse.

She closed the front door carefully because of the blackout, then switched on the light. Turning she caught sight of herself in the hall mirror and gasped with shock. One side of her face was red and swollen and her left eye was almost closed, the surrounding skin already darkening. Maggie came out into the hall.

'Oh, it's you love. I thought I heard the door but...' She broke off as Judy turned, and one hand flew to her mouth. '*Oh*! Oh, my dear Lord. What's happened to you? Here, come in and sit down.'

Judy told her and Bill the same story she'd concocted for her friends at the theatre – an attack in the blackout – attempted theft. Bill fetched her a nip from his precious bottle of brandy and Maggie hurried out to the kitchen to put the kettle on for a 'nice cuppa'. 'For the shock,' she explained. 'Are you sure you don't want to have a doctor look at that face?' she asked with concern. 'You could have concussion or your nose could be broken.'

But Judy assured her that she would be fine. Once they were all drinking tea Maggie looked up and asked, 'Where's Sid then? Where was he when this happened?'

Judy shook her head. 'I don't know. Isn't he here?'

'Didn't he come to meet you?' Maggie and Bill exchanged glances. 'We thought we heard him come in a while ago,' Bill said. 'Then he went out again. Must be half an hour since.'

'We thought he'd gone round to the theatre to meet you,' Maggie said. 'Maybe he's waiting for you upstairs.'

Judy's heart sank. 'I'll go and see.' She rose to her feet but staggered a little as a dizzy spell hit her. Maggie got up and took her arm.

'I'll come with you,' she said, glancing at Bill. 'Can't have you falling down the stairs.'

In the bedroom every trace of Sid was gone; his kitbag and all his belongings were missing. Judy looked around the room helplessly.

'Maybe he was called back unexpectedly,' she said lamely. 'This was his last day anyway.'

Maggie took her shoulders and turned her to look into her eyes. 'Judy love,' she said quietly, 'did he do this to you - was it him?'

'No! I told you, I....'

'Don't cover for him, love,' Maggie said with a shake of her head. 'We heard him, ranting and raving at you of a night, couldn't help hearing - specially the night he woke poor little Charlie. I could have wept for the kiddie – trying so hard to defend her mum.' She gripped both Judy's hands. 'I'm right, aren't I?' When Judy slowly nodded with tear-filled eyes, Maggie pulled her close and hugged her. 'My poor little love. You deserve better than him. Never you mind; you've got me and Bill now. We'll take care of you.'

Next morning Judy awoke with a painful lump on the back of her head and one eye black and blue with bruising. Her face was still swollen too and she wondered how she could possibly appear at the theatre looking such a sight. Charlie and Suzie were terrified when they saw her at breakfast. Judy assured them that it was an accident and not nearly as bad as it looked, but Suzie cried, upset to see her mother's face so damaged and disfigured. Maggie offered to take the girls to school and when Judy refused she found a pair of sunglasses, left behind by one of Sea View's summer visitors. Judy put them on gratefully and set off with the girls to school. Charlie's little mouth was set in a tight line on the way and she held tightly to her mother's hand.

When Suzie skipped ahead to greet a friend she whispered, 'Mum, did Dad hit you?'

Judy shook her head. 'I told you, I fell over and hit my face against the wall.'

'You've fallen over a lot lately,' Charlie said. After a moment she asked, 'Where is he?'

'His leave was finished. He's gone back.'

Charlie nodded, her chin thrust out. '*Good!*'

Judy bent down to look into her daughter's eyes. 'Charlie, listen to me. You're not to say anything about this to anyone. Do you understand?'

Charlie pouted. 'Yes, Mum.'

Judy went round to the theatre as soon as it was open that morning. Mr Gresham was shocked at her injuries. He agreed that she could not be seen in public with such bad bruises. 'I don't want you to be embarrassed,' he said. 'Would you like to take a few days off?'

Judy shook her head. 'I'd rather be at work. Isn't there something else I can do?'

The manager hesitated, rubbing his chin, then he said. 'I'm without a secretary at the moment. Carol is expecting a baby and she's been a bit under the weather. Could you handle some filing and a bit of tidying up – maybe answering the phone and taking messages?'

Judy nodded eagerly. 'I'd love to.'

Upstairs in his office he showed her the filing system and explained how it worked. 'I've been meaning to take a day off to go to head office,' he told her. 'But all this has been getting on top of me – taking up all my time.' He smiled ruefully. 'I know it's a mess but do what you can, anyway.'

Looking round Judy thought she had never seen anything quite so untidy. The cleaner had been in and vacuumed the carpet but the desk was invisible under a pile of papers. Slowly and carefully she went through them, filing everything in its appropriate place. She familiarized herself with the bookings chart and the accounts book, and then set about reorganising the jumbled desk drawers. When the telephone rang she answered it as efficiently as she could.

'Good morning. Summerton-on-Sea Little Theatre,' she heard herself say with a little stab of pride. 'Mr Gresham's office. Can I help you?'

By the time the manager returned just after lunch she had filed away all the loose papers, made a note of bills to be paid and written out receipts ready to be signed and posted. She tidied the office and reorganized Mr Gresham's desk; took down messages, neatly writing them on the telephone pad and, finally, dusted the places the cleaner had been unable to reach.

Standing in the doorway on his return he looked surprised. 'Well, well, what a transformation! I only hope I'll be able to keep up your excellent standards.' He looked at her. 'I suppose you can't type, can you?'

Judy shook her head. 'Sorry, no.'

He shook his head. 'Mmm – pity.'

Judy worked in the office for the rest of that week and when her bruises had faded enough for her to resume her old duties she was quite disappointed. Working with the kindly Mr Gresham and being in charge of the office when he was out had been the most satisfying job she had ever done.

The London blitz was relentless. Every day the news was bad. Not only of London but of other major cities that were being bombed.

Bill, his ear close to the wireless at every news bulletin, shook his head. 'Makes you wonder how long it'll be before Hitler makes a stab at invasion,' he said gloomily.

Maggie shook her head at him. 'We'll have none of that talk in this house, Bill Hurst,' she said sternly. 'We'll worry about that when and if it happens and not a minute before!'

Judy continued to worry about Auntie Lily and just after Christmas, when there was a bit of a lull in the bombing she announced her intention of going up to London to fetch her back. Maggie was horrified.

'You can't!' she said. 'It's too dangerous. You've got two kiddies to think of.'

'The raids are mainly at night,' Judy pointed out. 'If I catch an early train I can get over to Hackney, pick Auntie Lily up and be on a train back before the raids start.'

Maggie wasn't happy about it and neither was Bill but they could both see how determined she was.

'I can't just sit back and do nothing.' she told them. 'She's always been like a real grandma to me. I can't bear the idea of her alone up there in the blitz night after night.'

Seeing that she was adamant, Maggie made her sandwiches for the journey and Judy caught the six o'clock train from Summerton station on Sunday morning. It was after midday when she arrived at Liverpool Street.

Stepping out into the street she was horrified at the bomb damage. It was far worse than she had imagined. Clearly there had been a raid the previous night and some of the bombed buildings were still smoking. Everywhere looked so different. So many of the familiar landmarks had gone, but the buses were running and she took one to Hackney. She alighted at the bus stop and looked around her. The devastation was unbelievable; so bad that she felt disorientated, but bit by bit, going by buildings that were still standing, she picked her way to Clare Street where she had grown up with Christine and Harry and Auntie Lily.

Turning the corner she came to a sudden stop. It was as though her feet were glued to the ground. She could hardly believe her eyes. The whole street was laid waste. Nothing was left apart from piles of bricks and blackened, broken beams. Her heart began to pound and a huge lump thickened her throat. No one could have survived this, she told herself. Picking her way through the sooty puddles left by the firemen's hoses, the blackened rubble and the bomb craters, she tried to find number 28, Auntie Lily's house. Here and there were pathetic reminders of the people who had

lived there, a broken doll; a smashed picture, even a piece of knit-
ting, still attached to its needles. There was no way of singling out
any particular house. She was bending to pick up what was left of
a child's hair ribbon when she heard her name called.

'Judy! *Judy* love!'

Turning, she was astonished to see her parents standing at the
end of the wrecked street. Harry held out his arms to her and she
flew into them.

'*Dad! Mum*!' She was crying openly now, sobbing into Harry's
shoulder. 'Poor Auntie Lily. I came to get her – take her back with
us, If only she'd listened to me.'

'I know, love,' Harry soothed. 'I know.'

They found a café, its windows boarded up but still open for
business. Over a pot of tea Harry explained. 'We're on leave and
we came to see Lily yesterday. We were going to try and persuade
her to come to Norfolk with us when we came to see you. It was
going to be a surprise.' He shook his head. 'But we were too late.'

Christine took up the story. 'When we saw the street had been
bombed we thought there might just be a chance she'd gone to
the shelter, so we found the local ARP warden. He sent us to the
church hall that's being used as a community centre. It was where
they'd taken all the bombed-out survivors. We asked around and
found Mrs Jeffs who lived next door. She told us that Lily never
went to the shelters – didn't believe in them, she said; wouldn't
leave her home. They all tried really hard to get her to go but she
wouldn't budge.' Christine took out her handkerchief and dabbed
at her eyes. 'Stubborn old girl,' she said. 'Nothing would ever
change her, rest her soul.'

'Did they – find her?' Judy asked fearfully.

Harry nodded. 'Your mum and I went to the mortuary and iden-
tified her.' He grimaced. 'Well, as best we could. At least it would
have been instantaneous. She wouldn't have known anything
about it.'

'And the – funeral?' Judy asked.

'There was a mass burial for all the victims this morning.'

Judy gasped. 'So soon!' She looked at them. 'You went? You
stayed over last night?'

Harry nodded. 'We spent last night down the Underground; never got a wink of sleep.'

'You must come back to Summerton and spend the rest of your leave with me.' Judy said.

Harry nodded. 'That was what we intended. We were going to send you a telegram to say we were on our way.' He looked at his watch. 'And we better get moving before the raids start again.'

CHAPTER FIVE

Maggie and Bill were surprised when Judy returned with her parents in tow but they welcomed them with their usual warm hospitality. They were greatly relieved to see Judy back safe and sound, though sad to hear the news about Auntie Lily and horrified at Judy's description of the devastation in London.

Introductions were made all round and the children were excited to see their grandparents. Maggie rustled up a makeshift meal of eggs and chips and over it they all listened to Christine and Harry's news.

'We've been entertaining the troops at camps up and down the country,' Harry told them. 'You should have seen some of the places we've stayed at. One week it'd be some lovely posh guest house, the next we'd be in a draughty hostel with hot and cold running cockroaches!'

Christine laughed. 'Not to mention some of the transport we've had – anything from luxury coaches to removal vans.'

Maggie and Bill were intrigued and wanted to know if anyone famous had been on the bill with them.

'All the big stars are required to do six weeks a year for ENSA,' Harry told them. 'But so far we haven't worked with any of the big names. Maybe when we go abroad…'

Christine shot him a look. '*If* we go, that is.'

'Is it likely?' Judy asked anxiously.

Harry pulled a face. 'Well – it's on the cards that after this leave we might get an overseas tour, but it's not definite, so don't go saying anything. You know – careless talk etcetera.'

After the uncomfortable and traumatic day and night in London

Christine and Harry were grateful for hot baths and a comfortable bed but before they retired Christine went to the kitchen and handed Maggie their emergency ration coupons.

'We don't intend to deprive you of your precious rations,' she said. 'It's so kind of you to put us up at short notice like this.'

Maggie smiled as she gratefully slipped the coupons into her apron pocket. 'Not at all. We're well used to visitors. It's been our life for the past thirty years. It's lovely to meet you, Christine. Judy has told us so much about you that we feel we know you both already.'

Christine smiled. 'It's a relief to know the three of them have somewhere nice to stay. She's written so much about you in her letters, and about her job at the theatre and how much the children like their school. It's such a relief not to have to worry about them.'

'They're like the family we never had, bless them.' Silently Maggie wondered if Judy had written about Sid and his disgusting behaviour, but she said nothing. Knowing Judy she guessed that she would have kept quiet about it.

The next morning Harry went along and booked two seats for the following night's performance at the Little Theatre.

'We must get a look at the place where you're working,' he told Judy. 'Then we can visualize you there when we're away.'

'A while ago I did some work for the front-of-house manager in his office,' Judy said. 'I really enjoyed it.'

'Why were you working in the office?' Christine asked.

Judy blushed. 'Oh – just to help out,' she said. 'Mr Broughton's secretary is expecting a baby and she's been quite poorly. She'll be leaving soon.'

'Maybe you'll get her job,' Harry said.

Judy shook her head. 'No, I'd have to be able to type,' she told him.

'Then why not learn?'

Judy stared at her father. 'Me! Learn to type and do shorthand?'

'Well, why not? 'Specially if it earns you a better job. There must be some evening classes.'

'You're forgetting; I work in the evenings,' Judy pointed out.

Harry shrugged. 'Of course you do. But think about it, love. It wouldn't be a bad idea if you could manage it; a chance to better yourself.'

The trip to the theatre was a great success. The repertory company were playing a Noel Coward comedy that week and Harry and Christine came home in high spirits. Judy joined them as soon as she finished work and while Maggie was making a bedtime drink in the kitchen Harry wandered into the large room at the front of the house that was normally reserved for the visitors. Finding an upright piano in there he opened the lid and ran his hands over the keys. The piano was slightly out of tune but the sound of music soon brought Judy to the door.

'Dad, we don't come in here,' she whispered. 'It's the visitors' lounge and it's not in use for now.'

But Maggie had heard the music too and hurried through the hall to join her. 'That sounds lovely,' she said. 'It's so long since anyone played the piano.' She smiled shyly at Harry. 'What if we have our cocoa in here and you give us a tune?'

'We'll do better than that,' Christine, chimed in, joining them in the doorway. 'We'll give you a little taste of our new act if you like.' She slipped an arm round Judy's shoulders. 'You haven't heard us do our routine, have you?' She looked at Harry. 'That all right, love?'

He grinned. 'You bet. Don't want to get rusty, do we?'

Bill joined them and put a match to the gas fire; Maggie brought in the tray of cocoa and biscuits and Christine stepped up to join Harry at the piano.

'Ladies and gentleman, may I present the Musical Mitchells,' she said. 'Songs old and new at the piano for your entertainment.' She nodded to Harry who began to play.

Judy had only heard her mother sing in the kitchen before and now she was surprised by her strong soprano voice. She sang *A Nightingale Sang in Berkeley Square* and the *White Cliffs of Dover* as well as some pre-war songs. They finished with *We're Gonna Hang out the Washing on the Siegfried Line* with Maggie, Bill and Judy joining in enthusiastically. At the end they all clapped.

'Well, that was champion and no mistake,' Bill said. 'I reckon you must go down a treat with the boys.'

'Well, they do seem to like us,' Christine said modestly.

'Come and have your cocoa now,' Maggie urged. 'I reckon you deserve it; performing for us when you're on holiday.'

On the following day, when Charlie was proudly showing her grandparents her painting book, Suzie came out with a disturbing remark. Charlie was showing them the rainbow she had painted with her mother's help on their first day in Summerton-on-Sea.

'We saw a real one in the sky the first evening,' she explained. 'Mum says a rainbow means promises.'

'It didn't keep the promise you asked for,' Suzie piped up.

Harry laughed and pulled his little granddaughter onto his knee. 'Naughty old rainbow,' he said. 'What promise was that, then?'

Suzie glanced at her sister. 'She wanted it to promise that Dad wouldn't shout at us any more – but he *did*.'

The smile vanished from Harry's face. 'When was that, sweetheart?' he asked gently.

'When he came home,' Suzie said. She was eyeing her sister warily, seeing the telltale glint in Charlie's eye. 'He hit Mum too,' she added defiantly. 'And made her face go all funny.'

'You're not supposed to *tell*!' Charlie shouted. 'Mum said not to say anything.'

Harry gave Suzie a hug. 'She didn't mean to us, Charlie,' he said. 'We're family. You didn't do anything wrong, Suzie love. Off you go and play now, the pair of you.'

When the children had gone he looked at his wife. 'If I had that bastard here now I'd wring his scrawny neck for him,' he said angrily. 'I wish I'd never insisted on him marrying her. I reckon this has been going on for some time. You heard what that child said.'

Christine nodded. 'I know. I've had my suspicions. Well, at least he'll be out of the way for some time if he gets sent abroad,' she said. 'Don't say anything to Judy for now. We don't want to upset her, do we? We might not see them all again for some time.'

But later, when she was helping Maggie in the kitchen she tried to draw the older woman out, wondering if she knew about Sid's behaviour.

'Sometimes I wonder if all is as well as it could be with Judy and Sid,' she said. 'She's a loyal girl and I know she'd never complain but there have been times when I've wondered if her life was as happy as she made out.'

Maggie was peeling potatoes at the sink and she hesitated, her hands suddenly still. 'I have to say this, Christine,' she said at last. 'I can't help it but I don't like that man at all. I know he's fighting for his country, but the way he was with Judy and those precious babies when he was here on leave made my blood boil – Bill's too.'

She turned to face Christine. 'I'm not one to pry or interfere but we couldn't help hearing him yelling at her, poor girl, in their room of a night.' She paused. 'And then there was that awful black eye and swollen face on his last night. She *said* she was attacked in the blackout coming out of work, but she all but admitted it to me in the end. Not that I hadn't guessed. It was a funny thing to me that he left so sudden like, without saying as much as a goodbye or by-your-leave.'

She turned and put the potatoes into a saucepan. 'There – I've gone and said too much, haven't I? Now you'll go away and worry about her.'

Christine shook her head. 'At least if he's been posted overseas he won't be bothering her for some time,' she said. 'And don't worry; you were right to speak up. I'm grateful that she's got people like you and Bill to look after her. That takes a load off our minds, believe me.'

Later she tried to talk to Judy about Sid's behaviour but she refused to be drawn.

'I daresay he worries about us all,' she said, averting her eyes. 'It can't be easy, being away from your wife and kids.'

'Does that mean he has the right to abuse you when he comes on leave?' Christine asked angrily. 'What can he possibly have to complain about, shouting the odds and throwing his weight about?'

Judy bit her lip. 'He gets jealous – thinks I'm looking at other men.'

'And have you ever given him reason to accuse you of cheating on him?

'Of course not, Mum. I've been too busy taking care of the girls.'

'Yes, as he well knows. It's just an excuse to control you.'

'I did try to stand up for myself,' Judy said. 'To make him see that it wasn't the way a husband should behave. But that only made him worse.'

'Oh, Judy. Come here.' Christine gave her daughter a hug. 'I wish your father had never made you marry him,' she said tearfully. 'I know he does too now. At least you've got Maggie and Bill to take care of you for now and maybe your dad and I won't be away for too long. But if he does come home on leave again don't you put up with it.'

Judy smiled. 'I won't. Don't worry about us, Mum. We'll be fine.'

Christine and Harry stayed for a week but before they left Harry had another word with Judy about the typing lessons.

'Do think about looking into it, love,' he urged. 'You're a bright girl. You'd soon pick it up and you could earn much better money if you had a proper skill. You never know when you might need to be independent.'

Judy knew that he was thinking about Sid and his unreasonable behaviour but she didn't pursue the thought. 'I have been thinking about it, Dad,' she said. 'But it's difficult to find the time.'

Harry hugged his daughter. 'I wish we didn't have to be apart like this,' he said, still thinking about his unspoken worry. 'After the war's over we'll get it all sorted out, don't you worry.'

Judy and the children were sad to wave them off at the station, not knowing when she'd see them again. The Hursts missed them too.

'Your mum and dad were a real tonic,' Maggie said. 'Just what we needed to cheer us all up. It'll be a long time before I forget those lovely sing-songs we all had.' She slipped an arm round Judy's shoulders. 'You're going to miss them, but don't worry. You've still got me and Bill.'

The same night at the theatre Judy confided in Sally about the typing lessons Harry had suggested.

'If only I could type I might get Mr Gresham to give me Carol's job when she leaves,' she said.

Sally's eyes widened. 'My mum used to teach shorthand and typing,' she said. 'I bet she'd give you some lessons.'

'Oh, do you think she would?' Judy's heart gave a leap.

'I'll ask her.' Sally looked thoughtful. 'If you came in the mornings after you'd dropped the girls off at school I could take my David out for a walk in the pushchair. I'll ask Mum tonight,' she said resolutely.

Judy bit her lip. 'Would it be – you know – very expensive?'

Sally laughed. 'I'm sure Mum'd be only too glad to keep her hand in,' she said. 'She only gave up to be there for David and me. Tell you what, if she says yes just bring a jar of coffee and some milk.'

Mrs Carter was more than willing to give Judy some lessons and it was agreed that she should start the week after the Christmas holiday.

Claire Carter was a pretty, dark-haired woman in her early forties. She lived along with her husband, daughter and little grandson in a semi-detached villa on the outskirts of town. Judy took to her straight away. She had an easy-going, patient manner and made the lessons interesting and fun. Sitting together with her and her faithful Olivetti typewriter in the front room of 14 Sunnyside Drive Judy soon got the hang of the typewriter keyboard. The shorthand hieroglyphics were not quite as straightforward and took more studying, but by working hard at the homework Claire gave her she gradually began to master the new skill.

Sally would join them at the end of each lesson, after putting her little son down for his morning sleep. Over cups of coffee they would talk about everything, the war, their children, colleagues at the theatre and the difficulties of managing on the meagre rations. Judy looked forward to her lessons and began to feel her confidence growing day by day.

As January slipped into February and the days lengthened Judy realized that the time had come to speak to Mr Gresham about the job she coveted. Carol's pregnancy had clearly progressed to the stage when she would surely soon have to leave and there was no time to be lost. Screwing up her courage she went in to work early one evening and climbed the stairs behind the box office to tap on the office door. As she heard him call 'Come in' her heartbeat quickened. Would he think it was a cheek, asking outright for Carol's job? Well, there was only one way to find out. Taking a deep breath she opened the door and walked in.

Mr Gresham looked up and his eyebrows rose. 'Judy! This is a surprise. Is everything all right? I hope you haven't come to give me your notice.'

'No – nothing like that.' Judy cleared her throat. Suddenly her voice sounded all squeaky. 'It's just – I wondered – I've been...'

'Oh dear.' He smiled kindly. 'Surely it can't be as bad as all that. Come and sit down and tell me what's bothering you.'

Judy perched on the edge of the chair next to his desk and took another deep breath. 'Well,' she began. 'It's like this. When you asked me to help in the office, that time when I had a – when Carol was away, I enjoyed it very much. I've been taking typing and shorthand lessons since then and I wondered if you'd got anyone in mind for when Carol leaves.' *There* – she'd said it – burnt her boats. He could only say no, couldn't he? She held her breath.

'You've been taking lessons eh?' He looked impressed. 'That was very enterprising of you. You're right; Carol will be leaving in a couple of weeks' time and so far I haven't advertised the job.' Her spirits rose. 'But as a matter of fact my wife is an experienced secretary and she has offered to come in and help out.' Judy's hope plummeted. He smiled. 'But I'm sure she'd be more than happy to be excused the extra work. She's on all sorts of committees, you know: War Orphans and Widows– all that kind of thing.'

'So – you mean..?'

'I mean, yes, the job is still vacant. I take it you're interested.'

'Yes, I am – very.' She looked at him. 'Would you like to give me a test?' she asked tentatively.

'I don't think that will be necessary,' he said. 'I know you're more than capable of running the office. You were very efficient the week when you helped out in Carol's absence. And if you feel confident to handle the typing, which you clearly do, I'm happy. Shall we give each other a trial as we did before – say one month?'

Judy nodded enthusiastically. 'Oh, yes please. Thank you, Mr Gresham.'

He stood up and held out his hand. 'Right. That's settled then – saved me a lot of trouble. Nice to have someone you know you can get along with. You can start a week on Monday if you like, then Carol can show you the ropes before she leaves.'

When Judy arrived back at Sea View bursting with her good news Maggie and Bill were delighted. 'You deserve to get on,' Maggie said. 'I always knew you could do better than the job you were doing.'

'I'll be working normal office hours now,' Judy pointed out. 'It means I'll be here to put the girls to bed and read them a story.'

'And I'll pick them up from school at home time, so no need to worry about that,' Maggie assured her.

Bill was euphoric about the Italians' defeat at Tobruk and, a few weeks later, the capture of Benghazi.

'Field Marshall Wavell knows what he's doing,' he declared. 'If anyone can win the war for us it's him!'

Judy listened to him with a sense of foreboding. Sid was fighting in the Western Desert. She had received the odd postcard from him, heavily censored and telling her nothing much. He assured her that he was all right and said he missed her and the girls. All she could do was hope that the war would mellow him and that he would come home a nicer, more tolerant man.

CHAPTER SIX

When Carol left the staff and cast gave a leaving party for her. She had worked at the Little Theatre ever since she left school, six years before and was very highly thought of. All the staff and company had clubbed together to buy her a cot for the baby. It had been hand-made by the theatre carpenter, and the wardrobe mistress had created beautiful hangings and frilled padding for the interior. When she saw it Carol was moved to tears. Her husband was in the Navy, working on minesweepers and everyone knew how worried she was about him.

Judy and she had worked well together for her last week, Judy learning where everything was kept and with Carol's help familiarizing herself with the daily routine. When she got home on the first afternoon she told Maggie and Bill all about her new job.

'There's a lot more to it than I thought at first,' she told them excitedly. 'There's the upkeep and maintenance of the building as well as cleaning and keeping the furnishings in order. There's drink to order from the brewery and the wine merchants for the bar, all the wages to do – that's for the cleaning staff and usherettes as well as the maintenance man. He used to be called the fireman and all theatres had to have one.'

Maggie looked mystified. 'Why'd they want a fireman?'

'In the days when they used to have candles for footlights,' Judy explained. 'They were always setting fire to the curtains. Theatres were a big fire risk in those days – even after they had gas lighting.'

'Seems like you're learning a lot,' Bill remarked.

'I am,' Judy agreed. 'And then there's what Mr Gresham calls "hiring and firing", although the actors and actresses are taken on by the producer, of course. They have to audition.'

Maggie held up her hands. 'You've learned all that on your first day?'

'Oh, there's still a lot to learn,' Judy told her.

On the morning that she held her new post unaided for the first time Judy felt quite nervous, but Mr Gresham assured her with a very straight face that there was no one on earth who didn't make the odd mistake and that she would surely be forgiven – at least twice. (She never quite knew when he was pulling her leg.)

His routine was that he would spend an hour in the office first thing, dictating letters and giving her orders for the day, then he would be off, either to meetings or around the theatre, attending to the hundred and one administrative things that needed his attention. Later in the afternoon he would drop into the office again to sign his letters. So Judy had to make careful note of any messages and constantly check the diary to make sure that routine tasks didn't get overlooked.

She had been in her new job for about three weeks when suddenly, one morning, the door flew open and a young man in Air Force uniform burst in.

'Never fear, the gunner's here!' he declared loudly. Then, seeing that a startled stranger sat looking up at him from the other side of the desk he stopped short, colouring with embarrassment. 'Oh! Sorry. I thought my Uncle Bob was here.'

Judy couldn't help smiling at his confusion. 'Sorry to disappoint you,' she said. 'I'm just his secretary.' She still couldn't help feeling a little thrill of pride at her new title.

'Don't apologize,' he said, recovering with remarkable speed from his surprise. 'I'm all for a change of scene, specially when it's a pretty one.' He looked around. 'Where's old Carol then?'

'She's left to have her baby.'

'Oh yes, of course.' He perched himself on the edge of her desk. 'So now the dear old Unc has installed you, eh?. Well, he always did have good taste. What do I call you?'

'You don't have to call me anything.' She was a little annoyed at his cheek.

His eyebrows rose. 'Oh, come on. You have to have a name. I am a bit of a fixture round here, so we might as well introduce ourselves.'

'All right then. I'm Mrs Truman,' she said a little stiffly.

He pulled a downcast face. 'Aah, drat it – married! I might have guessed.' He grinned at her unrepentantly. 'Let me present myself – Flight Sergeant Peter Gresham.'

'How do you do.'

'Wow, we *are* formal, aren't we, *Mrs* Truman?' His blue eyes twinkled teasingly at her. 'Come off it; didn't your folks give you a Christian name?'

'Judy,' she told him, repenting a little. 'Look, your uncle is probably still around the theatre somewhere, if you'd like to go and find him.'

'I'm quite happy to wait for him here, thank you, Judy.' He peered at her. 'Is that a London accent I hear?'

She flushed. 'Yes. Me and my children were evacuated here.'

His eyebrows rose. 'Children too! And you hardly out of school. How many?'

'Two,' she said. 'Both girls.' She fidgeted with the papers on the desk. 'So if that's all, Mr Gresham…'

'Peter, please.' He looked at his watch. 'By the way, isn't it about coffee time?'

With a sigh Judy got up and put the kettle on, made coffee and found some plain biscuits left in the tin.

Peter took one and examined it disapprovingly. 'Rich tea! This the best you can do?'

'I'm afraid it is,' she told him. 'In case you haven't noticed there's a war on.'

He slapped his forehead. 'Well, damn me, so there is! I wondered why all those German pilots kept trying to shoot us out of the sky.'

She looked away, feeling rather foolish. 'You're stationed near here, are you?' she asked, glancing up at him over the rim of her cup.

'Not that far away. Bircham Newton. Bomber Command. My folks live here though, so I pop over when ever I get a few days' leave.'

As he drank his coffee Judy took a proper look at him. He was tallish – she guessed around five-ten. Slim too, though his shoulders were quite broad. He had nice dark wavy hair and was quite good-looking in a cheeky kind of way. *He probably thinks a lot of himself,* she told herself as she watched him help himself to the last of the biscuits.

'So – what does *Mr* Truman do?' he asked her.

'He's in the army – fighting in the Western Desert at the moment.'

'Mmm – tough. I'd hate to be cooped up in one of those sardine cans in all that heat.'

'Sardine cans?'

'Tanks,' he explained. 'A bomber is bad enough but *tanks*…' He shook his head. 'Phew! I get claustrophobia just thinking about it.'

'It can't be all that comfortable in a plane,' Judy replied. 'Are you a pilot?'

'*Me*?' He laughed. 'Nothing so glamorous! I'm a "Tail-End Charlie" – a rear gunner. A sitting target most of the time.'

To his delight she looked shocked. 'That sounds much worse than being in a tank,' she said. 'At least they're on the ground.'

The door opened and Bob Gresham came in. 'Peter! Mrs James in the box office said you were here.' He clapped his nephew on the shoulder. 'Good to see you, lad. I hope Judy here has been entertaining you.'

Peter slid off the desk and stood up straight. 'Yes, admirably, though I'm afraid I've kept her from her work.'

'Look, if you want to wait for me downstairs in the foyer I'll just have a quick word with Judy and then I'll join you.'

Peter put his cap on again and saluted. 'OK, Unc. Your wish is my command.' He looked across at Judy and winked. 'Thanks for the chat, Judy and the coffee and biscuits. See you around, eh?'

Bob Gresham grinned as his nephew closed the door behind him. 'He's a bright spark,' he said affectionately. 'My brother's oldest boy. Straight from college into the RAF. I don't know what these boys are going to do for a career once the war's over.'

'Do you want some coffee, Mr Gresham? I'm afraid your – er – Peter has eaten all the biscuits.'

He laughed. 'No, I'll pass on the coffee for now. I expect Peter will want to go for a liquid lunch. As for the biscuits, we can't grudge him those, can we? Not when he risks his life every night of the week.'

Judy thought a lot about Peter Gresham as she walked home that evening. She decided to ask Bill just what a rear gunner did. His uncle said he risked his life every night of the week, yet he seemed as though he hadn't a care in the world. Was that how servicemen in the front line coped?

When she arrived home Maggie was in a twitter. 'I've had a phone call from some people who stayed here the summer before the war started,' she explained. 'Two young couples, both on their honeymoons. They chummed up and now the chaps are on embarkation leave and they want to have a few days' holiday again together just as they did back then.'

'Oh, that's nice,' Judy said. 'When do they want to come?'

'Saturday,' Maggie said. 'They're from Southampton so they won't be here till late-ish.'

'That gives us plenty of time to get ready then,' Judy said.

Maggie looked as though she was regretting her decision already. 'I don't know. We haven't had any visitors since '39,' she said. 'There's the beds to air and the dining room hasn't been used for ages. And what on earth am I going to give them to eat?'

She sounded quite panicky and Judy patted her arm. 'I take it you've said yes?'

Maggie nodded. 'How could I refuse them, bless their hearts? We've got the rooms all right. But...' She bit her lip.

'Will they have bed and breakfast?' Judy asked.

'They asked for an evening meal as well,' Maggie told her.

'Well, don't worry. We'll manage between us somehow,' Judy said soothingly.

'Trouble is the rationing,' Maggie said. 'Bill and me planned to retire so we never gave a thought to how we'd manage with that.'

'They'll bring their emergency ration coupons like Mum and Dad did,' Judy said. 'There's only the four of them. Look, you and I will shop around and see what we can scrounge and I'll help you cook the evening meal when I get home from work.'

Maggie hugged her. 'What would I do without you?' She brightened, suddenly remembering something. 'Maybe the Broughtons can help. I don't really like asking but this is an emergency. I'll give them a ring.'

Farmer Broughton came up trumps. As luck would have it he'd recently killed a pig, and he supplied Maggie with sausages and some rashers of home-cured bacon. He also brought vegetables, eggs and a boiling-fowl, with which Maggie made a casserole and a huge pan of soup. Judy worked with her all Saturday afternoon, making the two double rooms at the front of the house as bright and comfortable as they could.

The Browns and the Pagets declared when they left that their second honeymoons had been as wonderful as their first and that Maggie Hurst was their fairy godmother. She waved them off with a tear in her eye, first extracting promises from them that they would return again as soon as they could.

'I couldn't have managed without you,' Maggie said slipping an arm round Judy as they watched the taxi draw away. 'You were a real natural. Anyone'd think you'd been in the business all your life.'

In fact, Judy had surprised herself during the visitors' short stay. She had enjoyed herself enormously despite the extra work. Bill had kept Charlie and Suzie quiet and occupied whilst she had helped Maggie to cook the evening meal. She had risen early each day to make morning tea and carried the two dainty trays upstairs, and when the evening meal was ready to serve she had doubled as waitress. She had even made out their bill, typing it professionally on the office typewriter, much to Maggie's admiration.

The guests were very appreciative and had given her an envelope at the end of the week, containing a sizeable tip. She had handed it straight over but Maggie had shaken her head and pushed it back into her hand.

'No! That's yours,' she said adamantly. 'You've worked hard for that. Take the kiddies out and enjoy yourselves.'

Bill had explained to Judy that many of the piers in south-coast towns had been blown up to foil an invasion, but luckily the pier at Summerton was still intact. Because of the lack of summer visitors, though, most of the usual entertainments had been curtailed. Only one show had resumed since the war began and that was the Marie Germaine puppet theatre. They had always set up their show at the pier head at the end of June each year but now they were only to be open during the school holidays as part of the town's Holidays At Home project. Their advertisement in the local paper read: *Puppet plays to delight young and old alike. Three performances daily.*

Judy read out the advertisement to Charlie and Suzie. 'Would you like to go on Saturday afternoon?' she asked them

'Oooh, yes please,' both girls chorused.

Now that she worked in the office Judy had Saturday afternoons off and this week she dressed the girls in their best summer dresses and brushed their hair neatly.

'If you're really good we'll have our tea out afterwards at the Tudor Tearooms,' she told them. Both girls danced up and down with excitement.

The entrance to the puppet theatre was decked with red, white and blue bunting. Judy paid for their admission at the door and they went inside. The little auditorium was almost full but they managed to find seats quite close to the front. A tiny stage had been erected, complete with proscenium arch and bright blue velvet curtains. As they settled down soft music began to drift out and the curtains were drawn jerkily back to reveal a brightly painted set.

The play was a version of *Cinderella* and soon the little girls were enthralled by the puppets in their colourful costumes. Judy watched their eyes grow rounder as they became completely absorbed by the music and atmosphere. To them it was as real as if they were watching real people perform. The audience, which was mostly made up of children, clapped excitedly when at last the little curtains twitched shut and the show was over.

'Did you like it?' Judy asked them.

Both girls nodded enthusiastically. 'It was lovely. Can we come again?' Charlie asked.

'We'll see. Only if you're very good.'

'I always hated hearing that, mainly because I found it so hard to live up to!'

Judy spun round, surprised by the voice behind her. She was even more surprised to see Peter Gresham, her boss's nephew, smiling at her.

'These two yours?' he asked.

Judy nodded. 'This is Charlotte and that's Suzie.'

He bent to shake hands solemnly. 'How do you do, ladies. Did you enjoy the show?' Both girls nodded shyly; even Charlie was struck dumb by this charming young man in the blue uniform.

'Do you often go to children's shows?' Judy asked him with a wry smile.

'Only when they're performed by my parents,' Peter told her.

'Your parents?'

'Yes. Marie Germaine is my mother.

'Oh. Is she French?'

He laughed. 'Gawd, no! Her real name is Mary German, at least it was before she married my dad. Marie Germaine sounds more theatrical. Besides, who wants to be called German at the moment?'

Judy smiled. 'I see. You're on leave again?'

'Only for a forty-eight.' He grinned at the girls and rubbed his hands. 'So – where are you off to now?'

'We're having our tea out at the Tudor Tearooms,' Charlie told him proudly.

He straightened up and regarded them with wide eyes. 'You don't say! What a coincidence! That's *exactly* where I'm going. Shall we all go together?'

To Judy's surprise Suzie reached up to take his hand. 'Yes please,' she whispered.

As they ate their tea, toasted teacakes and jam, followed by fancy cakes, Peter told Judy all about his parents' puppet theatre.

'They've been running it ever since I can remember. It was Mum to begin with: her father was a puppeteer; it goes back a long way in her family, and he taught her when she was a small child how to make puppets and string them and manipulate. Dad worked at the boat-yard back then. He used to be a master boat-builder, but she taught him all about puppets and they started the theatre and ran it in his spare time. When my brother and I grew old enough we became part of the show. Paul, my brother has always done the music – backstage with a gramophone, and we both helped with the voices. Later Mum and Dad taught us the art of manipulation.'

'So it's a family affair?' Judy said. 'Were you helping today?'

He laughed. 'Didn't you recognize the voice of the fairy godmother?'

Judy spluttered over her tea. '*No!* Not really?'

'Oh yes, really. I can cackle with the best of 'em.' His face grew serious. 'My brother Paul is eighteen so he'll be called up before long and I can't be relied on at the moment so it looks as though Mum and Dad will have to train someone else up. Either that or stop running the theatre.'

He insisted on paying the bill. When Judy protested he grinned and said. 'Let's call it making up to you for eating all the office biscuits at our last meeting.'

He also insisted on walking back to Sea View with them. At the gate he said. 'See you next time I'm home, Judy.'

'Maybe,' she said. 'And thanks for the tea. You really shouldn't have paid for us though.'

'Thank you for the company,' he said. ''Bye, Judy. Bye girls. See you around.'

Charlie and Suzie couldn't wait to tell Maggie and Bill all about their afternoon.

'It was about Cinderella,' Charlie said as Judy helped her off with her coat. 'She was all in rags at the beginning but then she went to the ball and met the prince.'

'The old lady turned into a fairy and magicked Cinderella a lovely dress,' Suzie chimed in. 'It was pink and all sparkly.'

'Yes and the prince was called Charlie like me,' Charlie added.

Judy laughed. '*Charming*. His name was Prince Charming.'

Charlie looked disappointed. 'Oh – well, anyway she had to run away 'cos it was midnight.'

'But he found her shoe and he looked for her and in the end she and Charlie got married,' Suzie finished triumphantly.

Charlie nudged her. '*Charming*, not Charlie,' she corrected. 'Mum said.'

Suzie looked at her mother. 'Mum – is Peter a prince?'

Judy shook her head. 'No, of course not.'

Maggie looked at her. 'Peter?'

'His parents run the puppet theatre,' she explained. 'He's Mr

Gresham's nephew, I met him when he was last home on leave from the RAF. He dropped into the office to see his uncle.'

'Did he now?' Maggie raised an eyebrow.

'He's ever so handsome,' Charlie said. 'He came with us to the Tudor Tearooms and he paid for our tea.'

'Well, fancy that!' Maggie exchanged a meaningful look with Bill which didn't escape Judy's notice. She'd always been so proud of her elder daughter's intelligent perception but there were times when she could have wished her less talkative.

CHAPTER SEVEN

Sea View had quite a few bookings over the summer of 1941. Servicemen on leave with their wives mainly, looking for a much needed break somewhere safe from the bombing. Maggie and Bill made them welcome and Judy helped as much as she could.

When the school holidays came round Charlie and Suzie spent most of their days playing on the beach. They played contentedly from early morning till Judy coaxed them home to tea. They loved the sea and revelled in the freedom to play in the sunshine. They grew brown and healthier week by week, mercifully oblivious in their youthful innocence of the ferocious and savage war raging throughout the world.

Bill continued to shake his head over the newspapers and BBC bulletins. The bombing on London and other cities was terrifying in its intensity.

Summerton-on-Sea continued to be comparatively safe. Occasionally the air-raid siren would sound late at night and Judy and the Hursts would listen apprehensively to the throbbing engines of the German bombers as they flew overhead on their way to a raid. But although it was nerve-racking it was rare for bombs to drop anywhere near the coast. Sometimes it was possible from the windows of Sea View to see British fighter planes attacking a squadron of German bombers over the sea; a spectacle which made Maggie shudder but which fascinated Bill. When the news broke that the Germans had invaded Russia he was full of foreboding. In the Western Desert the Desert Rats – of which Sid was now one – continued to fight Rommel's Afrika Korps, sabotaging his lines of supply and moving inexorably towards Cyrenaica.

Judy learned all the war news from the news bulletins and little or nothing first hand from Sid. His postcards, which arrived very infrequently, contained no information and what there was had always been heavily censored before they reached her. They were written in a stilted manner as though to a complete stranger and never asked after the children. They were in direct contrast to the ones she received from Harry and Christine, now touring RAF stations in Scotland. These were written mostly by Christine, who had a way with words. Her letters were full of amusing anecdotes and stories about their fellow performers and some of the interesting – occasionally famous – people they were appearing with.

Judy's job at the theatre continued to be rewarding and enjoyable. Peter dropped into the office at the theatre whenever he got leave, or managed to buzz over from Bircham Newton in his little car to snatch a few hours with his family. He was always the same, teasing her with his mischievous jokes. She came to look forward to his visits and always made sure that there were some biscuits in the office tin.

On one occasion when he was on a forty-eight hour leave he invited Judy to bring the girls to meet his parents and be introduced to their large cast of puppets.

Bob Gresham's brother, Steve and his wife, Mary lived in a rambling Victorian house on the edge of town. At the rear of the house was a barn, which they rented. Mary took Judy and the girls out to see it. As they climbed the wooden staircase she explained how they had come to rent it.

'It used to belong to a carpenter and when he put it up for rent we thought it would make a good storehouse for the puppets,' she said. 'There were so many that they took up several rooms in the house and we needed the space. But once we'd got it, it seemed a waste just to use it for storage, so we hit on the idea of making it into a private theatre. We give occasional shows here for friends and family and everyone seems to love it.'

At the top of the staircase was a little balcony with colourful flower boxes. The girls were enchanted. Mary opened the door to reveal a perfect miniature theatre with six rows of comfortable seats facing a tiny stage like the one they had seen at the pierhead.

She turned to the girls. 'Would you like to come backstage and see how it all works?'

They both nodded shyly and followed Mary through a curtain beside the stage. At the back was a platform on which the puppeteers stood to manipulate the puppets. There was also a bench on which stood a record player and a shelf of labelled records. Then there were hooks all along the back wall.

'The puppets hang on those,' Mary explained. 'And we have to hang them in order of appearance before the show starts so that we can quickly grab the next "actor" without a delay.'

'There's a lot more to it than you'd think,' Judy observed. 'It's all down to your skill that it all looks so effortless.'

Mary smiled. 'Well, thank you,' she said. 'But we have been doing it for quite a long time; in my case since childhood. It becomes second nature.' She pointed to the shelf of labelled records. 'Each play has its own music and each play has its own set of puppets.' She turned to the girls. 'Unlike real live actors who can play any part, the puppets can only do one character.' She smiled at the girls. 'And I'll let you into a little secret. There has to be a separate puppet for every costume change.' Charlie and Suzie looked up at her with round eyes. 'You see, once they are strung we can't take their costumes off.'

Judy laughed. 'Now I see why you have so many that you needed a special storeroom.'

Mary nodded. 'Come and see.' She opened another door at the back. There, hanging all around the small room on rows of hooks were dozens of puppets in every kind of costume imaginable.

'Steve and I make and string them all,' Mary told them. 'I know we call them puppets, but really they are called marionettes. Steve writes the plays and I make all the costumes and choose the music.' She looked at the girls whose mouths were open with amazement. 'Would you like to learn how to make them dance?'

'Ooh, yes please!' they chorused .

'Come and choose which one you'd like, then.'

Charlie chose a court jester but Suzie chose a princess in a spangled pink dress. The very one that had impressed her in

Cinderella. Luckily neither had complicated controls and with great patience Mary showed them how to work the strings and turn the little wooden dolls into the magical living characters they were so fascinated by.

Mary told them they were doing very well as they reluctantly handed the puppets back. 'I'll tell you what,' she said with a smile. 'Next time we give a barn show, as we call them, you and your mummy will have to come along. Would you like that?'

Both girls nodded enthusiastically.

Peter walked them home later, laughing as he listened to the girls' excited chatter about the lovely afternoon they'd had.

'Thank you for this afternoon,' Judy said as they reached the gate of Sea View.

He shook his head. 'Mum loves kids and she loves showing off her puppets too,' he said. 'And it gave me an excuse to be with you away from the office.'

Judy felt her cheeks colour and her eyes couldn't quite meet his as she said. 'I had a lovely time too, Peter. Thanks again.'

When she put them to bed that night Charlie and Suzie were full of their day out. They talked non-stop about the Greshams' lovely house and the enchanting barn theatre. But most of their enthusiasm was reserved for the puppets and the delight of learning how to manipulate them.

'Can we go there again soon, Mum?' Charlie begged.

'Ooh yes, can we?' Suzie echoed.

Judy laughed. 'It's not up to me,' she told them. 'Anyway, it's manners to wait till you're invited.'

'But Peter's mum did say she'd invite us to a show,' Charlie reminded her. 'When will that be?'

'I'm sure it will be soon,' Judy said, tucking them in. 'You'll just have to be patient.'

In late August Carol gave birth to a baby boy and a month later her husband's ship was torpedoed, going down with all hands. Judy went to see her, taking a small present for the baby and found her looking pale and drawn with grief. Her parents wanted her to move back in with them, she told Judy, but she was determined to keep her home and her independence.

'As soon as the baby is old enough to leave with Mum I intend to look for another job,' she told Judy, who felt guilty that she was holding down the job that Carol had loved. She wondered if Mr Gresham would ask her to leave, under the circumstances. She felt selfish, hoping that it wouldn't happen, but she needed the money. She received no money from Sid, a fact which she kept to herself. It was something of which she was vaguely ashamed, even though it wasn't her fault. She managed reasonably well on what she earned but if she lost her job she'd no idea how she'd cope.

She wondered if Mr Gresham would expect her and the girls to return to London as soon as the war was over. Going back was something Judy thought about a lot. She loved Summerton-on-Sea and more especially, living at Sea View with Maggie and Bill. The idea of returning to Hackney to live with Sid in near poverty, as they had before the war, dismayed her more than she cared to admit. She remembered with a shudder the lack of hygienic facilities and the creeping mould on the walls, created by the damp. Charlie had suffered from bad chests every winter ever since she was a baby.

Most of the girls she knew at the theatre had husbands in the forces, and they all longed for nothing more than their return and to resume a normal married life. For Judy it was very different. If she had ever been in any doubt she now knew without question that she did not love Sid. It was more than obvious that he did not love her either. Anything she might once have felt for him had been stamped out by his violent, controlling ways. Dad had forced them into marriage, which Sid had always resented, seeing it more as a punishment than a joy. And having married her he had always demanded that she repaid the debt he felt she owed him a hundredfold. At sixteen Judy had had little experience but she knew from her own parents' example that it was no way to conduct a marriage. If it hadn't been for her mother and Auntie Lily she wouldn't have had a clue when it came to bringing up babies or housekeeping.

The girls had no real bond with their father either. He had always failed to see that the respect he demanded of them had to be earned, not born out of fear. Most of the time she tried not to think about it; carrying on with life and pushing thoughts of the future into the background. But at the back of her mind there was always the nagging certainty that one day it would have to be faced.

Carol's newly widowed situation brought home to Judy the danger that Peter Gresham faced. She had asked Bill once to explain to her the role of a rear gunner and had been shocked by the perils that seemingly carefree Peter faced almost every day. Once when they were sharing coffee in the office she had asked him to tell her about it.

He gave her a wry smile. 'When a fighter plane moves in close for the attack, you sometimes get to look right into the pilot's face,' he said. 'It makes it personal. In that moment it's him or you, and there's always that split second of hesitation on both your parts. It's whoever fires first.' He paused. 'And, by God, it had better be you.'

They'd both been silent for a moment. 'War's a filthy business,' Peter said at last. She looked at him. He was so young; she guessed that, like her, he was in his early twenties – far too young to be facing sudden death every day. Sometimes, when he wasn't smiling, he looked drawn and very vulnerable. Without even thinking about it she had reached out to touch his hand. His fingers closed round hers and he squeezed them warmly, his bright smile returning.

In mid September the girls returned to school, leaving their beloved beach behind. They had grown so much during the holidays. Charlie was growing tall and beginning to fill out, whilst Suzie seemed as small and delicately built as ever. As she left them at the school gates on the first day of the new term Judy felt inordinately proud of her two beautiful children.

At the end of October Peter's plane was badly shot up during a bombing raid and he received a bullet wound to his left arm and shoulder. She learned about it from his grave-faced uncle one morning when he arrived late at the theatre.

'He was lucky – if you can call it that,' he told her. 'A couple of inches to the right and it would have hit his heart. It was thanks to the pilot's skill that the plane got home safely.' She learned that there were two other casualties besides Peter. They had all been sent to a military hospital near Norwich where Peter had had surgery on his injured arm and shoulder.

A couple of weeks later Bob gave her the news that his nephew had been moved to a convalescent home in the country.

'How would you like to come with me to see him on Sunday, Judy? I know it would cheer him up to see you. They've just told him that he won't be allowed to fly for quite a while after this and he's feeling a bit down.'

Judy felt her face flush warmly. 'Oh! I'd love to go. Thanks for inviting me.'

He nodded, smiling. 'I've managed to wangle a few extra petrol coupons so we'll drive over. I'll pick you up at about ten o'clock, OK?'

She nodded. 'That would be fine. I'll be ready.'

When she told the girls they begged to be allowed to go too, but she explained that children certainly would not be allowed. Maggie looked sceptical and later in the kitchen as they prepared the evening meal together she glanced at Judy.

'You think a lot of that young man, don't you?'

Judy turned away to hide the blush that coloured her cheeks. 'I think he's very brave,' she said.

'That's not what I asked,' Maggie persisted. 'I know he's attractive and you enjoy his company, love. And who can blame you. But do you think it's wise to see so much of him?'

'I can't help it if he drops into the office to see his uncle, can I?' Judy said defensively. 'And I couldn't refuse to go and visit him in hospital, could I?'

Maggie turned away with a rueful smile. 'No, of course not,' she said. 'I'm not criticizing you, Judy. Don't think that. But Peter is a free agent. And you're not.'

'You don't need to remind me,' Judy said bitterly.

'It's just that when Sid comes home he's bound to get to hear about your friendship with Peter, if it's only from the kiddies.'

'You think I've involved them too?'

'No, but they're bound to say something.'

'I can't go to work every day without seeing any men.'

'You know how he was last time,' Maggie went on, ignoring

Judy's defensiveness. 'You don't want to go through that again.'

Judy turned to face her. 'You think I shouldn't go and see Peter in hospital, don't you?' she said accusingly. 'And you think I should make myself scarce when he comes to the office. Maybe I should wear a bag over my head!'

Maggie looked startled. '*Judy!* There's no need for that, love. I'm only warning you – for your own good.'

Immediately contrite, Judy shook her head, tears filling her eyes. 'Oh, Maggie, I'm sorry. I shouldn't have snapped at you like that. Yes, I do like Peter – a lot; probably because he's so different from Sid. Apart from my dad he's the nicest man I've ever met. But I haven't forgotten that I'm married – to a man who's fighting for his country just as Peter is. I know nothing can ever come of my friendship with him and I'd never let it.'

Maggie put her arms round her. 'Oh, Judy love, I never meant you were doing anything wrong. I know you better than that. Just be careful not to let your feelings get out of hand, that's all. *Liking* can quickly become something else and I'd hate to see you hurt.'

Bob Gresham arrived on time on Sunday morning and found Judy ready and waiting. During the week she'd been wondering what to wear. Apart from a couple of plain skirts and blouses to wear for the office she hadn't bought herself anything new since before the war. And now of course even clothing was rationed. The previous afternoon she had suddenly made up her mind and gone into town armed with her new book of clothing coupons and the money she had been saving from her wages and the tips she had received from visitors. Looking round the shops she had spotted a pretty suit. It had a softly pleated skirt and a smart jacket nipped in at the waist with two patch pockets in the fashionable military style. It was in her favourite colour, a deep rose-pink, which complimented her fair colouring. At home she had washed her hair, brushing it into its soft, natural blond curls to tumble round her shoulders. When she was ready Charlie and Suzie stared at her in admiration.

'Ooh, Mum, you look lovely,' Charlie said.

'Yes,' Suzie echoed. 'As pretty as Cinderella.'

Bill smiled at her across the breakfast table. 'She's not wrong there. You look a right little bobby-dazzler!'

Maggie smiled but said nothing. Judy knew all too well what she was thinking but she told herself that it was no more than her duty to look nice for Peter, just as she would have done for Sid if it had been him.

The drive to Norwich was pleasant in Bob Gresham's car, a pre-war Rover. Judy had wondered if she would feel awkward and find conversation difficult but she needn't have worried. On their day out together Bob was relaxed and pleasant and chatted freely all the way about the theatre and his family. Maggie had made a packed lunch for them both, along with a flask of tea, and they stopped at the roadside to share it.

The convalescent home was a large country house on the outskirts of Norwich which had been requisitioned for the purpose. Although it was October the day was warm and sunny and many of the patients were sitting or strolling in the gardens. It was there that they found Peter sitting in a wicker chair, his left arm still in a sling. When he saw Judy his face lit up in the familiar sunny smile and he got up out of his chair to greet her and his uncle.

'Thanks for coming,' he said. 'They look after us really well here but it can get deadly boring, sitting around and doing nothing.'

Judy was looking at his arm. 'Does it still hurt?' she asked.

'Only when I laugh!' He grinned, sitting down again. 'The bullet did a good job – smashed a bone at the top of my arm on its way in.' He pulled a face. 'They call it the "humerus" by the way, so when I say 'only when I laugh' you can see why.'

Judy grimaced. 'It sounds horrible.'

He shook his head. 'The quacks have done a smashing job. There's so much metalwork in there that I daren't go near a magnet, but they reckon I'll get the full use back if I stick at the physio.'

'So – you won't be flying again for a while?'

'No, drat it. I expect I'll be flying a desk when I get to report back. That or what they call "light duties" which is another word for all the most boring jobs they can dream up.'

Bob Gresham got to his feet. 'I'll go and see if I can rustle up some tea,' he said, and walked off towards the house, leaving the two of them alone.

'I've missed your visits,' Judy told him shyly.

'Have you missed me too?' He reached for her hand. 'I've thought about you a lot since I've been crocked up.'

'Really?'

There was a small silence between them, then Peter asked, 'How are the girls?'

'They're fine. They wanted to come with me to see you. You've made quite a hit with them.'

'They're great kids.' He paused. 'Mum and Dad thought they were a credit to you. Their own dad must be really proud of them.' Judy didn't reply and he went on. 'You must have been really young when you had them, Judy. I guess that you're about the same age as me, and Charlie's – what, six?'

'Almost seven and a half,' she corrected.

His eyes opened wide. 'Wow! You must have been little more than a kid yourself when you had her.'

'I was. A silly, starry-eyed kid. We all make mistakes.' She blushed. 'Not that I've ever thought of Charlie as a mistake.'

'Course not.' He squeezed the hand he was still holding. 'Are you happy, Judy? Sometimes you look quite wistful.'

She shrugged. 'How many people are really happy, 'specially with a war on? Sometimes I wonder what happiness really is, but I do know that since we've been evacuated to Summerton we've had a nicer – a better life than ever before.'

He smiled. 'I'm glad. And after the war?'

She shook her head. 'I daren't let myself think that far ahead. Who can at the moment? When I think of what's happened to all the people I left behind in Hackney, trying to sleep down in the Underground stations and coming up next morning to find they've been bombed out – homeless. Hundreds of people have died. It makes me realize how lucky we are. I think that's the best we can hope for just now.'

At that moment Bob came back across the lawn carrying a tray of tea. He was smiling. 'What a lot of pretty nurses there are here,' he said with a grin at Peter. 'I bet they take your mind off your injuries all right.'

Peter laughed. 'Oh, you're right. They do.'

To her dismay Judy felt an involuntary little stab of jealousy at his lighthearted enthusiasm. It shocked her. Why should she bother if he found the nurses attractive? After all, he was a free agent. Maggie had been right to point out that fact to her. Had she also been right to warn her to be careful of her feelings? Or was she already too late?

CHAPTER EIGHT

At the beginning of December came the dramatic news that the Japanese had bombed Pearl Harbor in the Pacific. Bill was beside himself.

'Now the Yanks will *have* to come in with us,' he said. 'Between us we'll soon put paid to Hitler now!'

Maggie shook her head. 'What about all those poor people? How can you be pleased about a terrible thing like that?'

Bill shook his head. 'It's war, Maggie. I know it's terrible but this was just what we needed. You want old England to survive, don't you?'

'Of course I…'

'Suzie's going to be in the Christmas concert,' Charlie piped up from the open doorway

Suddenly diverted, Maggie and Judy turned to look at her.

'What did you say? Judy asked.

Charlie rolled her eyes dramatically. 'I *said* – Suzie's going to be in the Christmas concert at school.'

'She didn't say anything. Why didn't she tell me herself?'

Charlie grinned mischievously. 'She wanted it to be a surprise.'

'Then you shouldn't have told me. That wasn't very nice of you.'

'You had to know,' Charlie pouted. ''Cause you're going to have to make her a dress.'

Judy looked helplessly at Maggie. 'How do they think I'm going to manage that with clothes rationing?'

'We'll manage somehow.' Maggie smiled. 'I've got loads of old evening dresses up in the attic from when Bill and I used to go dancing. Between us we'll rustle something up.' She looked at Judy. 'Aren't you proud of your daughter?'

'Of course I am.'

'She's going to sing and…'

'I think you've said enough.' Judy held up a finger to silence Charlie. 'Let Suzie tell us herself. It's her news, after all.'

Suzie walked in at that moment, looking at her sister with a frown. 'You've *told*!' she accused her sister. 'I said not to.'

'Not all of it, I haven't,' Charlie said. 'I haven't told them what song you're going to sing.'

All three faces turned towards the younger sister, who blushed furiously.

'Well,' Judy said. 'Are you going to tell us?'

'I'm going to dance,' Suzie said triumphantly. 'As *well* as sing a song

Maggie beamed. 'Well I'm blowed!' she said. 'If that isn't the best news I've heard all week! Well done, luvvie!'

'I'm going to sing *The White Cliffs of Dover* and I want a dress like the one the princess wore in *Cinderella*.'

Charlie pulled a face. 'Well, *I* think it's soppy,' she said, turning to stomp off upstairs.

Suzie looked pleadingly at her mother. 'Can I, Mum? *Can* I?'

The weeks that followed were busy. Judy feared Suzie was going to be disappointed about getting a dress like the one the princess had worn in *Cinderella* but, rummaging in the attic, Maggie found a dress in just the right shade of pink. It was made of watered silk and had a long skirt which would yield more than enough material to make a dress for the diminutive Suzie. She also found a box of sequins and some crystal beads from her dressmaking days.

'I've got some old net curtains somewhere,' she announced, warming to the task. 'If we starch them we can make stiff petticoats to make the skirt stand out.'

She unearthed her old sewing machine and with Maggie cutting and stitching and Judy sewing on the spangles they created the perfect princess party dress for Suzie. Charlie looked on scornfully.

'She's going to look like a Christmas tree,' she said. 'Ugh! I'm glad I don't have to dress up like that!'

Charlie was never happier than when she was dressed in shorts and a plain cotton top. She hated frills, and fussy dresses didn't suit her anyway. By the end of the previous summer she had taught herself to swim, scaring the life out of Judy as she waded determinedly into the sea until it was chest high and splashing and spluttering until at last she managed a few triumphant strokes. Her favourite subjects at school were PT and games and in the summer she had excelled on the school sports day, winning most of the races.

'A proper little tomboy, she is,' Maggie said fondly. 'One of these days she'll be an athlete.'

Peter came home on leave for Christmas. His arm was still stiff and painful but he was determined to get the full use of it again so that he could go back to being a rear gunner. Although he didn't say so, Judy knew that his Uncle Bob hoped that wouldn't happen. Secretly she hoped so too.

Peter was a regular visitor at the office during his leave and when he heard that Suzie was to be in the school concert he begged to be allowed to go along to see her. The concert was scheduled for the evening of the day school broke up for the Christmas holidays and Peter joined Judy and the Hursts along with a reluctant Charlie, who couldn't understand why she couldn't stay at home to listen to the wireless instead.

The teacher who had produced the concert had done a wonderful job, patiently coaxing out all the talent she saw in her pupils. The school choir opened the concert with a rendition of *Somewhere Over the Rainbow*, which brought tears to many a mother's eyes. After that there were sketches and monologues. A little boy played a rather halting Chopin waltz on the piano and then at last it was Suzie's turn.

The curtains parted to find her standing centre stage in her pink spangled dress. She looked so tiny alone in the middle of the stage that Judy's throat tightened. She held her breath, her heart fluttering as she willed her daughter to do well. The teacher accompanying her on the piano nodded and she began to sing: *There'll be bluebirds over...* a little shakily at first but gathering in confidence as the song progressed. Peter, sensing Judy's emotional reaction, reached for her hand and gave it a surreptitious squeeze. But it was after the song had finished that the real surprise came, when

Suzie went into her dance routine. She moved as lightly as a piece of thistledown, pirouetting like a little ballerina. Judy could not believe her eyes. Clearly she had inherited the talent and grace of movement from Christine, her grandmother. But why had she never seen it in her before? She glanced at Charlie, sitting on her other side.

'Did you know she could dance like that?' she whispered as Suzie took her bow to rousing applause.

Charlie shrugged. 'She's always prancing about upstairs.' She looked at her mother. 'This is the first time she's ever let anyone see her doing it.' She pulled a face. 'Daft, isn't it?'

I'm the daft one, Judy told herself. I have a talented daughter and I never knew it.

They all walked home together and Maggie invited Peter in for a late night drink.

'It's only cocoa,' she said. 'But you're welcome.'

He grinned. 'Cocoa sounds just the job. Thank you, Mrs Hurst.'

Suzie was in a state of excitement as Judy saw both girls to bed. 'Did you like it, Mum? Do you think the other people did?'

'You were very good,' Judy told her. 'I never knew you could dance like that. Where did you learn how to do it?'

'I used to watch Grandma practising and I saw the ladies on the stage when we were in London,' Suzie told her. 'Sometimes you took us to the theatre with you when you went to work – remember?'

Judy did remember. The occasions when there was no one to leave the girls with had been very rare. She would smuggle them in and sneak them into a couple of vacant seats in the gallery with some sweets to keep them quiet. Suzie had been very young at the time. It was amazing that she had absorbed so much.

Later she walked out to the front gate with Peter. 'Thanks for letting me come with you this evening,' he said. 'I enjoyed it very much and the Hursts are a smashing couple. Bill and I had a good natter about the war while you were putting the girls to bed. You're lucky to have such a good billet.'

'I know I am,' she said. 'It was a very good concert, wasn't it?'

'Wizard! Little Suzie was terrific.' He paused. 'Judy, there's a

Christmas dance on at Bircham this weekend. Would you like to go?'

Her heart missed a beat. 'What – with you?'

He laughed. 'Of *course*, with me. Who else?'

She bit her lip. 'What I mean is, why *me*? You must know dozens of girls, Peter. Maybe a special one.'

He touched her shoulder. 'You're a special one to me.'

'I'm married, Peter,' she said in a small voice.

'I know that. I'm not planning to whisk you away on a white charger. It's just a Christmas dance. Where's the harm?'

She thought of Maggie's warning and wondered what she would say if she accepted Peter's invitation. She looked up at him and saw that his eyes were shining expectantly in the darkness.

'I'd really love to go, Peter,' she said. 'But would you mind if I had a think about it and let you know?'

'Of course not. But what's the problem?'

She took a deep breath. 'I live here with Maggie and Bill. They're so kind to us – more like family and I know they'd be willing to mind the children for me. But it's not fair to take them for granted. I'll have to ask them first.'

He nodded. 'Of course you do. I wasn't thinking. Just let me know. But don't be too long. The tickets are going fast.'

After Peter had left Judy went indoors and gathered up the cups and plates.

'I'll wash these,' she said. But she had no sooner run water into the sink than Maggie joined her, closing the kitchen door behind her.

'Is something up, love?' she asked, picking up a tea towel. 'I thought you looked a bit pensive when you came in just now.'

Judy glanced at her. 'Peter has just asked me to go to the Christmas dance at Bircham with him.'

Maggie's expression did not change. 'And you said..?'

'I said I'd ask you.'

'I'm not your mum. You don't have to ask my permission, Judy.'

'I'd need to ask if you minded sitting with the girls,' Judy said. 'I don't want to take advantage and I know you don't really approve of me seeing Peter.'

Maggie put the tea towel down and turned Judy to face her. 'It's Christmas, love,' she said. 'I can't grudge you a little bit of fun. You work so hard and you're a good mum to those kiddies. You deserve to go out for once and enjoy yourself. All I ask is that you watch your feelings for that young man. Now that we've met him I can see that he's a lovely boy. I'm sure he hasn't got a bad bone in his body. But you're both young and....'

'I know what you're saying, Maggie. You don't have to worry – I promise.'

'Then you go with my blessing. And have a lovely time.'

Peter was delighted when she told him she would go to the dance with him, and although she looked forward excitedly to the occasion herself Judy was worried that she had nothing to wear. There would be RAF wives and girlfriends there. She was sure they'd all look glamorous and she didn't want to feel out of place or to let Peter down. Looking round the shops in Summerton she couldn't see anything she liked or could even afford. Again Maggie came to the rescue, climbing once more into the attic to open the trunk containing her old evening dresses, all swathed lovingly in tissue paper. With a cry of triumph she pulled out a black silk evening dress with diamante straps.

Looking through a copy of *Vogue* Judy chose a style that could be adapted from the material. It had a flared skirt and a close-fitting bodice with a sweetheart neck and short sleeves. There were only a few days left but Maggie promised to do her best to try to recreate it. She was turning out to be very clever with her old sewing machine and now that everyone was required to make do and mend, her skill was coming in handy.

When the dress was finished and Judy tried it on she was delighted. The silky material hung beautifully, the skirt swirling round her legs as she tried a few dance steps. Maggie had even found a pair of silver evening shoes and a little bag to match at the bottom of the trunk.

'I can't think how my feet ever fitted into those,' she said with a laugh as Judy slipped them on. 'I used to be the same size you are now.' She pulled a rueful face. 'Must be middle-age spread, I reckon.'

Peter called for her in his ancient little car and gasped with admiration when he saw her.

'You look really lovely, Judy,' he said, his eyes shining as he took both her hands. 'I'm going to be the envy of all the other chaps.'

The dance was held in the officers' mess, which had been decorated with festive streamers. A huge Christmas tree stood at the end of the room, close to the platform where the band was playing. All the men were in uniform and Peter proudly introduced Judy to some of his friends and their girlfriends who were gathered at the bar. When he asked her what she would like to drink she shook her head.

'Oh, just a lemonade, please.'

One of Peter's friends laughed. 'Come on, Judy, it's Christmas. Have a drop of gin in it.'

She agreed and found that the drink made her feel much more relaxed. Peter was a good dancer and as he held her in his arms and she followed his steps around the floor she felt as though she was floating. Her spirits soared. It was so long since she'd felt so happy

In the interval a buffet supper was laid out in an adjoining room. Peter found two seats and then brought her a plate of food.

He looked at her. 'Having a good time?'

She nodded. 'I can't remember when I've enjoyed myself so much. This is the first dance I've been to for ages.'

'Did you go with your husband before the war – Sid, isn't it?'

Judy frowned and shook her head. The mention of Sid's name quickly brought her down to earth with a bump and suddenly she felt guilty.

Peter covered her hand with his. 'Sorry. Perhaps that was tactless of me.' He paused, glancing at her. 'You never talk about him, Judy. You told me the first time we met that he was in the Western Desert and that's all I know.'

She nodded. 'Maybe the least said, the better.'

'Why do you say that? Most girls with husbands overseas talk of nothing else.'

She raised an eyebrow at him. 'Oh. You talk to other married girls, then?'

He grinned. 'Of course I do. A lot of the WAAFs here are married.' She felt his hand tighten round hers. 'What is it, Judy? Are things all right between you?'

At that moment the band struck up and Judy jumped to her feet, pulling him up with her. 'They're playing again. Let's go and dance.'

Peter didn't mention Sid again.

At last the evening came to an end and Peter drove her home. It was a slow drive in the blacked-out countryside with the car's headlamps half obscured to avoid being spotted from above. Just before they reached Summerton Peter drew the car to the side of the road and switched off the engine. Judy looked at him.

'What's wrong? We haven't run out of petrol, have we?'

He laughed. 'I hope I'm a little more subtle than that.' Reaching into the glove compartment he took out an oblong package tied with ribbon. 'I wanted to give you this. It's just a little Christmas present.'

Her heart sank. 'Oh, Peter! I haven't got you anything. I never....'

'Never mind that. Just open it.'

When she untied the ribbon and opened the box inside she found a delicate silver bracelet in the form of little hearts, linked together. She looked up at him. 'Oh, Peter! It's lovely, but you really shouldn't!'

'You don't like it.'

'No – I mean *yes*, of course I like it. I *love* it, but it's too much.'

'Not for you, it isn't. Nothing is too much for you.'

'Don't say that.'

'It's true. Ever since we met I haven't wanted to be with anyone else.'

'But you know I'm...'

'Married. I know. I also know that you're not happy.'

She stopped his words, biting her lip. 'Peter – stop. Don't say any more. I'm happy tonight. I've had a wonderful time. I can't remember when I've been so happy – so please, don't spoil it.'

'Would this spoil it?' He reached out to pull her closer and his lips found hers. Never in her life had she wanted so badly to be kissed by anyone and after a moment's hesitation she responded with all her heart. For a while they were both quiet as he held her close, then he said.

'In wartime we should take our happiness when and where we can – without guilt: without fear or worrying about a future we might never have.' He looked down at her. 'Agreed?'

She nodded, a lump in her throat.

'So – whatever comes we'll cherish this moment?'

'Of course,' she whispered.

'And you won't regret it tomorrow and stop seeing me?'

'I won't be able to, will I?' she said, half-teasing. 'I work in your uncle's office.'

'Too right!' He hugged her close. 'I've got you in my clutches.'

When they arrived at the gate of Sea View he looked at her. 'Well, I suppose this is where we say goodnight.'

'Yes. Thank you for a wonderful evening, Peter. And for my lovely present. I hope you have a wonderful Christmas with your family.'

'You too, Judy.' He laid a hand on her arm as she made to get out of the car. 'Before you go, there's something I should tell you.'

She turned. 'Yes?'

'The MO passed me A1 yesterday. That means that when I go back off leave I'll be flying again. I can't tell you anything but it looks as though there's a big show ahead and they need all the bods they can get.'

'Oh, *Peter*.'

'So – just in case anything happens I want you to know that I love you, Judy. I know that as long as you're married this isn't going any further but I can't help it and I want you to know just in case – well – just in case.' He kissed her briefly. 'Off you go now before I forget that I'm a gentleman. See you soon. Goodnight, my darling Judy.'

Maggie hadn't waited up and Judy was relieved. She wanted to be alone and relive every second of her wonderful evening. She knew she should be dismayed by Peter's revelation but she wasn't.

She'd known for some time now that she loved him too. Until now she had never known what love was. She'd had no idea that it could cut so deeply into the soul; that it could make you soar with happiness or drown with sorrow all in the space of one heartbeat. But she was married. She had exchanged vows with Sid – Sid who was fighting in the desert in horrible conditions for his country, for her and the girls. There was no way that she and Peter could ever be together. And there was the added possibility that he could be killed, as so many young airmen were. He could be lost to her for ever. She might never see him again.

She stared into the darkness of her blacked-out bedroom, allowing the tears to run, unchecked down her cheeks to soak into the pillow. '*I love you too, Peter*,' she whispered, wishing with all her heart that she'd told him so when she had the chance. However wrong – however futile, it was the truth.

It was the first week in January when Bob Gresham told Judy that Peter had been posted to Devonshire. He did not get home on leave again and in May the 'big show' he had spoken of turned out to be a massive air offensive by the RAF on Germany's ports and largest industrial towns. Enraged by the devastation of Lübeck and Rostock Hitler upgraded his own air offensive, bombing some of England's most beautiful cities. Exeter first, then Bath, Coventry, Norwich, York and Canterbury. Bill shook his head.

'They're getting too close for comfort,' he said gloomily. Maggie stared in horror at the newspaper photographs of the devastation of Exeter.

'Just look at that,' she said. 'A whole city very nearly been flattened in one night. Those poor people.'

Judy looked at her children and thanked God for their safety. She tried not to think about Sid and her parents facing danger every day, but deep in her heart it was Peter she was troubled for: Peter facing death or some hideously disabling injury night after night. Her heart ached for him till she thought it would break.

CHAPTER NINE

As the months went by Judy threw herself into her job and her children. The news was frightening and she dreaded Bill's gloomy prognosis as he pored over the wireless and the newspapers.

The postcards from Sid dried up completely. The news about the Eighth Army in the Western Desert improved slightly as the Eighth Army began to gain ground and Judy couldn't help wondering whether Sid had been wounded.

Bill had been greatly cheered by the news of the RAF's 1000-bomber raid on Cologne, which made Judy slightly resentful. Didn't he care about the deadly danger that Peter and all his fellow airmen were in? Maybe if he had a son in the RAF he would see things differently. In August the failed attempted landings in Dieppe brought a frown to Bill's face once again.

'They weren't ready,' he complained. 'This is a disaster – a bloody disaster. Hitler must be laughing his jackboots off!'

Maggie frowned at him and tutted. '*William Hurst*! Watch your language in front of the children.'

Peter wrote occasional brief letters. They were light-hearted and amusing, about everything but the war. He never mentioned the closeness they'd shared on the night of the Christmas dance. He always sent love to Charlie and Suzie as well as Maggie and Bill and he asked Judy to go and see his parents occasionally as a favour. His younger brother had been called up now and was in the army, so his parents had two sons to worry about.

Judy was shy about going to see Mary and Steve Gresham, but when she mentioned it to Bob he urged her to go, and to take Charlie and Suzie.

'They really took to you,' he told her. 'I know they'd be pleased to see you again. It's hard for them with both lads in the war now. The three of you would cheer them up.'

She went along with Charlie and Suzie one Saturday afternoon in October. Mary looked tense as she answered the door but her face lit up in a smile when she saw who her visitors were.

'Judy! How lovely to see you – and the children too. Come in and tell me what you've all been doing.'

She insisted that they stayed for tea and as there was a private puppet show arranged for friends that evening she invited them to stay. Judy looked doubtful, then the girls gave her no choice but to accept, both clamouring together:

'Ooh, can we, Mum?'

'Oh, *please!*'

Outnumbered, she gave in and they stayed, climbing the wooden staircase to the barn and squeezing into the little theatre along with a group of the Greshams' friends. The play was a fairy tale and the girls were enchanted, especially when a chorus line of frogs came on and performed a routine. Later, Mary asked them to go back to the house for a drink, but this time Judy was adamant.

'It's long past bedtime for these two,' she said. 'We've had a really lovely time, though. Thank you, Mrs Gresham.'

'Oh, Mary, please.' Peter's mother took both of Judy's hands and pressed them warmly. 'It's nice to have something to take my mind off the boys,' she said. 'Steve and I hardly sleep for worrying about them. Paul is still doing his basic training but heaven knows where he'll be sent after that.'

Judy nodded. 'I know how you must feel.'

For a moment there was silence as neither of them spoke of the dread they shared, then Mary took a deep breath. 'But there,' she said. 'We're not the only ones worrying, are we? There are hundreds of mothers and fathers and wives worrying about their nearest and dearest.' She looked at Judy. 'You must be worried about your husband – your mother and father too. How are they?'

'I haven't heard from my husband for some time,' Judy told her. 'But it's understandable with things as they are in the desert. Mum and Dad must be due for some leave soon, though. Mum wrote that their tour of Scotland is almost over and they might be going abroad soon.'

Mary shook her head. 'Well, let's hope they manage to spend some time with you before they go.' She looked at the girls. 'Look at these two, they're asleep on their feet, bless them. You will come and see us again soon, won't you?'

Both girls nodded vigorously.

'Say thank you for having us,' Judy whispered, giving Charlie's shoulder a surreptitious push.

'Thank you for having us,' they said in unison. Charlie added, 'I liked the frogs best. They were really funny.'

'I liked the fairies,' added Suzie.

Charlie pulled a face at her. 'You always like the sissy stuff,'

Judy put a hand behind each girl, pushing them towards the door. 'Come on, stop arguing you two. Time we went home.'

When the three of them arrived back at Sea View Maggie was bubbling over with excitement. 'We've had a phone call,' she said, hardly able to wipe the smile from her face. 'Guess who's coming?' She looked at the girls. 'I bet you can guess.'

Charlie pulled a face. 'It's not Dad, is it?'

Suzie piped up. 'I bet it's Granny and Granddad.' She turned a hopeful little face up to Maggie. 'Is it? *Is it?*'

Maggie nodded, laughing. 'Yes, bless your heart, you're right. They'll be here some time tomorrow and they can stay for a whole week. Isn't that good news?'

The girls began dancing round the kitchen with excitement. Judy smiled.

'Did they say any more? Are they going overseas?'

Maggie shook her head. 'I don't know. It was your dad who rang from a phone box and he didn't have much change. We'll hear all their news tomorrow. It's a good job we've got a room vacant. I shan't take any more bookings while they're here. I daresay they'll be needing a good rest.'

'It'll be so good to see them,' Judy said. 'It seems ages since they were here last.' She looked at the two girls, almost beside themselves with excitement. 'Come on, you two. I think you've had enough excitement for one day; upstairs with you both!' She clapped her hands and chased them, giggling, into the hall. In the doorway she turned. 'Thank you, Maggie. I really appreciate all that you do for us.'

Maggie shook her head. 'Get away with you! Having the three of you here with us and meeting your family has been a treat for Bill and me. It's given us a new lease of life.' She watched as Judy ran up the stairs after her two little girls and sighed. She'd had mixed feelings when she heard that Peter Gresham had been posted to Devonshire on the other side of the country. The day after the Christmas dance Judy had looked so alive. Her eyes shone and there was a lightness to her step. Maggie had noticed the delicate silver bracelet that she had begun to wear, too, and guessed that it had been a present from Peter, but she pretended not to notice it. They were in love. There was no getting away from the fact and Maggie wished with all her heart that Judy was free to follow her heart. Peter was perfect for her and Judy was like the daughter that she and Bill had always longed for. She'd give anything to see her free of that brute she was married to. But married she was, and in Maggie's book vows were vows and not to be broken. Brute, the man might be, but say what you might he was fighting for his country along with the best of them. Besides, there were two kiddies to think of. She sighed and turned away towards the kitchen. 'Ah well, what will be, will be,' she muttered under her breath.

Harry and Christine arrived the following afternoon and when Judy came home from work they were already enjoying cups of tea and slices of Maggie's home-made Victoria sponge. They were pleased to see Judy looking well and astonished at how much the girls had grown since their last visit. Bill brought out photographs he had taken of Suzie in the spangled dress she'd worn for the school concert.

'Quite the young lady!' Christine looked at them for a long while. 'You say she sang and danced?' She looked up.

Judy nodded. 'She surprised us all. I had no idea.' She looked at Suzie. 'After tea why don't you put on your dress and dance for

Granny and Granddad,' she suggested. 'Show them what you did in the concert.'

Suzie shook her head shyly and Charlie chimed in, 'I bet you've forgotten how to do it!'

'No I haven't!' Suzie countered hotly.

'Go on then. I dare you.'

'All right. I *will*!'

Upstairs, helping Suzie to change, Judy silently applauded her elder daughter for her unwitting encouragement. As she fastened the buttons at the back of the dress she couldn't help noticing that Suzie was already growing out of it. She was thoughtful as she brushed the little girl's hair. In no time at all they'll be grown up young women, she told herself with a pang of regret.

Suzie performed her song and dance perfectly, and when she'd finished her admiring little audience clapped enthusiastically. Later, after the girls were in bed and Christine was helping Judy to wash up in the kitchen she said, 'I know she's my granddaughter but she really does show promise, Judy. Where did she learn to dance like that?'

Judy smiled. 'She gets it from you. I never inherited your talent or Dad's but it seems to have come out in Suzie. She told me she watched you practising and on the odd night when I had to take them to work with me she watched the chorus line and tried to copy them. She wasn't much more than a baby at the time. I never had any idea she was interested, although Charlie says she was always prancing about, as she put it.'

'You really should send her to dancing classes,' Christine said.

Judy coloured. 'I'd love to, Mum, but I can't afford it.'

Christine put down the plate she was drying and looked at her daughter. 'You get a good salary from your job at the theatre, don't you? With that and what you get from the Army...' She paused as Judy turned away. 'What is it, Judy? You've got a pay book, haven't you?'

Judy sighed. 'No. Sid said it was better that he sent me money himself. I'd get more that way.'

Christine frowned. 'But that money comes from the Government.'

'I know, but he said he'd chosen to do it differently.'

Christine looked unconvinced. 'So, how much does he send you?' When Judy hesitated she threw up her hands. 'Oh, *Judy!* He doesn't send you anything, does he?'

'He used to but it's stopped. I haven't heard from him for ages,' Judy said. 'He could be wounded – *dead* even, for all I know.'

'I think you'd have heard if he was.' Christine pulled the corners of her mouth down. 'Mmm, well, the least said, the better, I suppose. But if I were you I'd look into it. They're his kids after all and you can't bring them up on fresh air.'

'I wouldn't know where to start, Mum.'

'The War Office might be a good place,' Christine said, but even as she framed the words she knew she was wasting her breath. 'Tell you what,' she said, seeing the look of dismay on her daughter's face. 'Let your dad and me pay for dancing lessons for little Suzie. We've nothing else to spend our money on at the moment. Let's go and get it arranged while we're on leave.'

The dancing lessons were arranged for Suzie the following day and Harry insisted that, to make it fair, they would put the same amount of money in a bank account for Charlie.

The week went all too quickly. The girls listened with saucer eyes as Harry regaled them with stories about the strange and remote places they had performed in.

'Once when we were up in Orkney we were billeted in a real castle,' he told them. 'It had battlements and turrets and every-thing. Some people said it was haunted, but Granny and I never saw any spooks, did we?' He turned to his wife, who frowned at him.

'Leave off, Harry, you'll give them nightmares,' she admon-ished. 'Take no notice of him,' she told the girls. 'There's no such things as ghosts anyway.'

'Sometimes there wasn't even anywhere for us to perform,' Harry went on unabashed. 'Once we did our act on the back of a lorry with the tailboard down. I kept thinking that the piano was going to roll right off the end, and me with it.'

Their stories kept the girls, Bill and Maggie amused but Maggie insisted that Harry and Christine had a proper rest while they were on leave. She cooked them the best meals she could manage on the rations and suggested that they relax as much as possible.

Harry was amused. 'Anyone'd think we were invalids,' he said, laughing. But even he had to admit that the rest and the sea air helped to refresh them.

When Bill asked Harry confidentially where they would be sent next Harry shook his head.

'They don't actually tell us,' he said. 'But the rumour mill has it that a load of mosquito nets has been ordered, so it's on the cards it'll be Egypt.'

Bill let out a low whistle. 'A bit of a change from Orkney, eh?' He leaned forward and lowered his voice. 'If you see that Sid Truman over there give him one on the quiet for me, will you.'

Harry gave a wry smile. 'If only I had the chance.'

All too soon it was time to wave her parents off once again. Judy and the girls went to the station with them and as Harry boarded the train he gave Judy a quick hug.

'I can't tell you how proud your mum and I are of you,' he whispered. 'You're bringing those kids up a treat on your own, and now you've got yourself a good job. I said you could do it, didn't I?'

'Only because of your encouragement, Dad.' She kissed his cheek. 'And Maggie and Bill's help of course.'

As the guard blew his whistle Harry joined his wife on the train and Judy waved them off with a heavy heart. When would she see them again, she wondered; would they be safe on the other side of the world? Outwardly they seemed to be enjoying their travels with ENSA. As Harry said, they were seeing places they would never have seen if it hadn't been for the war. But it didn't convince Judy that life was all fun for them and their fellow performers. Some of the conditions they had to suffer were squalid and uncomfortable, to say the least, and there was always danger, working as they did in what were potentially enemy targets. How much longer could the war last? And what would become of them all once it was over?

*

Business at the Little Theatre began to pick up noticeably, mainly due to the arrival of the Americans, who were now stationed at the new USAF base about twelve miles from Summerton-on-Sea. The olive-green uniforms became a familiar sight around the town and trade at local shops, pubs and cinemas improved. 'The Yanks', as the locals quickly learned to call them, seemed very fond of children and one day Charlie and Suzie came home in a great state of excitement. That afternoon three crates of oranges had been brought to the school. They arrived on an army lorry, Charlie explained. And a nice soldier who 'talked funny' gave two of the big boys some chewing gum for helping to carry the crates. The girls had two oranges each, fruit that they could barely remember eating before. Judy made them share half an orange between them each day, so as to make the treat last.

Suzie took to her weekly dancing classes at Miss Paige's dancing school like a duck to water. She had only been attending for a few weeks when Gladys Paige sent Judy a note, asking if she would call in to see her.

'I believe you are a secretary at the Little Theatre,' she said as Judy sat opposite her in her tiny office.

Judy nodded, wondering what her job could possibly have to do with Suzie's dancing lessons. 'That's right.' She cleared her throat. 'I hope there's nothing wrong.'

'No, of course not,' Miss Paige said reassuringly. 'Suzanne is a dear child and shows great promise. I just wondered how you would feel about her appearing in public.' Seeing Judy's look of bewilderment she hurried on. 'You'll be aware of course that the Little Theatre Company is putting on the usual pantomime this Christmas. It's to be *Dick Whittington* this year and I've been asked to provide a troupe of little girls to take part and I'd like Suzanne to be in it. I think it would be good for her confidence.'

Judy could feel her colour rising. *Her Suzie* – on the stage! Mum and Dad would be so proud when she wrote to tell them. Suddenly she was aware that Miss Paige was waiting for an answer. 'You seem hesitant,' the dancing teacher ventured.

Judy shook her head. 'Oh no! I was just a bit surprised, that's all. After all, she's only been coming to your classes for a few weeks.'

'That's true, but I'm sure she can do it, otherwise I wouldn't suggest it. I'll have to provide two troupes, performing on alternate nights, because of the regulations regarding child performers, of course.' She looked at Judy, 'You're happy then?'

'Yes. I'm thrilled, and she will be too. She loves your classes so much – looks forward to them all week and she practises all the time at home.'

'I'm so pleased. I think we'll be able to hire most of the costumes but can I call on you if we need any dressmaking help? I hear you have a very obliging landlady.'

Judy smiled. 'I'm sure Mrs Hurst and I will do what we can.'

Back at Sea View she couldn't wait to break the news. Suzie went pink and bit her lip as though she was about to cry.

'*Me*? Can I really dance on a real stage in the pantomime, Mum?'

'Miss Paige thinks you can. You do want to, don't you? Because if you don't no one is going to make you.'

'*Yes*! I want to.' Suzie jumped up and down excitedly. 'You will let me, won't you, Mum?'

'Of course. It's all arranged. All you have to do now is work hard on the routines and enjoy it.'

'And we'll all come and see you,' Maggie told her, as excited as Suzie herself. 'And when you hear us clapping it'll be just for you!'

Charlie pulled a face, though secretly she was as pleased as the others. 'Dancing about like a daft twerp; I'm glad I don't have to do it.' She looked at her sister's crestfallen face and added, 'Still, we'll have something to show off at school about now, won't we, Su?'

As the third year of the war drew to a close Bill was rejoicing again. In November the Eighth Army had made a significant stride forward by taking El Alamein. Mr Churchill made a speech on the wireless, declaring it to be, 'not the beginning of the end but perhaps the end of the beginning.' And for the first time in months there were smiles on people's faces. A few days later all the church bells rang out for the first time since 1940 in celebration of the hard-won victory. There was a special thanksgiving service at the parish church and Judy, Maggie and Bill went along with the children.

It was when they arrived home that the blow fell. As they approached the house a telegraph boy stood at the door, his red bicycle propped up against the gate. Maggie and Bill glanced at each other as the boy stepped forward.

'Mrs Truman?'

'Yes?' Judy held out her hand and the boy handed her the small orange-coloured envelope.

'Any reply?' he asked, standing a little apart as he waited.

Judy quickly tore the envelope open and read the brief message inside, then she looked up at him, her face ashen. 'No,' she said quietly. 'No reply.'

CHAPTER TEN

Bill quickly unlocked the door and ushered them all inside. Maggie slipped an arm round Judy's shoulders and told the girls to go upstairs to play. Suzie obeyed at once but Charlie was looking up anxiously at her mother's face.

'Mum, are you all right?'

Judy nodded, managing a smile. 'I'm fine. Do as Auntie Maggie says and go upstairs. I'll come up in a minute.'

As Charlie reluctantly followed her sister up the stairs Maggie peered into Judy's face. 'Is it bad news, love?'

Judy silently handed the telegram to Maggie who scanned the brief message.

'Oh Lord!' She slipped an arm through Judy's. 'Come on through to the kitchen and sit down, love.'

Bill produced a tot of his coveted brandy. 'Here, get this down you, girl.'

As Judy sipped the brandy Maggie silently passed the telegram to her husband. As he read he mouthed the words.

Shipped home with injuries. Southampton Military Hospital. Come soon. Sid. He looked at Judy.

'You're going?'

She nodded. 'I must. He needs me.'

Maggie bit her lip hard. She longed to say what was in her mind. Judy hadn't complained but she knew the girl hadn't heard a word from that husband of hers for months. Now that he'd been injured he was asking for her.

'Southampton is an awful long way,' she said at last. 'But if you want to go don't worry about the girls. They'll be fine with us. And

I'm sure your Mr Gresham will manage without you at the theatre for a few days.'

Judy nodded and took a deep breath. 'I'll ring him now, if you don't mind me using the telephone.'

"Course not girl, just help yourself,' Bill said. 'Tell you what, I'll get the time table out while you're doing that and look up the trains for you. And if you want to phone the hospital…'

'No,' Judy shook her head. 'I'll just go. As soon as possible if that's all right with you both.' She looked around. 'I'll ring Mr Gresham and then I'd better go up and tell the girls.'

Upstairs in the room the girls shared she sat on the edge of the bed. 'Listen, I want you to be very good girls because I have to go away for a few days,' she said. 'Your dad has been hurt and they've sent him back to England to a hospital in Southampton to be made better. He needs me to go and see him.'

Suzie began to cry. '*Mum!*' She threw her arms around her mother. 'You will come back again, won't you?'

Judy drew her close and kissed the top of her head. 'Of course I will, sweetheart. It's not for long and you'll be fine with Auntie Maggie and Uncle Bill.'

'I'll look after you. Don't cry, silly,' Charlie told her sister. 'Where's Southampton?' she asked.

'It's a city in the south of England. It's quite a long way away.'

'Are there any bombs there, like London?' Charlie asked fearfully.

'No,' Judy lied. 'Don't worry. I'll be quite safe.'

Bill told her that she would have to catch a train to London and change there for Southampton. 'The journey might take you a long time, love,' he said. 'I reckon you'd best get a good night's sleep and start first thing in the morning. There's a train for London at seven.'

Judy shook her head. 'I'll go now, as soon as I've packed a few things.'

Bill shook his head. 'You won't get all the way to Southampton in half a day.'

'Maybe not, but I'll have to try,' Judy argued. 'If I stay till morning I won't sleep anyway.'

Judy caught the first available train. Maggie made her a packed lunch which she ate on the train. It was a slow journey. The train seemed to stop at every little station on the way, so that it was early evening and dark by the time she arrived at Liverpool Street.

The station was seething with troops. She queued up for a cup of tea at a trolley manned by the WVS, studying Bill's written instructions as she drank it. She saw that she must make her way over to Waterloo to catch the connection for Southampton. There was a train at eight o'clock and the journey would take about five hours. It would be into the small hours before she arrived and she had no idea where she would go then. She decided to worry about that when it happened. If she was lucky she'd be able to get some sleep on the train. But as she began to descend to the Underground the familiar wail of the air-raid siren began and in minutes she was surrounded by people, all rushing to stake their claim to a place to sleep on the platforms below. She stopped a man hurrying past.

'Excuse me, which platform do I need for Waterloo Station?'

He stared at her. 'There's a raid on, luv. Didn't you 'ear the siren? All the trains stop when there's a raid.'

She felt panic rise in her throat. 'A bus then. What number bus?'

He laughed drily. 'You'll be lucky!' And before she could ask him any more questions he was swept away by the mass of humanity jostling all around her. Fighting against the tide and holding fast to the handrail to avoid being knocked over, she made her way back up to the street. As she emerged from the station she heard the roar and thrum of planes overhead, then suddenly a long whistle and a deafening bang. She sprang into a doorway, shivering; her hands over her ears. *Oh God*, she prayed. *Please God don't let me be killed.* She thought quickly about Charlie and Suzie and the lie she had told about there being no bombs. She thought about Sid, lying in hospital with terrible injuries, and last of all about Peter. Was this to be her punishment for falling in love with him?

A passing air-raid warden spotted her huddled in the doorway and stopped. 'I'd take cover if I was you, duck,' he said. 'You're not safe there.'

'Is there a bus to Waterloo?' she asked him, her teeth chattering with fear as another bomb dropped, so close that the ground trembled under her feet. He shook his head.

'There'll be no more buses till the All Clear goes.'

'But I have to get to Southampton tonight.'

'Not tonight you won't.' He took her arm. 'Come on now. Be sensible. Go down the Underground and wait for the all clear, duck. Better safe than sorry, eh?'

Reluctantly she obeyed him and walked back into the station. As she reached the bottom of the staircase the sight before her brought her to a halt. Never in her life had she seen so many people crammed into one space. And most of them looked as though they were used to it. They'd brought their rolled up mattresses, sandwiches and flasks, books and magazines. People of every age were there, old and young; most of them were good-humoured and sharing what they had. There were babies in carry cots and toddlers in push-chairs; even children doing their homework. An old woman sitting on a mattress near her feet looked up at her with a smile.

'You look a bit lost, luv.' She moved over to make a space. 'Sit with me if you like. I'm on me own.' Opening a bulging canvas bag at her side she took out a packet of sandwiches, offering it to Judy. 'Go on, 'ave one, duck. I've got plenty. It's only spam but it keeps yer belly from rumbling.'

'Thank you.' Judy joined her on the mattress and took a sandwich gratefully. It seemed ages since she'd finished Maggie's packed lunch. 'You're very kind. I was on my way down to Southampton but it looks as if I'll have to wait till morning now.'

'Southampton, eh?' The woman chewed on her sandwich with toothless gums.

'Yes. My husband is in the military hospital there.'

'Sorry to hear that, duck. What's yer name by the way. I'm Ivy. Ivy Watson.'

'Judy Truman.' She looked round. 'Is it always this crowded?'

Ivy grinned. 'Crowded? This is nothing compared to some nights. If we're lucky the raid won't last long. If not we're 'ere for the night, so might as well get on with it. Sometimes even if the All Clear goes and you goes back up top, you just gets orf to kip and the bleeders are back again. Might as well stay put, I always says.'

'Don't you worry about your home?' Judy asked.

Ivy shook her head. 'Not any more. Been bombed out twice. I live in one room now along with what I could pick out of the rubble.'

'I'm so sorry.'

Ivy shrugged. 'Don't be sorry, luv. I'm still on me two feet and that's more'n some poor buggers can say.' She peered at Judy. 'I reckon you're a Londoner yerself, ain't you?'

Judy smiled. 'Yes, from Hackney. My two little girls and I were evacuated to Norfolk back in '39.'

Ivy nodded. 'Good. Best thing an' all. You wanna stay there.'

After a while someone at the far end of the platform began to play a penny whistle and one or two people started to sing the words of *We'll Meet Again*. Immediately everyone joined in, Ivy included. She nudged Judy and winked. 'Sing up, luv. Keeps your spirits up, it does.'

The sing-song went on for some time, running the gamut of every kind of music Judy could think of. They sang hymns, popular songs; songs from musical shows and films; even snatches of opera. By the time they were finished Judy's throat was quite dry. Ivy fished a bottle out of her capacious bag and handed it to her.

'Here, 'ave a drop of this. It's me home-made elderberry wine from before the war. Used to pick the berries when we went down Kent, hop-pickin', I did, then I'd make the wine when we got 'ome.' She cackled. 'My Alf used to say it'd cure anything from bunions to baldness.' She pushed the bottle into Judy's hands. 'Go on, 'ave a good swig. It'll 'elp you get orf to kip.'

Judy put the bottle to her lips and tipped it up, coughing as the acrid liquid hit the back of her throat. 'Th-thank you,' she spluttered, handing it back. 'It's very – nice.'

'Powerful, init?' Ivy cackled gleefully. 'Better than some of that gut-rot the pubs deal out these days.' She gulped down a surprising amount of the potent brew, smacking her lips appreciatively as she rammed the cork back into the bottle. 'Well, dunno about you but I reckon I'm going to try an' get orf for a bit.' She lay down on the mattress and after a few moments she began to snore.

Judy dozed on and off in the hours that followed, all the time conscious of the thuds that reverberated even down here in the Underground. When she heard the distant whine of the All Clear she decided to try her luck above again. Glancing regretfully at the sleeping form of Ivy she found herself in a quandary. She was reluctant to wake the old woman, yet it seemed so rude to just disappear after all her kindness. She fished in her handbag for a pencil and an old envelope, scribbling a brief note on the back:

Dear Ivy. Thank you for your kindness. Love Judy. After a moment's hesitation she added, *Good luck and God bless.* Then she slipped the note into Ivy's bulging holdall for her to find later.

She'd read a lot about what the papers called the 'spirit of the blitz'. Now she'd encountered it at first hand.

Above ground it was barely light and everywhere seemed eerily silent. The landscape had changed since before the raid so that there was a slightly surreal feel to everything. There was broken glass and masonry everywhere and the bus stop seemed to have disappeared. The street was deserted and there was no one about to speak to so she began to walk, not knowing whether she was going in the right direction, just feeling that she had to do something. Suddenly a black cab pulled up on the opposite side of the road and the driver called out to her.

'You all right, luv?'

She nodded. 'I have to get to Waterloo to catch a train for Southampton.'

'Then you're walkin' in the opposite direction,' the man said. Seeing her distressed expression, he said, 'Come on, hop in. I'll take you there.'

Judy crossed the road hesitantly. She didn't have money to spare for taxis. 'It's very good of you,' she said to the driver. 'But - I haven't...'

He grinned. 'S'all right luv, it's on the 'ouse. It's on me way 'ome anyway. Come on, get in. It's cold and it's a fair old walk from 'ere to Waterloo.'

The taxi driver told her he'd been on his way home last night when the raid began and had to take cover in the nearest shelter, not knowing whether his taxi would still be in one piece when he emerged.

'That would've been me livelihood up the spout, so I've been lucky this time,' he told her. 'And between you'me things've picked up nicely since the Yanks arrived.'

On the way they had to negotiate bomb craters in the road and fire engines where men were still battling to put out houses still burning from incendiary bombs. The driver took it all in his stride, still talking nineteen to the dozen.

'They keep on talkin' about a second front,' he remarked. 'Can't come soon enough if you asks me, not after Dunkirk. I wish I could 'ave a go at them meself but I'm fifty-one this year. Still, I reckon if it goes on much longer even blokes my age'll get a turn.'

At Waterloo Station Judy alighted, thanking her gallant rescuer for saving her the long walk. Buying her ticket, she was told that a train for Southampton was due to leave from platform six in half an hour's time. At eight o'clock a convoy of Army lorries drew up outside, discharging a cargo of soldiers who teemed onto the concourse, each of them laden with full kit. When the train bound for Southampton steamed into platform six it became clear to Judy that they were all catching the same train.

The journey was hellish. Most of the time she stood in the corridor shoulder to shoulder with soldiers. Once a kindly soldier offered her his kitbag and she gratefully perched on it until her back began to ache and she was glad to stand up again. By the time she arrived at Southampton Central station she was dishevelled and exhausted. She bought a cup of tea and a sausage roll from a buffet trolley and ate it standing up before walking out into the street, hoping that the hospital wasn't too far away and that there was a convenient bus to take her there.

The hospital had been extended by a series of Nissen huts which, Judy was told on enquiring, constituted the military wing. She had no idea which ward Sid was in so she went into the first hut she came to and asked a passing orderly if he knew where she could find Private Truman. He shook his head.

'Would he be in a surgical or a medical ward?'

She shook her head.

'Well, d'you know what kind of injuries he's got, miss?'

'No. I only heard he was here yesterday. I've come all the way from Norfolk.'

'And you would be...?' He looked at her enquiringly, his head on one side.

'I'm his wife.'

'Right, I see. So you'll have his number and details. I'd ask at the main hospital if I was you. That's where they do all the admissions.'

As Judy walked across towards the main building she felt so tired that she was beginning to doubt whether her legs would carry her much further. And she still had to find somewhere to stay. Suddenly a loud voice behind her called her name.

'*Jude!*'

Only one person ever called her that. She spun round to see Sid walking towards her. He wore the blue uniform of a military hospital patient and was walking with a stick. He caught up with her, shaking his head and frowning.

'Blimey, you took your time!'

'I came as soon as I got your telegram,' she told him. 'I got stranded in London last night. There was an air raid and I had to shelter down the Underground.'

'Never mind that. You're here now.'

She stared at him. 'I expected you to be in bed. The telegram said you were injured.'

'And I *am*!' he interrupted irritably. 'Just because I'm on me two feet don't mean I'm A1,'

'So how long have you been here?'

'Three weeks.'

She stared at him. 'Three *weeks*! Why wasn't I informed?' she asked, bemused.

He shrugged. 'Search me. I sent you the wire yesterday because they can't find me a place in a convalescent home so I need you to take me back with you till I get my discharge.'

'They're going to discharge you – from the Army?' Judy asked.

He shook his head. 'Not a chance; from hospital, I mean. Soon as I've been passed fit they'll send me back to my unit, then back over there or somewhere even worse, more's the pity!'

'What happened to you?'

'We were transporting explosives up to the front line and our convoy got shelled. I copped a bloody great piece of shrapnel in my back and another in me leg.' He scowled at her, shifting his weight and leaning heavily on his stick. 'How long are you gonna keep me standin' 'ere answerin' all your questions? Talk about the bloody third degree! I've had two operations – twenty-eight stitches in me leg and God knows how many more in me back. It still hurts like hell.'

'I'm sorry, Sid. I wasn't thinking.'

'That's your trouble, you never bleedin' *do* think!'

She tried to take his arm but he shrugged her off. 'Leave off. I'm not a bleedin' cripple. They wouldn't let me make the journey alone. That's the only reason I sent for you, not because I need proppin' up.' He turned back towards the hospital. 'I'll just get my kit together and we can be off.'

'Off? Where to?'

He sighed and gave her a pitying look. 'You never listen to a word I say, do you? Back to that gaff of yours in Norfolk of course.

'Today – *now*?' Judy felt on the point of collapse. Her throat thickened and tears stung her eyes. 'I can't turn round and go straight back, Sid,' she said. 'I've got to have a sleep and something to eat first. It's taken twenty-four hours to get here and I've had a terrible journey. The trains were packed; I spent last night down the Underground and I haven't had a wink of sleep. I've had nothing to eat but a couple of sandwiches since breakfast yesterday. Can't we at least find somewhere to stay for the night?'

'Still moanin' then!' he accused. 'It's all you ever do. You wanna try bein' out there to the dessert. Boilin' heat; no sleep; shells and bullets comin' at you from everywhere. I've had that every day for months. You'd have something to moan about if you had to be there.' He looked at her white exhausted face. 'Oh, all right, have it your way. One more night in hospital won't hurt me, I suppose. We'll go first thing tomorrow.' He looked at her as he turned back. 'Well, what are you waitin' for? You'd better start lookin' for a bed for the night, hadn't you?'

*

Judy learned from the hospital receptionist that there was a hostel in the next street for the wives and relatives of patients. She went along and enquired and was lucky to get their one remaining room, which she shared with the wives of two other wounded men.

Before she turned in she telephoned Maggie from the pay-phone in the hallway to ask if it would be all right to bring Sid home with her. It took some time to get through but Maggie sounded surprised to hear from her. She was so grateful to hear that Judy was safe and sound that she gladly agreed to put Sid up until his medical discharge.

One of the girls Judy shared the room with, whose name she learned was Kathleen, had red-rimmed eyes and an ashen face and Judy learned in a whispered conversation with her other companion that Kathleen's husband's plane had been shot down and he was so badly burned that he wasn't expected to live. Poor Kathleen cried pitifully all night long, but Judy was so tired that even the poor girl's sobs could not keep her awake.

Next morning she collected Sid from the hospital. He was annoyed that he was obliged to wear his 'hospital blues' until his discharge.

'I wanted to wear me proper uniform,' he told her. 'I've got a stripe to show off. I'm Bombardier Truman now,' he said proudly. 'Promoted on the field.'

'Ah, that would be why that orderly didn't recognize your name when I asked,' she said.

His head snapped round. 'Orderly, what orderly?'

'When I arrived yesterday – at the military huts. I asked for Private Truman. I told him I was your wife.'

'What did you say that for?'

'Because I am. And because he asked me what relative I was.'

Sid glowered. 'Nosy bastards. They're all the same.'

Judy had been dreading the journey back to Norfolk but as it turned out it was relatively uneventful. Sid's 'hospital blues' assured them a seat as everyone respected a wounded soldier.

They crossed London in safety, although Sid was appalled to see the damage created by the blitz, and the last leg of the journey to Summerton-on-Sea was fairly peaceful. Judy guessed rightly that most of the movement was going in the other direction.

'Dunno what you made so much fuss about,' Sid commented as they alighted from the train. 'Trouble with you is you don't know you're born. Talk about a cushy number! No one'd know there was a war on down here.'

CHAPTER ELEVEN

When Sid undressed, Judy was pleased to see that his wounds were healing nicely. All his stitches had been removed and the swelling and inflammation were going down. She still didn't understand why she had not been informed before about his being wounded and shipped back to England but Sid shrugged the matter off, saying that the powers that be had more to bother about than informing soldiers' wives every time their husbands got what he now referred to as 'a little scratch'.

Maggie and Bill made Sid welcome in spite of their instinctive distrust of him.

'No getting away from the fact that he's been wounded fighting for King and country,' Bill told his wife as he helped her prepare a meal in the kitchen. 'He's only here for ten days, so we'd best put up and shut up.'

'It's Judy and those kiddies I worry about,' Maggie said.

Bill shook his head. 'You never know, being wounded might have made him a changed man. Nothing like a brush with death to make you glad of what you've got.'

Maggie said nothing but she told herself that she wasn't going to hold her breath on that count. She'd seen the truculent look on young Charlie's face when her father arrived. As for little Suzie, she looked scared stiff whenever he was around.

It turned out that if Sid was a changed man it was only for the worse, at least as far as Judy was concerned. Their first argument arose when he made it clear that he expected her to stay at home from work to look after him. When she told him she couldn't he went into one of his characteristic bad moods.

'What've I come here for if it isn't to be with my missis?' he complained.

'I know and I'm sorry, but we're so busy at the theatre,' Judy told him. 'It's pantomime time again and there's such a lot of extra work.'

'So some stupid pantomime is more important than your old man, is it? Just you tell that boss of yours that I've been risking my life for the likes of him. The least he can do is give you some time off to be with me.'

'He already has,' Judy reminded him. 'So that I could go down to Southampton to collect you.'

'*Collect me!*' Sid shouted. 'You make me sound more like a bleedin' *parcel* than your husband.'

Judy winced. 'Could you not keep swearing in front of the children.'

'In *front* of them?' He looked round in an exaggerated way. 'I don't see them, do you? They turned invisible or what?'

'They can hear you. They're only in the next room.'

'Well if they can hear me good luck to them. They'd better get used to hearing folks swear. I won't have you bringing them up posh. Once we get back to the East End it'll all be normal again and you don't want the other kids makin' fun of them, do you?'

Judy's heart sank. Remembering the way they lived before the war was like a nightmare. One she hoped she'd never have to live again.

Since Sid's arrival the girls had kept out of his way as much as they could and he was beginning to notice, so that evening Judy suggested that Suzie might like to show her father how she could dance.

'She was in the school concert last year,' Charlie told him. 'She's going to be in it again this year.'

'*And* I go to dancing classes at Miss Paige's dancing school,' Suzie piped up proudly. 'I'm going to be in the pantomime troupe at the theatre where Mum works too.'

Sid's eyebrows rose but he made no comment. He gave Suzie's performance a cool reception and later, in their room he demanded to know where Judy got the money from for dancing classes.

'Mum and Dad came on leave a few months ago,' she told him.

'Mum was impressed with Suzie's dancing and she and Dad offered to pay for her to have lessons.'

'Oh, they did, did they? Well that stops here and now!' Sid told her with a scowl. 'I'm not having any kid of mine cavortin' on a stage for folk to gawp at, and I'm not having other people payin' for luxuries for her either.'

'It's not a luxury. It's part of her education,' Judy argued. 'And they are her grandparents. Mum says she's got talent.'

He grunted. 'Huh! *Mum says*! D'you want her to be a common bloody chorus girl like *her* then?'

Judy's heart quickened and she felt her colour rise. She hadn't forgotten Sid's mother's insulting remarks about what her mother did for a living. 'It's a perfectly respectable profession. She could do a lot worse,' she countered.

'In that case why not get her some whoring lessons while you're about it?'

Judy's heart gave a lurch and a sudden spurt of anger blurred her vision. 'How *dare* you speak like that about my mother?'

His suggestive snigger tipped her over the edge and before she could stop herself she raised her hand and slapped him hard across the cheek.

The surprised expression on his face was almost comical, but a moment later it was replaced by one of searing anger. His hand shot out, grasping her wrist and twisting it behind her back until she cried out with pain.

'Don't you *never* do that to me again,' he hissed between clenched teeth. 'If you ever raise your hand to me again I'll bloody *kill* you – *understand,* you vicious little cow?' He let go of her wrist and threw her hard against the wall. 'And you cancel them poncy bloody dancin' lessons tomorrow, right? If you don't then I will. Got it? I'm havin' no kid of mine makin' a show of herself!'

On the way to school next morning Judy explained gently to Suzie that she would have to miss her dancing lesson this week. She had no intention of cancelling the lessons or Suzie's appearance in the pantomime. The child was so excited about it. She simply couldn't do it to her. As soon as Sid had returned to his unit the lessons and rehearsals for the pantomime would resume. She had never been more determined about anything in her life.

Maggie was busy preparing for Christmas again, chivvying Bill to get the decorations down from the loft and baking puddings and a big cake with all the dried fruit she had managed to save during the year. Someone had given her a recipe for mock-marzipan, made from soya flour, and she was determined to try it out. She was relieved that Sid was due to report back to the hospital for discharge on 10 December and would not be with them for the festive season.

'He'd put a damper on anyone's Christmas,' she told Bill as he staggered down the stairs with the big box of paper-chains and streamers.

He shook his head. 'Not so loud. He'll hear you,' he whispered.

'No he won't. He's gone to the pub. I wondered how long it'd be before he started drinking again,' Maggie said with a sniff. 'I'll be glad to see the back of him, I don't mind telling you.' She took the box from his hands and added, 'And don't trot out all that about him defending King and country, Bill Hurst. I don't care if he turns out to be General Montgomery's right-hand man, I still don't like him and I never will!'

Life at the theatre was busy. Rehearsals for Dick Whittington were in full swing. Life wasn't easy for the director. Most of his male actors had been called up or had joined ENSA. He was left with very young men, barely trained, or older actors past the conscription age.

Material for costumes and refurbishment was hard to come by, especially with clothes rationing. The theatre seating needed reupholstering, and there were countless maintenance jobs and very few tradesmen to attend to them. It was part of Judy's job to try to find solutions to all these problems. Every Monday morning there was a meeting which included all the executive staff and, as she took the minutes, Judy had become adept at recognizing which of the tasks would come her way.

At the following Monday's meeting the wardrobe mistress Roberta Sutton, or Bobby as everyone called her, brought up the question of costumes. The costumes were to be hired. The main need was for a gauze curtain for the transformation scene and Bobby Sutton thought she knew where some scrim might be obtained.

'I just need someone to come with me and help carry the stuff,' she said looking round the table. 'It'll be on a huge roll. Jim Granger would have come. As stage manager he's got all the necessary measurements but he's in bed with flu at the moment.' All eyes turned in Judy's direction.

'I'll go with you if you like,' she volunteered. 'Just let me know when you want to go.' She looked at Bob Gresham. 'Is that all right?'

He nodded with a smile. 'Poor Judy. You're getting to be everyone's dogs' body, aren't you?'

Bobby came up to the office later and asked Judy if she would be free to accompany her that afternoon at four o'clock. 'I've got the measurements,' she told her. 'It shouldn't take long.'

'I usually pick the girls up from school at four,' Judy said. 'But don't worry, I'll make other arrangements.'

In her lunch hour she went home to Sea View. She found Maggie in the kitchen and asked if she would pick the girls up.

Maggie nodded. 'You know I'd be glad to, love.' She paused. 'But maybe Sid would like to do it. It's his last day and he hasn't really seen much of them since he's been here, has he?'

Judy found him lying on their bed upstairs reading the *Daily Mirror*.

'I've got to do an errand for the theatre this afternoon, so could you pick the girls up from school, she asked him.

'*Me*?' he said, outraged that he should be asked to do such a thing. 'Pickin' up kids from school is women's work. What's wrong with her ladyship downstairs?'

'She thought you might like to be asked,' Judy told him.

'Why me?'

'Because you're their father and because you haven't spent much time with them during your leave.'

He sat up. 'Oh, that's what she thinks, does she? Havin' a snide little go! Well, for your information, and *hers*, I'm not on leave. I'm convalescent.'

'You're fit enough to go to the pub though,' Judy said. She knew that his 'hospital blues' and the stick he no longer needed but nevertheless used, brought him plenty of free drinks along with the sympathy, and she guessed from the arrogant mood he came home in each night that he milked the situation for all it was worth.

'I'll do what I like with my own time,' he told her. 'Anyway, why can't you go?'

'I promised Bobby I'd go and help carry some material.'

He was off the bed in an instant. 'Bobby! And who might this *Bobby* be when he's at home?'

'Bobby is a woman!' Judy laughed. 'She's the wardrobe mistress. Her name is Roberta but everyone calls her Bobby.'

'Don't think you can pull the wool over my eyes,' he sneered. 'It's that bloke who was all over you that night I met you out of work, isn't it?'

'Of course not. I told you...'

'You'd better be tellin' me the truth, otherwise there'll be hell to pay and you know it.' He threw himself back onto the bed and snatched up the paper again. 'And you can tell her downstairs that it's not *her* place to tell me how to treat my own family.' As she turned to go out of the room he said, 'Oh, and by the way, I found out where that dancing school is and I went to see the stuck-up cow who runs it this morning.'

Judy's heart sank. 'Why did you do that?'

'Because I knew *you* wouldn't, that's why. I told her Suzie wouldn't be comin' any more and to leave her out of this poxy troupe she's plannin'.'

'How *could* you, Sid? She's talked of nothing else ever since she was chosen. She's going to be so upset and disappointed.'

'If that's the only disappointment she ever gets she'll be bloody lucky,' he said. 'She's gonna have to learn to roll with the punches.'

'She's seven, Sid.'

'Never too young to learn,' he said, and went back to reading the paper.

All afternoon as Judy helped Bobby carry the roll of scrim back to the theatre she was silent, her heart heavy as she thought about the shattering disappointment that was due to hit Suzie later. But when she arrived home Sid was waiting for her, his face white with anger. He held an envelope in his hand.

'Upstairs,' he said. 'You've got some explainin' to do.'

Judy followed her husband upstairs in fear and trepidation. Even his back bristled with anger. She couldn't imagine what accusation he had to throw at her this time.

In their room he slammed the door shut and waved the envelope under her nose. 'Y'know what this is, do you?'

She shook her head. 'Of course I don't know. I haven't opened it.'

'*I* have, though!' He pulled a Christmas card out of the envelope and thrust it in her face. 'Who's *Peter*?' he demanded.

Judy felt her colour rise. 'He's my boss's nephew. He's in the RAF.'

'Oh yes! And what does he mean by sendin' you his love and wishing he could be with you for Christmas?'

She shook her head. 'I'm sure he sent the same message to his family.'

He responded by ripping the card in half and throwing the pieces in her face, 'But you're not his *family*, are you? You've been havin' a fling behind my back, haven't you, you slut? Jumpin' into bed with all and sundry, I bet. And me out there fightin' for you – gettin' shot up and nearly killed!' He grabbed her by the neck and pushed her against the wall. 'That Bobby this afternoon. I bet you been sleepin' with him right under my nose.'

'I told you, Bobby is a woman. And it's not true, what you're saying.'

He turned the key in the door and pocketed it, turning to her with the merciless expression she had come to dread on his face. 'Right. It's my last night so now you can entertain *me* like you been entertainin' the troops.'

What followed was painful and humiliating but Judy gritted her teeth and forced herself to put up with it. She didn't dare cry out in case the children or the Hursts heard her, but Sid's assault on her was both brutal and degrading. He only stopped when Maggie tapped on the door to say that supper was ready.

'Get up!' he demanded. 'Make yourself look decent and we'll go down to eat. And take that stupid look off your face. Whatever we do up 'ere is nobody else's business – right?'

Judy got unsteadily to her feet. She began to take off her torn dress and replace it with a skirt and jumper that would hide the bruises on her arms and neck. She said nothing. When she was dressed and her hair combed he inspected her.

'*Smile!*' he hissed at her. 'We've been enjoyin' our last evening together so take that miserable dyin'-duck look off your face.' He grasped her shoulders, making her flinch. 'If one of them downstairs even so much as asks you what's the matter you'll get more of the same so just remember that.'

Downstairs in the kitchen Maggie had made a rabbit casserole with plenty of vegetables. She glanced warily at Judy as she and Sid came into the room but she said nothing. Judy for her part tried her best to appear normal, although inside she was still shocked and shaking. Although Maggie's casserole was delicious she had to force herself to eat and make light conversation, longing for the meal to be over so that she could escape the look of unease in Maggie's eyes. But Sid had not finished yet.

When the meal was over Judy looked at the girls. 'Up to bed with you now,' she said. 'I'll be up to tuck you in soon.'

As they got up to leave the room Sid said, 'By the way, Suzie, you won't be going to no dancin' classes any more. You're not gonna be in the pantomime either. I won't have a daughter of mine showing herself off in public. It's not right.'

The expression of shock on Suzie's face tore at Judy's heart strings. The little girl's eyes filled with tears as she looked from her father to her mother and back again. 'Oh, Dad, *please!*'

He held up his hand. 'Don't start the waterworks. It cuts no ice with me. I said no and I mean no. I've been to see that teacher of yours and it's all finished and done with, so you might as well get used to the idea.'

Suzie burst into tears and ran to Judy, who put her arms around her. Maggie's eyes filled with tears and Bill cleared his throat loudly and walked out of the room. Suddenly Charlie, who had been silent all through supper, flew at Sid, pummelling him as hard as she could with her small fists.

'I *hate* you!' she shouted. 'You're the worst dad in all the world. You always spoil everything. I hate you. *I hate you*! You're a – a – *bloody bugger!*'

Sid grasped both her hands in one of his and lashed out at her legs, thrashing her till red weals appeared on her thighs. 'Don't you dare swear at me, you little bitch.' He dragged her, kicking and screaming to the door and pushed her through it. 'Get upstairs to bed!' He glowered across the room at the sobbing Suzie. 'You too. Go on – get to bed out of my sight!'

When Suzie had scuttled fearfully past him to follow her sister there was silence in the room. Sid looked from Judy to Maggie defiantly. 'OK. Either of you got anything to say?' he challenged.

Maggie walked silently out of the room, her face saying everything that was in her heart, leaving Judy facing her husband. Suddenly, in spite of the trauma of what had just happened she found she was deadly calm.

'*Why*?' she asked. 'Why take out your bad temper on the children?'

'I won't have my own kids swearing at me,' he said, slightly defensively.

She shrugged. 'I thought that was how you wanted them to be,' she said. 'You've certainly done your best to set them an example.' She walked to the door. 'I'm going up to them now, and I'll be sleeping in their room tonight.' She walked out of the room, surprised that he made no attempt to stop her.

Upstairs she found Charlie trying to console her sister. Very calmly she undressed them both and then herself. Climbing into bed she cuddled them both close, soothing their tears away until at last they slept.

Sid's train left very early next morning. Maggie did not get up to make him breakfast. Judy rose at half past five and cooked him some of the bacon and eggs that Farmer Broughton had brought them a few days before. When he came down he was wearing his uniform, complete with the new stripe. As he ate she said nothing, drinking a cup of tea and then putting on her coat and leaving the house with him, bound for the station. On the way neither of them spoke

On the platform Sid dropped his kit-bag to the ground and lit a cigarette. He glanced at Judy. 'What's up? Cat got your tongue?'

She looked him straight in the eye. 'Far from it. There's a lot I have to say to you, Sid,' she said.

He shrugged. 'Go on then, get it off your chest.'

'A man could go to prison for what you did to me last night,' she told him quietly.

He smirked. 'But we're married. I'm entitled to do as I like whether you like it or not.'

'You're not entitled to abuse me. I don't like it, Sid and I won't put up with it any longer. I don't want to be married to you any more,' she said. 'I've had enough.'

'Suits me,' he said coldly.' I never wanted to marry you in the first place. I'm not even sure those kids are even mine, 'specially now I know what a cheatin' slut you are.'

She shook her head. 'You know there's no truth in that. Not that you've ever treated either of them like your own.' She looked at him. 'Everything you say, it's just excuses to brutalize your wife and children. Does it make you feel manly to hit women and children?'

He shrugged, drawing hard on his cigarette. 'Don't exaggerate.'

'It's over, Sid. I want a divorce.'

'Oh, that's a nice way to send a man back to the front line, I must say!'

'I mean it.'

'Just because I try to discipline the kids you've lost control of? Just because I was a bit rough with you last night?' He was all bluster now. In the distance a train whistle sounded and the shape of the engine could be glimpsed through the morning mist, winding its way round the bend in the track. Sid hauled his kit-bag onto his shoulder and gave her a long look.

'Don't you think I'll ever let you divorce me,' he said. 'We're married and we will be till I decide different, so don't you forget it.' He threw down the stub of his cigarette and ground it out with his boot. 'If there's any chuckin' out to be done I'll be the one doin' it!'

The train drew into the station with a hiss of steam and a grinding of brakes. Doors flew open and passengers alighted.

Sid looked at her. 'S'long then,' he said. 'You'll hear from me when I've made me mind up.' Without a backward glance in her direction Sid walked away and got onto the train. As he did so Judy turned and walked out of the station.

CHAPTER TWELVE

When Judy arrived back at Sea View it was still early. Maggie was up and waiting for her. She wore her blue dressing-gown and had a hot breakfast waiting and the kettle on ready for a pot of tea. When Judy walked in she looked up expectantly.

'He's gone, then?'

'Yes.' Judy sat down at the table, feeling suddenly exhausted. 'I'm sorry about last night, Maggie. You and Bill shouldn't have to see and hear things like that in your own home.'

Maggie put a hand on her shoulder. 'Don't give it another thought, luvvie. It wasn't your fault. I couldn't help feeling sorry for the kiddies though. They don't deserve to be treated like that.'

'No, they don't.' Judy took a deep breath. 'And neither do I; which is why I've just told Sid that I want a divorce.'

Maggie gasped. '*Never!*' She sighed. 'Well I can't say I blame you, even though I've always said that "for better or for worse" is a sacred vow and should be kept. I've never seen any man behave to his wife and children like he did.' She put a plate of bacon and eggs in front of Judy. 'Just you get that down you. You look like a wraith. I'll swear you've lost more'n a stone since you fetched him back from Southampton.'

Judy smiled. 'Thank you, Maggie. I don't know what I'd do without you.' She took a mouthful of bacon and realized suddenly how hungry she was.

'So how did he take it?' Maggie asked, pouring two cups of tea and sitting down opposite Judy. 'I'd like to have seen the look on his face.

'At first he didn't seem to care,' Judy told her. 'But then he changed his tune and said we'd stay married until he decided different.'

'Bluster!' Maggie declared. 'He wouldn't want to lose face – *you* divorcing *him*. I can't say I know a lot about the ins and outs of it, but I'd say you had plenty of grounds, not the least of which is cruelty. Don't you think I haven't seen those bruises.'

Judy sighed. 'I daresay you're right, but to be honest I haven't got the strength to deal with it at the moment. What I have to do first is to go and see Miss Paige and try to put things right with her so that Suzie can still be in the panto.'

'Oh yes. You're right there,' Maggie said. 'The look of that little angel's face last night will haunt me for ever. Bless her heart. How could he be so mean?'

'I'll go round and see her in my lunch break,' Judy said. She looked at her watch. 'I'd better go and get the girls up now, ready for school.

With Sid gone Judy felt as though a great weight had been lifted from her shoulders. There was plenty to do at the office but as soon as her lunch break came round she put on her coat and made for Miss Paige's.

The dancing school was held in a church hall and Miss Paige lived with her elderly mother in a small terraced house a few doors away. Judy knocked on the door, hoping that she wasn't disturbing their lunch. After a short wait the door was opened by a smiling Gladys Paige. When she saw that her caller was Judy her smile vanished.

'Oh! Mrs Truman.'

'May I come in, Miss Paige? I need to talk to you.'

'I really don't think there is anything more to be said,' the teacher said stiffly.

'Oh, but there is. Please, I have to explain – about Suzie.'

With a resigned sigh the teacher held the front door open and stood aside for Judy to pass. She pushed open a door to her right into an empty room. 'We can talk in here.' She closed the door and looked at Judy. 'Please – have a seat.'

Judy sat down on the edge of the settee and began. 'First I have to apologize for my husband's behaviour,' she said. 'He didn't tell me exactly what he said to you but I imagine he wasn't too polite.'

Miss Paige sat up very straight on a chair opposite. 'The word impolite hardly describes it,' she said, making Judy's heart sink. 'He all but accused me of taking money under false pretences and being an immoral influence on little girls.'

Judy winced. 'I'm so sorry. All I can say is that he was badly wounded in the Western Desert and he hasn't been quite himself since.'

The teacher's outraged expression softened a little. 'I see. Well, of course I understand, but that isn't really an excuse for speaking so insultingly.'

'Of course it isn't.' Judy cleared her throat. 'I'm here to ask you if you'd consider taking Suzie back,' she said. 'It isn't her fault. She was so happy to be chosen for the panto troupe and she loves your classes.' She paused. 'My parents did pay for a whole year's classes and....'

'But I gave your husband the money back.'

Judy stared at her. 'You gave it back?'

'Yes, minus payment for the first term, of course. He demanded it; quite forcibly actually. Didn't he tell you?'

Judy stood up, her heart beating fast. 'No, he didn't. I think there must be some kind of mix-up. I – I'll get back to you.'

Miss Paige stood to face Judy. 'Suzie is a dear little girl and she shows a lot of promise,' she said. 'As long as it's what you want I'll be happy to take her back, just so long as there are no further repercussions.'

'There won't be, I promise, and thank you,' Judy said, edging towards the door. 'It's very good of you, Miss Paige and, again, I'm so sorry for what happened. I'll get back to you as I said.'

All afternoon at work Judy racked her brain to think of a way of paying for Suzie's dancing lessons. Sid's effrontery in pocketing the money that Christine and Harry had paid was staggering. Suzie had only had one term's worth of lessons. There was the rest of the year to be paid for. She couldn't ask her parents to pay again. Yet how could she disappoint Suzie? She'd assured her this morning on the way to school that she'd be going back to her dancing lessons and both girls had gone into school in a happier mood than she'd seen them in since before Sid's convalescent leave.

When she met the girls out of school it was all they wanted to know.

'Did you see Miss Paige?' Suzie asked. 'Did she say it was all right?'

'What did Dad say to her?' Charlie wanted to know. 'Was he nasty? I bet he was. I said he was a bl...'

'*That's enough,*' Judy interrupted. 'I don't want to hear you saying those words again, Charlie. Do you understand?'

Charlie pouted. 'Dad says them all the time.'

'That doesn't make it right,' Judy told her. 'Don't let me hear it again.'

'So what did Miss Paige *say*?' Suzie asked, tugging at her mother's hand.

'It was all just a silly mistake,' Judy said unconvincingly. 'I'll sort it all out so don't worry.' But even as she said it she wondered if she was going to have to let Suzie down yet again.

When the girls were in bed that evening she repeated to Maggie and Bill everything that Miss Paige had told her about her encounter with Sid. Their shocked faces said it all.

'So there are no fees left,' Judy said. 'I've had no money from Sid for months and what I earn won't stretch to dancing classes.'

Bill stretched out a hand to stop her. 'Now just you stop worrying,' he said. 'I'm sure when Harry hears about this he'll send you the money straight away, but in the meantime we'll lend it to you so that Suzie can go back straight away.'

Judy swallowed hard at the lump in her throat. 'Oh, Bill, That's so kind, but I can't accept your offer. I can't ask Dad to pay over again.'

'Then we'll *give* you the money,' Maggie said firmly. 'You've more than earned it with all the help you've given with the summer visitors; helping me round the house too. You deserve a little reward and you're more than welcome to the money.' She looked at her husband. 'Isn't she, Bill?'

He nodded. ''Course you are, love.'

'It will only be for the three terms,' Judy said. 'And I'll only accept it as a loan. I won't ask Dad. I'll save up a bit each week and pay you back.'

Maggie smiled. 'Well, we'll see about that. The important thing is getting little Suzie back to those classes.'

The two weeks in the run-up to Christmas were hectic. At work Judy was busy and at home she and Maggie worked in their spare time on the costumes for Suzie. Some were hired and required alteration for the minuscule Suzie; others had to be made from scratch and all the children's mothers were busy. Maggie spent most of her time in the kitchen, cooking, and both she and Judy struggled to find presents in the shops for the girls. This Christmas finding luxuries like toys was even harder and many of the shops had little to offer. Suzie had set her heart on a doll and Judy eventually found one tucked away in Summerton's only department store. Maggie decided that her present to Suzie would be to make a complete wardrobe of clothes for it. Charlie was more difficult. She hated what she called 'soppy things', loving to be out of doors enjoying physical activity. When the first snow began to fall Bill thought he had the answer and he set to work on his big surprise for Charlie; he hammered away for hours in his shed, making a super wooden sledge, which he secretly looked forward to helping her play with.

Rehearsals for the pantomime were going well and in the final week the little girls who were to take part were taken along to the theatre to rehearse on stage. Suzie could hardly contain herself.

'There are real footlights, Mum,' she said as Judy collected her from the stage door after the first rehearsal. 'I can't wait for it to be Boxing Day.'

Judy laughed. 'Let's get Christmas over with first,' she said.

Christmas Day was a great success. Suzie was enchanted by her doll and the array of clothes that Maggie had made and Charlie couldn't wait to try out her sledge. Maggie's Christmas fare, planned and saved for all year, went down well and when at last it was time for bed the girls were sad it was all over.

'Tomorrow is a big day,' Judy reminded them as she tucked them in. 'The first performance of the pantomime.' She stroked

Suzie's baby soft blonde hair back from her forehead. 'Get to sleep now. You want to look your best tomorrow, don't you?'

'A story, Mum!' Charlie demanded. 'Read us a story before you go downstairs.'

Judy opened their favourite book and read a story from it. By the time she had finished Suzie was already fast asleep. She put the book away and looked at a still wide-awake Charlie. 'Try to sleep now,' she said, tucking her in more firmly.

'OK.' Charlie sighed. 'Mum, how long will the war last?'

Judy shook her head. 'I don't know, love. It might still be a long time.'

'I hope it is.'

'Why do you say that?' Judy asked. 'War is a terrible thing. We're lucky here but some people have to sleep every night in air-raid shelters. Sometimes when they wake up their houses have been bombed to bits.'

'I know.' Charlie reached out a hand to hold onto her mother's. 'But when the war is over we'll have to go back to Hackney, won't we? And Dad will come home to stay.' She looked at Judy with wide eyes full of dread. 'I don't want to go back there, Mum. I don't want Dad to live with us.'

'Shhh.' Judy stroked her daughter's cheek. 'It's Christmas, no time to be thinking things like that.' She paused, longing to take away Charlie's fears. 'Maybe, just *maybe* we won't have to go back.'

Charlie's eyes filled with hope. 'Won't we, Mum? Won't we *really*? Can we stay here at Sea View with Uncle Bill and Auntie Maggie for ever and ever?'

Judy shook her head. Had she said too much; given the child false hope? 'No one really knows what will happen in the future, so it's useless to worry about it,' she said. 'But we can look forward to tomorrow. The pantomime will be wonderful, so go to sleep now.'

As she made her way downstairs she thought about what Charlie had said. It was all wrong that a nine-year-old child should feel like that about her father. Charlie and Suzie deserved the same loving childhood with two parents that she'd had. What if Sid refused her a divorce? What if he insisted that they remain married and living under one roof? Could he do that? What rights did she have as an abused wife? She had no idea. All she knew was that, like Charlie, she could take no more.

The first night of the pantomime went well. Judy and Charlie sat in the front row of the stalls along with Maggie and Bill. Judy was nervous for Suzie before the curtain went up but the moment the troupe of little girls came on her nerves melted away. Suzie looked so happy and she never put a foot wrong in any of the routines. In the interval Maggie turned to her.

'She's a little natural,' she said. 'Bill and I couldn't be prouder if she was our own granddaughter.' She took Judy's hand and gave it an affectionate squeeze.

Charlie, sitting on her mother's other side, grinned with satisfaction. 'Wait till after the holidays when we go back to school,' she said. 'Our Suzie's famous now, isn't she?'

The day after Boxing Day it was business as usual for Judy. The takings at the box office had been good: the opening night of the pantomime almost a sell-out. She was busy with the books when she heard the office door open and close. Thinking it would be Mr Gresham she did not look up, but when no one spoke she raised her eyes from her work and gasped to see Peter standing looking at her.

'*Peter!*' She rose to her feet. 'I thought you couldn't get home this Christmas.'

He smiled. 'I arrived late last night. It's good to see you, Judy.'

She pulled out a chair for him. 'Sit down. You look exhausted. Would you like a coffee?'

'Thanks.' He sat down and she saw now with concern that his skin looked grey and there were fine lines around his eyes.

'It's good to see you too.' She switched on the kettle and spooned coffee and dried milk into two cups. 'Does your Uncle Bob know you're home?'

'Not yet.' He looked up at her. 'I've missed you, Judy.'

She handed him his cup. 'I've missed you too.'

'Mum said your husband was wounded.'

'Yes. I had to go down to Southampton to fetch him home for convalescence. He went back before Christmas.'

'Was it bad?'

She didn't know whether he meant Sid's injuries or his behaviour; she had never mentioned his manner towards her so he must be referring to his wounds. She took a sip of her coffee. 'He caught quite a lot of shrapnel in his back and leg. He was lucky that it didn't damage his spine.'

He looked at her. Her hesitation hadn't escaped him. 'You and the girls must miss him.'

She made a noncommittal sound and buried her face in her coffee cup.

'Judy, I've only got today and tomorrow. Can I see you? Could we go somewhere for a drink this evening, or maybe something to eat?'

Her heart leapt. There was nothing she wanted more than to be with Peter, even if it was only for an hour. She smiled. 'That would be lovely.' She reached out her hand towards him. 'Peter, you look so tired. I heard about the bombing raids on the news. Has it been bad?'

He sighed, taking her hand and pressing it between both of his. 'Bad doesn't anywhere near describe it. We live on the edge every night, all of us. What we do is a mixture of mass murder and self-preservation. Every night when we get back there are friends who've bought it, sometimes several. Every night you expect it to be your turn. One day...'

'Peter, *don't*!' She looked at his haunted eyes and longed to put her arms round him, wipe the horror from his mind. 'I wish there was something I could do,' she finished lamely.

He smiled at her, the old Peter making a brief appearance. 'You can, just by being you, by being here. Shall I come and pick you up tonight?'

She paused, thinking about Maggie and some of the things she'd said about her friendship with Peter. But somehow she felt that

Maggie would understand, under the circumstances. 'Yes,' she said with a smile. 'Pick me up – about half past seven.'

CHAPTER THIRTEEN

Judy was ready when Peter arrived to pick her up. She'd been open with Maggie about where she was going and the older woman had said nothing. Privately she felt that Judy deserved an evening out. She guessed that her feelings for Peter were deeper than mere friendship but in her mind she reasoned that no one could blame her for being attracted to a man who treated her like a woman instead of a punch bag. She kept her thoughts to herself, but when Judy came downstairs with her eyes sparkling and dressed in her best her heart sank a little. Was the girl heading for heartbreak? She took a deep breath and decided that in a world where there was so much heartbreak maybe it was fair enough to take the risk for the sake of a few hours' happiness.

Peter drove out to a tiny thatched pub on the edge of a village. Although it was dark Judy could see the swinging sign outside. It depicted a woman in Tudor costume and the name, The Queen of Hearts. Peter drove round to the yard at the back and switched off the shielded headlights. It took a few moments for Judy's eyes to adjust to the sudden gloom, but when they did she saw that Peter was looking at her intently.

'Judy, have you forgotten what I told you on the night of the Christmas dance last year?'

She was glad of the darkness to hide her sudden rush of colour. 'No, I haven't forgotten.'

'I want you to know that it wasn't just the romantic atmosphere of the occasion.' He grinned. 'Or the drink. I meant it. I really did.'

'I know.'

'So...?' He leaned closer. 'Any regrets about it?'

'Only one,' she whispered.

'What's that?'

'That I didn't say it back – that I loved you too. Because I do.'

'Oh, Judy darling.' He drew her close and kissed her. 'You have no idea how many times I've heard you say that in my dreams.' He picked up her wrist and pressed his lips against the bracelet he'd given her. 'You still wear it. I noticed the day before yesterday when I came up to the office that you had it on.'

'I wear it every day,' she told him. 'It reminds me of you and the times we've spent together.'

'All too few times.' He pulled her close and kissed her again.

'I wished and wished I'd told you that night,' she told him when they moved apart. 'But I felt that I didn't really have the right; that it was wrong.'

'Because you're married?'

'Not just that.'

'Then what?'

'Because – because I'm not good enough for you.'

'Don't say that. Don't *ever* say that.'

For a moment neither of them spoke, then Peter said: 'It's cold. Shall we go inside and have that drink?'

Inside the pub there was a welcoming log fire. It was quiet, just a few locals playing darts in the adjoining bar. They took their drinks to a table near the inglenook fireplace and settled down.

'How long is your leave, Peter?' Judy asked.

He lifted his shoulders. 'I've got to report back tomorrow.'

'It doesn't seem long enough to get the rest you need.'

He smiled. 'That's what Mum says but there are so few of us. A couple of days are better than nothing.' He took a deep draught of his drink and looked at her. 'So – tell me about him – about Sid.'

Her heartbeat quickened. 'What do you want to know?'

'So much. All of it. It's time you got it off your chest.' He looked at her. 'Whenever the subject comes up you quickly change it,' he said. 'Why do you do that, Judy?'

She flushed. 'I thought we'd come out for a quiet drink.'

'There you go, changing the subject again.' He leaned closer. 'You're not happy, are you, Judy? There's something badly wrong with that marriage of yours.'

She bit her lip, reluctant to admit to the shaming treatment she put up with. 'All right, if you really want to know, he's violent,' she blurted. 'He's cruel and hard and he doesn't love me or the girls. We were forced into marriage. He never wanted me and he's proved it almost every day since. When we've been together, that is.' She looked at him defiantly. 'There, are you satisfied now?'

His eyes softened and he reached out to take her hand. 'I'm so sorry. I never meant to force you into a painful admission.'

She picked up her glass and took a long drink from it. 'It's all right. It's true, all of it. The reason I don't like talking about it is because it makes me feel guilty and ashamed.'

'You have nothing to feel guilty or ashamed about.'

'I have. I caused it. It's all my fault. I told you I wasn't good enough. I should never have had anything to do with him in the first place. My parents never trusted him.'

'Then they shouldn't have let you marry him.'

She looked at the floor. 'Dad was angry. Charlotte was on the way. He couldn't see any further than the disgrace...'

'Oh God.' He moved closer and put an arm around her. 'Judy, you say he's violent. Does he hit you?' He took her silence for affirmation. 'You don't have to put up with that, you know.'

She turned to look at him. 'It was bad when he was here last time; so bad that I told him I wanted a divorce.'

'You did? Good for you.'

'But he said I would only get one if and when he was ready.'

'Bluff.'

'Maybe. Peter, can we stop talking about it now?'

He smiled. 'Of course. Are you hungry?'

'A bit.'

'Then you shall be fed.' Smiling he got up and went to the bar where he charmed the landlady and made her laugh. Coming back to the table he smiled at her.

'We're in luck. She says she'll make us some sandwiches. She's got some ham and chicken. They don't go short out here in the sticks. I said plenty of mustard on the ham. Is that all right?'

She laughed. 'It's fine.'

The sandwiches, served to them by a smiling landlady who

obviously took them for a young married couple, were delicious, made with home-made bread and home-reared chicken and ham. When they had eaten Peter said, 'I feel a lot better for that.'

Judy nodded. 'Me too.'

He leaned forward. 'Judy, don't be cross, but when I was talking to the landlady I asked her if they had rooms vacant here.' He held up his hand. 'I know what you're thinking so *don't*. I want you so much and tomorrow I'll be gone again. When I said I loved you I meant it with all my heart. This might be our only chance. It might be...'

'*Don't!*' She stopped him with a hard squeeze of his hand. 'Please don't.'

He looked at her. 'So – do I tell her we're staying?'

Judy was fighting with her conscience. Spending the night with Peter would be wrong. It would be unfaithful to her marriage. But what marriage? All she knew with Sid was fear and dread. Fear of his brutality and dread of being tied to him for ever. Yes, she had to face the fact that it was true. And there was no denying that she did love Peter. Why should she deny them both this one night when they wanted so badly to be together?' Slowly she nodded. 'Yes, tell her.'

The room was small but cosy. The landlady had lit a fire in the fireplace which warmed the whole room. Judy looked at the big double bed and then at Peter. He held out his arms.

She had never known such tenderness; such sweet passion. She'd wanted it to last for ever. Now, lying in the crook of Peter's arm as he slept, she fought the urge to sleep herself, wanting to savour as many of the hours left to them as she could. In the light of the dying fire she looked at his sleeping face, all the lines of fear and exhaustion smoothed out. He looked so young and vulnerable that she wanted to wrap him in her arms and hold him there for ever; safe and loved. She could still see the scar on his shoulder where he'd been shot by the enemy fighter. It reminded her of the risks and the traumas he lived through every day with so many others. Friends who hadn't made it back from the nightly bombing raids. Others badly injured, some maimed for life. How could she bear it if anything happened to Peter? She closed her eyes tightly and forced herself not to think about it.

Examining her innermost thoughts she found that she felt no guilt. She deserved Peter's love as he deserved hers. It was merely a quirk of fate that they hadn't met before. Sid didn't care about her anyway, except as a possession, something to be tamed and controlled, like an animal. She owed him no loyalty after the way he had treated her and the girls.

In the early hours they woke and loved again. This time Judy wept quietly afterwards, knowing that in a few hours they would drive back to Summerton. His leave would be over and he would go back to that hell on earth, whilst all she would have would be the memory of this night.

Early next morning before it was light they rose and dressed, went downstairs and paid the bill. The landlady, wearing her dressing-gown, unlocked the back door for them.

'Good luck both of you!' she called as they got into the car. 'Happy landings!'

Neither of them spoke until they were on the way back to Summerton. Peter turned to her

'Thank you for last night,' he said. 'I'll treasure the memory for the rest of my life.'

Looking at him she was stunned to see that there were tears in his eyes. 'Me too, darling,' she said. 'Whatever the future holds no one can take that away from us.'

'I love you so much,' he said huskily.

'I love you too,' she said, her head on his shoulder. 'And I always, *always* will.'

CHAPTER FOURTEEN

As 1943 dawned Bill became more and more excited and optimistic about Britain's change of fortune. Towards the end of January the news that the Russians had liberated Stalingrad had him glued to the wireless at every bulletin. Meantime Bomber Command's nightly raids on Germany were stepping up.

'Those RAF boys deserve a medal, every one of them,' he pronounced as he pored over the daily paper. 'They're doing us proud and no mistake.'

Judy listened to his excited pronouncements with mixed feelings. So many planes were lost every day; so many young men killed. Could Peter possibly come through this alive and well?

'It won't be long now!' Bill announced confidently. 'You mark my words, we'll be hearing that the second front has started soon and after that it'll just be a matter of time.' He threw an arm around Maggie's shoulders. 'We'll get that cottage in the country yet, girl. Roses round the door and the lot.'

Judy thought about it with a heavy heart. Where would that leave her and the girls? When Maggie and Bill sold Sea View and moved on to their much deserved retirement, she and the girls would have no choice but to go back to Hackney and whatever awaited them there.

There had been no word from Sid since he went back to his unit. Not that she'd expected to hear from him after what had passed between them just before he left. In a way it was a relief but Judy worried about the future. With her job at the theatre and partly government-subsidized rent here with Maggie and Bill she could just about manage, but when the war was over, when Maggie and Bill were ready to move on and they were obliged to return to London, what then? The thought kept her awake at night and nagged away at her all day like an aching tooth.

Maggie noticed her preoccupation and although she didn't like to pry she felt she had to ask. 'Are you all right, love? You've been very quiet lately, like you've got something on your mind. You look so down,' she said.

Judy shrugged. 'Just worried about the future,' she said. 'There's been no word from Sid and I wonder what's going to happen.'

'Well, whatever happens he'll have to face up to his responsibilities; be a man and support his family,' Maggie said. 'How long is it since you heard from him?'

'Not since he went back last December.'

Maggie shook her head. 'Then you'll have to get word to him somehow. Would you like Bill to write to someone on your behalf? It's disgraceful, the way he's treated you.'

'*No!*' Judy felt her heartbeat quicken. 'No, Maggie. You don't understand. It's not as simple as that. There's something you don't know – something I haven't told you.'

Maggie looked at her. 'What is it, love?'

'It's Peter. We – we're in love.' Judy couldn't meet the other woman's eyes.

Maggie smiled. 'Well, I can't say I'm surprised.'

Judy looked at Maggie, her eyes full of anguish. 'I love him, Maggie. I love him so much. We love each other. I didn't know it was possible to be loved like that. That night, just after Christmas…'

'I know.' Maggie held up her hand. 'I heard you come in early next morning and I guessed. This makes it even more important that you get in touch with Sid.'

Judy's eyes brimmed with tears. 'I don't know where to start. Peter's in so much danger, I can't give him anything else to worry about. Then there are his parents. What will they think? Their son and me – a married woman with two children. They'd be disgusted with me.'

'They'll be nothing of the kind,' Maggie said sternly.

'But if Sid sticks to his word and refuses to divorce me I won't have any choice but to stay married to him and go back to London.'

'You *can't*!' Maggie looked horrified. 'Imagine what he'd put you through, especially if he found out about Peter.'

Judy sighed. 'Then what? I can't continue to bring up two children alone on what I earn.'

Maggie stood up again and put her arms round her. 'You're a good girl, Judy. You and those kiddies have been like family to me and Bill. I know what you've done is wrong and I won't pretend otherwise, but you don't deserve to be tied to a man like Sid Truman for the rest of your life.' She lifted the hem of her apron and dabbed the tears from Judy's cheeks. 'There now, don't cry and don't worry any more. It's not good for you. We'll think of something, don't you fret.'

'It's such a relief to talk about it,' Judy said.

'You should have told me before. Still, never mind. We'll think of something.'

News of the Allied victories kept Bill in good spirits, but Maggie managed to capture his attention a few nights after her talk with Judy. She'd had an idea and she wanted to put it to him. When he heard it he had reservations. He loved Judy and the girls like a father but as for Sid— as he pithily put it: 'I wouldn't spit on him if he was on fire!' There was no way he would ever lift a finger to benefit him. At last they came to a compromise and on Sunday evening after the girls were in bed they invited Judy to sit with them while they put their plan to her.

'Bill knows about you and Peter,' Maggie said.

Bill looked at the floor and cleared his throat. 'Don't think we're judging you, girl,' he said. 'Because we're not. We haven't lived to be our great age without understanding a bit about human nature and we know it's not in you to do anything immoral.'

Judy smiled. 'Thank you, Bill. It's very good of you to say that.'

'We want to help,' Maggie put in. 'Neither of us want to see you go back to that husband of yours to keep a roof over your heads, and we've come up with a plan. As you know, we were about to retire when the war started. This business is getting too much for us.' She glanced at her husband. 'Well, to cut a long story short, we're going to start looking for that dream cottage right away. At our age why wait?'

Judy's heart sank. They were going to sell up.

Maggie hurried on. 'But we're going to keep this place on and we'd like you to accept the position of manager.'

'*Me*?' Judy stared at them. 'But – how will that work? Surely you'll need to sell Sea View to pay for your cottage.'

Bill shook his head. 'We've got a bit saved,' he explained. 'And we'll still take a percentage of the earnings from here; a small percentage to pay for the overheads. The rest will be yours, plus the salary we'll pay you as manager.'

Judy was speechless. She looked from one to the other helplessly. 'I don't know what to say,' she stammered. 'It's so generous. I can't believe you'd be so kind to us.'

'There is one condition,' Maggie put in quickly.

Judy held her breath. 'Of course. Whatever you say.'

'You know our opinion of Sid. Bill and I agree that we couldn't let him benefit from this in any way. Not after what we've seen of him. You've already told him you want a divorce, so we want you to set things in motion right away.'

'How do I go about that?' Judy asked. 'I wouldn't know where to start.'

'We'll help,' Bill promised. 'I'll have to see the solicitor about drawing up a proper legal contract for you. We want everything to be done properly. While we're there we can ask about the divorce as well.'

'I'll have to give in my notice at the theatre,' Judy said.

Maggie laughed. 'No hurry about that, love. We haven't found this dream cottage of ours yet.'

Letters came from Peter quite regularly, sometimes long and loving, sometimes short and scrappy. She could always tell when he was exhausted and traumatized after bombing raids, though he never mentioned the war or what he was doing. Judy wrote back. She tried to make her letters light-hearted too and never once did she mention her impending divorce or her concerns about it.

Once again the summer term came to an end. As the school holidays came closer the girls were full of what they would do with the long weeks of freedom that lay ahead. Mary Gresham had invited them both to lend a hand at the pier puppet theatre and they were looking forward to it.

Sea View was fully booked for the rest of the summer with servicemen and their wives and families looking forward to enjoying a few days' peace and quiet. On the day before school broke up Charlie's teacher sent a message home for Judy via Charlie to ask to see her.

'What have you been up to?' she asked as she read the brief note that Charlie handed her.

'*Nothing!*' Charlie said indignantly. 'I'm always good, I am!'

Judy laughed. 'Well, there's a novelty.'

She went along to see Charlie's teacher the following Friday after school. Mrs Thompson was an older woman who would probably have retired had it not been for the war. Since Charlie had been in her class she had done particularly well. The teacher greeted Judy with a smile and offered her a chair.

'Charlotte is a good girl,' she said. 'Very hard-working and very bright.'

Judy nodded. 'She loves school and is never any trouble about doing her homework.'

Mrs Thompson smiled. 'That's good to hear.' She paused. 'I asked you to come and see me this afternoon because I wanted to ask how you'd feel about Charlotte being put in for her scholarship examination a year early.'

Judy was taken aback. 'Well, I don't know. Do you think she's ready?'

'More than ready. She's already at least a year ahead of her class-mates. I feel sure that she'd pass without any trouble. The point is that once she started at the high school the work would be that much harder. I'm not concerned that she'd cope with the work. I just wonder if she'd flourish under that kind of pressure. It would be awful to see her lose interest. She doesn't have to sit the exam for another year but it seems a shame to hold her back. You know your own child, so what do you think?'

'She loves her work,' Judy said slowly.

'I know she does, and the extra year at high school would be beneficial to her later,' Mrs Thompson went on. 'I can visualize her going on to college – even university if she continues as she is at present.'

'I think maybe it would be best if I asked her how she feels about it,' Judy said at last.

'There's just one other thing,' Mrs Thompson said. 'What are your plans once the war is over? If you're planning to return to London...'

'No.' Judy shook her head. 'I've been offered a very good job here in Summerton-on-Sea and I'm planning to take it and stay on.'

'I see. Well in that case there isn't a problem. It would be a pity to have to transfer her.'

All the way home Judy glowed with pride. She knew that Charlie loved school but she'd had no idea that she was so gifted. She felt a stab of guilt. She had made so much of Suzie's talent as a performer that Charlie must have felt resentful, yet she had never once showed it. She would make sure she made up for it now. In the kitchen she told Maggie what the teacher had said and asked if she'd distract Suzie after tea so that she could talk to Charlie.

'Of course I will, love.' Maggie beamed. 'Would you believe it? Our little Charlie going to university!'

Judy took Charlie down onto the beach, where they sat on the sand. 'There's something I want to talk to you about,' she said.

Charlie picked up a handful of sand and let it slowly trickle through her fingers. 'Is it about Dad?'

'No. It's about you. You know I went to see your teacher this afternoon?'

'Yes.'

'She asked me how I'd feel about you taking your scholarship exam next spring. A year early.'

Charlie looked up, her cheeks colouring. 'What did you say, Mum?'

'I said I'd talk to you. I know you love school and you're good at the work, but do you think you're ready for high school?'

Charlie's eyes sparkled. 'I want to go, Mum. Can I? You won't say no, will you?'

'If you want to go of course I won't stop you,' Judy promised. 'But the work will be harder than it is now. The other girls will be older. You might find it hard to keep up.'

'I won't. Mrs Thompson already gives me special work the others don't do.'

'Well, if you think you can manage and you really want it...'

'I do. *I do*! But...' Charlie's face fell. 'Dad won't come home again and stop me going like he stopped Suzie going to dancing, will he?'

'No. I won't let that happen.'

'But what if the war ends and we have to go back to London?'

'That's something else I wanted to talk to you about. Uncle Bill and Auntie Maggie are going to retire, move away to a smaller house. They have offered me the job of managing Sea View.'

'So does that mean we can stay here?' Charlie face lit up. 'For keeps?'

Judy smiled. 'For keeps.'

'And live at Sea View?'

'Yes.'

Charlie considered this for a moment, her face solemn. 'But what about Dad?' she said at last.

Judy bit her lip. This was something she'd been dreading. 'He might not want to live with us any more after the war.'

'Really? Is it true?'

The look of hope on the child's face tugged at Judy's heart strings. No child should feel like that towards her father. 'We'll have to wait and see.' Judy tipped Charlie's chin up and kissed the end of her nose. 'I'm so proud of you, my clever girl.'

Charlie put her arms around her mother's neck and hugged her. 'I love you, Mum. I hate it when Dad hits you.'

Judy held her close. 'I'm going to make sure it never happens again,' she promised

Judy went to bed that night with a feeling of optimism. She had been offered a new job – one that she looked forward to. The tide of war seemed to be turning. Her children were doing well and the long summer holidays stretched ahead. It seemed there would be sunshine all the way.

The following morning she was up early, taking cups of morning tea upstairs to the visitors, and some for Maggie and Bill too, before leaving for work. She had just come downstairs when the front doorbell rang. She went to answer it, wondering who could be visiting at the time of the morning.

Steve Gresham stood on the doorstep. His face was grey. Judy's heart plummeted.

'Steve?'

'Can I come inside for a minute, my dear?'

'Of course.' Judy held the door wide. 'I've just made some tea. Would you like a cup?'

He shook his head. 'I don't know how to tell you this,' he said. 'But Peter made us promise you were to be one of the first to know, should it happen.'

'*Happen*?' Judy felt for the edge of a chair and sat down. Steve put out a hand to her.

'Are you all right?'

'Yes.' She looked up at him. 'Please, tell me,' she said faintly.

'Peter's plane was shot down somewhere over Germany last night,' Steve said softly. 'At the moment he and all the crew are reported missing.' He swallowed hard. 'I daresay we'll learn more in a few days' time. For now all we can do is pray.'

CHAPTER FIFTEEN

Somehow Judy got though the summer. No news came about Peter, and Mary and Steve carried on with their puppet shows down at the pier, battling on bravely.

'At least it keeps us from thinking the worst,' Mary told Judy when she picked up the children one afternoon. 'We just live from day to day.' She smiled. 'How are you, dear? You look very peaky.'

Judy longed to tell Mary that she loved Peter and how much it hurt her, not knowing whether he was alive or dead. Ever since the morning she had heard the news about him she had hardly slept. She also lived in dread that Sid might come home again and that there would be a confrontation about the divorce. The constant anxiety made her ill. She felt utterly exhausted most of the time; she couldn't sleep and had little appetite. Maggie was worried about her. She refused to allow her to help with the visitors and tried her best to get her to eat and take more rest.

'You must try and buck up, love,' she said, seeing Judy push her plate away almost untouched yet again. 'You've hardly eaten enough to keep a mouse alive for weeks. You'll be ill yourself at this rate.'

It was early September, a week before the children returned to school when Bob Gresham arrived in the office one morning, looking more relaxed than he had for weeks.

'Peter's been taken prisoner,' he told Judy. 'He's in a POW camp somewhere in Germany. Mary and Steve had word from the International Red Cross yesterday afternoon. He and the flight engineer from his crew were captured trying to get across the border into Switzerland.'

Judy felt faint with relief. 'Is he all right?'

'As far as we know,' Bob went on. 'They'd been travelling and hiding up for weeks, which is why we hadn't heard anything. We're allowed to send parcels through the Red Cross, and Mary's already started putting one together.' He smiled. 'You know what she's like. She told me to tell you that if you want to include anything just let her know.'

Judy hurried home that evening, hardly able to wait to tell Maggie and Bill the good news. They were both overjoyed.

'Well, at least he'll be out of danger now till the war's over,' Bill said philosophically. 'No more flying. That's something to be grateful for. So many of those poor young lads aren't coming home at all.'

Judy's appetite returned immediately she heard that Peter was alive. The colour began to come back into her cheeks and she was much more her old self again, much to Maggie's relief. Often at night she dreamed that Peter was home again. They were married and the four of them were a family. Then she'd wake to the reality that it wasn't true and the depressing realization that there was a great deal to go through yet before they could even think of being together.

Bill was as preoccupied as ever with the war news. Italy surrendered unconditionally; the allies had taken Palermo and the Germans had been routed at Kursk. Places that were on the tips of everyone's tongues now were places few had even heard of before but that did little to dampen Bill's enthusiasm for the victory he was convinced would come soon.

The children returned to school and by early October the summer visitors had dwindled to nothing. When the bookings at Sea View finally came to an end Maggie began her end-of-season cleaning marathon, constantly grumbling about the state of the house.

'We always used to spend the autumn and winter doing maintenance and decorating, but you can't get the paint and wallpaper now,' she told Judy one evening after the girls had gone to bed. 'It's a crying shame.'

Bill shrugged. 'Well, if we can't, neither can anyone else,' he pointed out. 'Our home looks no worse than anyone else's, so why worry?'

Maggie rolled her eyes to the ceiling. 'Typical male point of view,' she said. 'No doubt you'll start moaning when the roof falls in on us!'

Bill shook his head. 'Trust you to exaggerate!'

'Believe me I'm not exaggerating,' Maggie protested. 'Most of the sheets want turning sides-to-middle and the pillow cases are so thin you can see through them.' She looked at Judy. 'When they're hanging on the line you can see the sun shining through them.'

'Well just thank heaven that the sun's shining,' Bill said. 'Anyway, it won't be long now before you can buy all the sheets and pillow cases you want! You see if I'm not right.'

A month later Judy received a telegram from her parents. They were back in England and arriving home the following afternoon. She was so excited. It was so long since she had seen them.

She took the girls to the station to meet them the following afternoon and when they stepped down from the train there were hugs and kisses all round.

'Just look at these two!' Harry exclaimed. 'I can't believe how much they've grown. Look at this young Charlie. She's almost up to my shoulder.'

'What did you expect?' Christine said. 'After all, it's almost two years since we've seen them! I can't believe it. Such a big chunk out of all our lives.'

'We're going to live at Sea View for ever and ever,' Suzie piped as she skipped along beside them. 'We're never going back to London at all.'

Charlie nudged her. 'Mum said not to say anything, big mouth!' She looked up at her grandparents' astonished faces. 'It was supposed to be a surprise,' she said.

Christine looked at Judy. 'Is that right?'

'Maggie and Bill want to retire and they've offered me the job of managing the guest house,' Judy told them. 'I was going to tell you all about it later.'

'And Sid?' Harry asked, one eyebrow raised. 'Where does he come into all of it?'

Judy shook her head. 'Maybe we can talk about that later.' She nodded in the girls' direction and, taking the hint, Harry took both girls by the hand and walked ahead. 'What about you two?' he asked them. 'I want to hear all about what you've been doing.'

Charlie and Suzie both tried to talk at once, each of them eager to tell their grandfather about their latest successes.

'I haven't heard from Sid for months,' Judy told her mother as they walked behind. 'I've no idea where he is. I think I told you he was wounded.'

Christine nodded. 'You wrote in one of your letters that you'd had to go down to Southampton to fetch him.'

'After his convalescence he went back to his unit. I've heard nothing since.'

'But that's terrible.'

'It was a nightmare while he was here,' Judy went on. 'He was violent and nasty. He cancelled Suzie's dancing lessons and pocketed the money you and Dad paid for them. He accused me of being unfaithful. I'd had enough, Mum, so before he went back I told him I wanted a divorce.'

'Good for you. What did he say?'

'He said it would happen when he was ready and not before.'

Christine shook her head. 'Something will have to be sorted out. He can't just walk out on you.' She looked at Judy. 'It's really good to hear you've been offered the job of managing the guest house, but what's to stop Sid from turning up on your doorstep when the war's over and demanding to move in?'

'Bill and I are going to see a solicitor,' Judy explained. 'It's to have a proper contract drawn up for me as manager of Sea View, but Bill says we can ask about the divorce while we're there.'

Christine sighed. 'Those two have been so good to you.'

'I know. I don't know what we would have done without them.'

'And I think it's a good idea of Bill's to ask about the divorce. Something has to be done about it. You can't go on like this.'

After the girls had gone to bed that night Bill and Maggie sat down with Judy and her parents while Bill set out the plans that he and Maggie had made.

'We want to buy a cottage and retire,' he explained. 'And we can't think of anyone better to manage this place for us,' he said. 'We know that she's more than capable and it will give her and the girls a home and an income.' He looked at Judy. 'I might as well tell you now that we're also planning to leave the house to you in our will so that you and the kids will be all right should anything happen to Maggie and me.'

Judy blushed. 'Oh, Bill!'

'That's very generous of you both,' Harry said. 'She's a lucky girl.'

'We've no one else to leave it to,' Maggie put in. 'And Judy and the girls have been like the family we never had. It's a pleasure to think they'll be settled here.'

'But we have made a stipulation,' Bill added. 'We want her to set the divorce in motion. It's her decision and we agree with it. Don't think we haven't given this a lot of thought,' he added. 'Maggie and me have always believed that marriage is sacred. You're meant to keep the vows you make in church, but we've seen for ourselves the kind of man Sid Truman is. The last time he was here his behaviour was atrocious and there's no way we ever want to see him benefit from our actions, so that's where the solicitor comes in.' He looked at Judy. 'I've made an appointment for Monday afternoon at half past four,' he told her. 'If that's all right with you, Judy, we'll go along and set things going.'

Later, when she and her mother were alone, Judy told Christine about Peter.

'I know I was wrong to spend the night with him,' she said. 'But I don't regret it. He's a prisoner of war now and I probably won't see him again until the war is over. I love him, Mum. I always will, and he loves me too. I didn't know what love was till I met Peter. It might be that we can never be together but I'm willing to wait for him for as long as it takes.'

Christine hugged her tightly. 'I hope it all works out for you, love. He sounds so nice and if anyone deserves some happiness you do.' She smiled. 'Perhaps this is a good time to tell you what your dad and I have planned for after the war. Both of us are tired of travelling. We'd like to settle down somewhere nice. What we thought was that we'd look for somewhere where we could start a dance-and-music school.'

Judy was delighted. 'Oh, Mum, that's a lovely idea!'

Christine smiled. 'I'm glad you think so, and with you planning to stay here in Summerton maybe we'll find a place here too.'

But although the idea was exciting, they both knew that they had a long way to go before their dreams could be realized.

Judy was nervous as they climbed the stairs to Mr Kennedy's office on Monday afternoon. When the receptionist showed them into his office the solicitor rose from behind his desk to greet them.

'Mr Hurst and Mrs Truman, good afternoon.' He shook hands with them both and Judy immediately felt more at ease. He was an elderly man with smooth grey hair and kindly blue eyes behind rimless glasses. He sat down behind his desk and invited them to take the two chairs opposite. Opening a file in front of him he glanced at it, then looked up at Bill.

'You want me to draw up a contract of employment for Mrs Truman?' he said.

Bill nodded. 'And my wife and I want to add something to the will we made with you some time ago.'

'I see. Well, that should be quite straightforward.'

The employment contract was quickly drawn up and signed by Bill and Judy. The solicitor explained that a codicil, leaving Sea View to Judy in the event of both Hursts' deaths would be required and would take a little time to draw up. Mr Kennedy looked up.

'Is that all, then?'

Bill cleared his throat and glanced at Judy. 'There is just one more thing, Mr Kennedy,' he said.

At that point Judy felt that she needed to take over. This was her problem and she didn't intend to leave Bill to deal with it. Laying a restraining hand on his arm she spoke up, 'I want to divorce my husband.'

The solicitor looked at her over the tops of his spectacles. 'I see. I take it that he is in full agreement with this?'

Judy shook her head. 'We've only discussed it briefly. I have reason to believe he might - might...'

'Contest it?' The solicitor nodded. 'On what grounds do you wish to divorce him?'

Judy swallowed hard. 'Cruelty,' she said softly.

'Mental or physical?'

'Both.' Judy felt her colour rise and looked down at her hands, twisting nervously in her lap.

'I can vouch for that,' Bill put in stoutly. He could see how humiliating this was for Judy and it was making him angry. 'Sid Truman has stayed in our house on leave and each time we have witnessed him being violent to his wife and young daughters.'

'How very regrettable.' Mr Kennedy looked up. 'I take it he is in the services.'

'Yes. The Army,' Judy said.

'And where is he serving at present?'

Judy glanced at Bill. 'I'm not sure. He was in the Western Desert when I last heard from him.'

'So you don't know where he is at present?'

'Not really, no.'

'But you've been receiving your Army wives' pay?'

'No.'

'That makes things rather difficult. You see, I can't serve divorce papers on him if I don't know where he is.'

Bill cleared his throat. 'Wouldn't it be possible for you to find out?'

'I can certainly try.' Mr. Kennedy looked at Judy. 'I'll need his full name, rank and number.'

She licked her lips. 'Bombardier Sidney Arthur Truman, Royal Artillery 15083508.'

The solicitor made a note on his pad. 'And you say you last heard from him – when?'

'Last December when he returned to his unit. He'd been convalescing after being wounded.'

'I'll see what I can do.'

Christine and Harry were waiting eagerly to hear the outcome of the visit when Bill and Judy got home. They were disappointed that there would be a delay whilst Sid's whereabouts were obtained.

'Never mind,' Harry said. 'It shouldn't be too difficult to find him, not with his name, rank and number.'

On the morning that they left a telephone call came from Mr Kennedy. Bill answered the phone.

'I'm sorry, but Mrs Truman has gone to the station to see her parents off,' he said. 'Can I give her a message?'

'Yes. I'd like her to call in to the office to see me.'

'Oh. Have you found her husband?' Bill asked.

The solicitor paused. 'I'm afraid there are some complications,' he said. 'I'll explain to Mrs Truman when she comes in to the office. It's a matter of some urgency. Do you think she would be free to come this afternoon?'

Bill was intrigued. 'I should think so. She was going straight on to work, so I'll ring her there and call you back.' Bill cleared his throat. It all sounded very mysterious. 'I'll come along with her then, shall I?'

'I think that on this occasion it would be better if I saw Mrs Truman alone,' the solicitor said. 'I have a free slot at four o'clock, so if you could let me know if that will be convenient...'

'Yes, yes of course I will.'

In the kitchen Bill and Maggie speculated on why the solicitor wanted to see Judy urgently, and alone.'

'You don't think he's been killed, do you?' Maggie asked.

Bill shook his head. 'Judy would have been notified,' he said. 'After all, she is his next of kin.'

'Well don't you think you should get on the phone and tell her about the appointment?' Maggie said.

Bill went into the hall and dialled the number of the theatre. 'Judy, Mr Kennedy wants to see you,' he said. 'He says it's urgent and he can give you an appointment at four o'clock this afternoon. I said I'd ring back and let him know.'

'I'll have to leave work early but I'm sure it'll be all right,' Judy said. 'You can tell him I'll be there.' She paused. 'Bill, did he say anything else? Has he found out where Sid is?'

'He didn't say,' Bill told her. 'He was a bit cagey about it if you ask me. He wants to see you on your own too. I hope everything's all right, girl.'

'I'm sure it will be, Bill. I'll tell you everything when I get home. Thanks for ringing.'

There was no problem about leaving work an hour early and Judy presented herself at Mr Kennedy's office with five minutes to spare. Waiting in the outer office she had time to speculate on what the solicitor had to tell her. But she was completely unprepared for what was to come.

The receptionist's telephone rang and she turned to Judy with a smile.

'You can go in now.'

Mr Kennedy rose from his desk to greet her and indicated a seat opposite. When she was seated he looked up.

'When you were last here, Mrs Truman, you told me you hadn't heard from your husband since last December. Is that right?'

'That's right. It was December the tenth, to be exact. I saw him off on the train.'

'And he was meant to be rejoining his unit?'

'Yes.'

Mr Kennedy examined his notes and then said, 'I'm sorry to have to tell you this, but in response to my enquiries I am informed that Bombardier Sidney Truman deserted from the Army ten months ago. He hasn't been traced since.'

Judy gasped. '*Deserted*?'

'You're sure you've heard nothing from him?'

'Not a word.'

The solicitor sighed. 'It seems very strange that the military police haven't paid you a visit.' He peered at her over the tops of his spectacles. 'The wife is usually their first contact. You say you've had no enquiries about his whereabouts at all?'

You say? Judy felt her colour rise. Did the man think she was somehow involved in Sid's disappearance? Was he accusing her of hiding him?

'I've heard nothing at all,' she said firmly. 'If I knew where he was I wouldn't have asked you to find him, would I?'

He nodded. 'Of course not. I apologize if I sounded as though I doubted your word, but there is something very odd here. You say you don't have a pay book and have received no money from your husband?'

'That's right. He told me he preferred to send me the money

direct.'

Mr Kennedy looked sceptical. 'But he has reneged on that?'

'Most of the time, yes.'

'Forgive me for asking, but do you have your marriage certificate with you?'

Her 'marriage lines' were something Judy always kept in her handbag. She opened it now and produced the tattered envelope containing the certificate. She handed it across the desk.

Mr Kennedy examined it carefully. 'Well, as far as I can tell that seems to be in order,' he said at last, handing it back. He looked at her, his face grave. 'Is there is anyone you can think of who might be shielding your husband, Mrs Truman? If there is, I advise you to get in touch with them without delay. At the moment he is what is termed absent without leave and as such he is already in a lot of trouble. But as long as he is missing there is no way that we can obtain a divorce.'

CHAPTER SIXTEEN

Christmas came and went. Once again Suzie was in the school concert and Judy tried very hard to concentrate on the children and to put Sid's absence to the back of her mind until after the festivities. Soon after Christine and Harry had gone back she received a letter to say that there were rumours that their next stop might be somewhere in the Far East. Her heart sank. It sounded like a very long way away and she wondered how long it would be before she saw them again.

Nothing was heard either from or about Sid and, as the weeks went by, she grew more and more worried. She had no idea what to do. Every time there was a knock on the door she expected it to be him, demanding to be taken in and sheltered; she had no idea what she would do if this should happen. When she expressed her fears to Bill he left her in no doubt as to what would happen.

'I'd have to get straight on to the authorities,' he said without hesitation. 'Concealing a deserter is a crime. I'd have no choice, so don't you worry your head about that.'

But it did little to stop Judy from worrying. Ever since she'd visited the solicitor she'd hardly slept. Lying awake she thought of various possibilities and at last she made her mind up about what she must do. She confided her intention to Maggie and Bill.

'I'm going to have to go down to Gravesend and see Sid's mother.' Even as she said it her heart plummeted. 'I'm not looking forward to it and I'm not sure how much help she'll be, but Charlie's exam is only a few weeks away and I have to do this before that.'

'What's she like, this Mrs Truman?' Maggie asked.

'She's not a pleasant woman,' Judy said. 'I haven't seen her for years but I doubt if she's mellowed with age.'

Maggie frowned. 'Do you really have to go and see her? Isn't there anyone else?'

Judy shook her head. 'No, she's my only hope; the only person I can think of who might know where Sid is,'

'I realize it won't be very pleasant for you,' Bill put in. 'Would you like me to come with you?'

Judy was touched. 'No, Bill. This is something I have to tackle by myself.'

He shrugged. 'I don't like to think of you putting yourself through this, but until we find out where he is and what's happening our hands are tied.'

Judy nodded. 'Exactly. So if you don't mind looking after the girls for a couple of days…'

'You know you don't have to ask,' Maggie interrupted. 'They're like our own grandchildren and no trouble at all, bless them.'

'In that case I'll ask Bob for a few days off and go – maybe next week.'

Things at the theatre were quiet after the pantomime's short season was over and Bob Gresham was quite happy for Judy to take a couple of days off. She came home and explained to the girls that she had to go away for a couple of days.

'Can't we come too?' Charlie begged.

'No, love, I have to go on my own,' Judy told her gently. 'Besides, you have to go to school. You can't stay away now, can you? Not with your exam coming up.'

She packed a few clothes, intending to find some accommodation in a bed and breakfast somewhere, and caught the first train on Monday morning.

Gravesend had suffered quite a bit of bomb damage but Judy found that Liberty Street was still standing more or less intact. She knocked on the door of number thirty-four and waited. From within she could hear children's voices and a woman's strident shout.

'Shurrup, can't yer! There's someone at the flamin' door.'

A moment later the door was flung open and Annie Truman's bulk filled the doorway. She looked much the same as Judy remembered her, greasy grey hair pulled back into a knot at the back of her head and a grubby pinafore worn over a sagging skirt and jumper. She stared challengingly at Judy.

'Yeah? Watcher want?'

'It's Judy, Mrs Truman. Sid's Judy.'

The woman frowned and leaned closer. '*Sid's Judy*,' she mocked. 'Don't talk rubbish. Sling yer 'ook!' She began to close the door but Judy put out her hand. 'Mrs Truman – *wait*, please. I need to speak to you. It's important.'

Something in Judy's tone made the woman hesitate, peering at her with short- sighted eyes. 'Who are you?'

'I'm Sid's wife, Mrs Truman. Don't you remember? I'm the mother of his two daughters.'

'Sid's wife my foot!' Annie Truman's mouth folded into a tight line. 'I remember you now. You're that slut he brought 'ome once, reckoning to be up the duff.'

'Sid and I were married over ten years ago, Mrs Truman.'

'You're a liar!'

'Is Sid here?'

'No, he ain't!'

'Do you know where he is?'

At once Annie's expression was guarded. 'What's it to you?'

'Because, as you must know, he's deserted from the Army. I haven't seen him for over a year. He must have been in touch with someone.'

'Huh!' Annie folded her arms across her vast bosom. 'An' you reckon I'd tell *you* if I knew where e was?'

'I told you. Sid and I are married. He's my husband.'

'Clear orf!' Annie said menacingly. 'I've told yer. Sid ain't got nuthin to do with you, so bugger orf before I call the lads.'

Her tone was so vicious that Judy took a step backwards. At that moment a young woman squeezed past Annie with a small child in a pushchair.

'I'm going to the shops, Annie,' she said with a sidelong glance at Judy. 'I shan't be long.'

Annie ignored her, relaxing her bulk again. 'Look,' she said leaning forward and staring at Judy in a threatening manner. 'I got a bleedin' 'ouseful 'ere. They all got bombed out an' I had to take 'em in so if you think that you and your two brats are gonna move in 'ere you got another think comin'!'

'I don't want to move in with you,' Judy said as patiently as she could. 'But I need to know where Sid is.'

'An' you won't be findin' out from me, so sod orf!' She slammed the door in Judy's face, opening it a crack to bellow, *'And don't bleedin' come back 'ere if you know what's good for yer!'*

Judy turned away feeling angry and frustrated. She might have known it was useless to come here and ask Annie to tell her where her eldest son was. She might be impossible but she obviously wasn't going to betray her own flesh and blood.

At the end of the road was a greasy-spoon café and as Judy passed she thought she saw someone gesturing to her through the steamy window. Looking closer she saw that it was the young woman she had seen coming out of the Trumans' house. The girl was beckoning her. After a moment's hesitation she pushed open the door and went inside. The girl was seated at a table in the corner, her sleeping toddler in the pushchair beside her. She smiled at Judy and pointed to the vacant chair opposite.

'I often pop in here for a cuppa and a bit of peace and quiet. Like a cuppa?'

Judy sat down. 'I'd love one, thanks.'

The girl went to the counter and returned almost immediately with two cups of tea. 'I'm Molly,' she said. 'Molly Truman, Jack's wife. Jack's in the Navy. The flats where we were living got bombed, so we had to move in with Annie.'

'It can't be easy,' Judy said.

Molly smiled ruefully. 'You're not kidding. It's bloody mayhem, if you'll pardon my French.' She took a sip of her tea.

Judy smiled. Molly seemed a nice girl, certainly a cut above the Trumans. 'Is that your little girl?' she asked.

Molly nodded. 'Yes, that's Elaine. Jack's only seen her once.' She leaned forward. 'Did I hear you say you was Sid's wife?'

Judy nodded. 'That's right. I've got two little girls, Charlotte, who's ten and Suzanne, nine.

Molly looked surprised. 'Blimey! You must've been a kid when you had them.'

'Sixteen.'

'Really?' The girl looked thoughtful. 'Sid must be a good bit older.'

'More than ten years.' Judy looked at the girl's pensive expression and asked. 'Why do you ask?'

Molly looked doubtful. 'I'm not sure if I should say anything or not,' she said hesitantly, 'but there's this woman who's been round Annie's a couple of times. She's in her late thirties, I'd guess. She's called Joan and she's got two boys. One's just been called up and the other one's fifteen.' She raised her eyes to meet Judy's. 'It sounds as though I've been earwiggin' but the walls are so thin in them houses that you can't help overhearing. The thing is, she calls herself Mrs Truman too and I know she's not married to either of the other two brothers.'

'So – what are you getting at?' Judy asked.

Molly looked awkward. 'Well – she's been quizzing Annie about Sid's whereabouts too.'

Judy frowned. 'But *I'm* Sid's wife.'

'She wears a wedding ring,' Molly said. 'Look, I'm sorry to say this, love, but I reckon Sid must have another family you don't know about.'

'That can't be right!' Judy was stunned. Her first reaction was that there must be some mistake, then a lot of things began to fall into place. The fact that she'd never had a proper pay book from the Army; that none of his family had come to their wedding; Sid's long absences and the lies he told; the fact that he hardly ever gave her any money. She looked at Molly. 'Do you know where she lives?'

Molly looked scared. 'Oh, now look, I only told you 'cause I thought you should know. I didn't mean to make no trouble.'

Judy shook her head. 'I don't want to make trouble for anyone, and I wouldn't drop you in it, so don't worry. She's probably as much in the dark about it as me, but I have to know the truth.' She looked at the girl's doubtful expression. 'You must see that, Molly.

I've got two children so I must know. If you know where she lives please, will you tell me?'

'Annie'd kill me if she found out.'

'She need never know.' Judy leaned forward. 'Just give me the address.' She opened her handbag, and took out a slip of paper, and pushed it across the table. 'Write it on there and then you can truthfully say you didn't tell me.'

'She lives in Tilbury. I only know the name of the road, not the number.' Molly scribbled something down and quickly stood up. 'I'd better go.' She looked uneasy. 'It wouldn't do for me to be seen talking to you.' She laid a hand on Judy's sleeve. 'Good luck,' she said quietly. 'An' I hope I ain't spoken out of turn.'

When Molly had gone Judy looked at the slip of paper. Tilbury was an area she didn't know, except that it was on the other side of the river. Gathering up her coat and bag she went out into the street and headed for the Underground.

As she sat in the train Judy's thoughts were in turmoil. Had Sid really married her bigamously? She had difficulty coming to terms with the possibility. It was something that up till now she thought you only read about in the Sunday papers. Could it be that this woman was someone Sid had once known and had fathered two children with? Either way it was vital that she should find out.

Coming out of the Underground station Judy saw that the area had been badly bombed. It looked run down. The streets were dirty and the whole place had an uncared-for look. Making enquiries, she found the street Molly had named and knocked on the first door she came to. A woman answered, a small child clinging to her skirt. She eyed Judy suspiciously

'Yes?'

'I'm looking for Mrs Joan Truman,' Judy said. 'I'm not sure which number she lives at.'

The woman took a step outside and pointed down the street. 'Number forty-one, right at the end there.'

'Thank you.' Judy set out to walk the length of the street. It had clearly been bomb-damaged but most of the houses were occupied, having been hastily patched up by the local council. Taking a deep breath she knocked on the door of number forty-one.

The woman who answered looked tired and careworn. 'If you're selling something you're wasting your time,' she said wearily.

'I'm not selling,' Judy put in quickly before the woman could close the door. 'I'm looking for Sid Truman's wife. Would that be you?'

The woman sighed wearily. 'I've got no idea where he is if that why you're here,' she said. 'If he owes you money I'm sorry but I haven't seen him for years. I told the MPs that.'

The military police! So they had been here? Once again Judy saw the woman beginning to close the door. 'Please,' she said, putting out her hand. 'I *must* speak to you. It's very important. Can I come in for a minute? I'm not after money or anything like that. I just need to speak to you. It's important.'

The woman frowned and gave a resigned sigh. 'Oh, all right.' She opened the door. 'Come in, but if it's got anything to do with Sid you're wasting your time.'

Relieved, Judy stepped through the door directly into the living room. Although she could see that the house was shabby it was clear that the woman took a pride in the little she had. The room was clean and tidy. The deep cracks in the walls and ceiling had been patched up and hastily colour-washed. On the mantelpiece stood two framed photographs, one of a young man in RAF uniform, the other of a younger boy in school uniform.

'Your sons?' Judy asked.

The woman nodded. 'Good lads, both of them. I had hoped the war'd be over before either of them had to go, but there it is.' She looked at Judy. 'What is it you want?'

Judy took a deep breath. 'You say you've had a visit from the military police?'

'Yes. They reckon Sid's deserted. I wasn't all that surprised. I knew something must've happened when the money stopped coming. They seemed to think I'd know where he was.' She gave an ironic laugh. 'That's a laugh! I've only seen him a couple of times since the war started. Not many more before it, either. Always coming and going, Sid. A proper fly-by-night; said he had a job travelling. Never took no interest in the boys, never mind me.'

'But you were definitely married?'

'Oh yes, we was married all right! We got married when my Jimmy was on the way. Both really young, we were. No more than kids. Biggest mistake of my life.' She stared at Judy. 'Who are you, anyway?'

'I think you should sit down,' Judy told her. 'You see, Sid married me too; almost eleven years ago in Hackney. I've got two daughters aged nine and ten.'

Joan Truman sat down suddenly as though her legs had suddenly collapsed under her. She stared at Judy disbelievingly, seeming lost for words. Judy opened her handbag and took out the envelope containing her marriage certificate. 'Here is the proof,' she said, handing it to Joan. 'Please believe me when I tell you that this is as much a shock to me as it is to you. I had no idea he already had a wife and family.'

Joan sat staring at the certificate for a long time; when she looked up again her face was white with shock. 'I always knew he was a bastard but I never thought he'd stoop to something like this,' she said. 'Eleven years ago and I never guessed!'

'When did you last see him?' Judy asked.

'After he'd been wounded,' Joan told her. 'He said he'd been to a convalescent home and he had a few days' leave before going back. I woke up one morning and he'd gone. Not so much as a goodbye or a by-your-leave. I've heard nothing since. That's what I told the MPs and that's God's honest truth.'

'He wasn't in a convalescent home, he was with me,' Judy told her. 'The girls and I were evacuated to a little seaside town in Norfolk. He sent for me and I had to travel all the way down to the hospital in Southampton to pick him up. He went back just before Christmas a year ago and said he was reporting back to his unit.'

Joan was silent for a moment. 'Looks like we've both been taken for a ride,' she said at last. 'Not to mention the Army. But what do we do about it?'

'Before he went back I told him I wanted a divorce,' Judy said.

'Can't say I blame you.' Joan shrugged. 'And I certainly don't want him back again.' She looked at Judy. 'You know what this means, don't you?'

Judy shook her head. 'No, what?'

'It means that you can wash your hands of Sid Truman,' said Joan. 'You don't need no divorce cause you and him were never married, not legally anyway.'

'And what does that make my children?' Judy asked.

Joan snorted. 'Bloody lucky if you ask me!'

CHAPTER SEVENTEEN

'Nothing that man does surprises me,' Bill said when he and Maggie had listened to Judy's account of what happened in Kent. 'Desertion *and* bigamy, eh? Looks like he'll be in for a long spell inside when they do eventually catch up with him.' He smiled and rubbed his hands.

'But the bright side of it is that we can start putting your future in place, Judy. I'll get on to Mr Kennedy tomorrow morning and hurry him up on that codicil thing.' He reached out a hand to Maggie. 'And you'n me'll start looking round at cottages for sale, eh, old girl?'

Maggie smiled. 'Don't go getting ahead of yourself, Bill Hurst. 'We might have to wait till the war's over. I don't think people are moving around much at the moment.'

'Be positive,' Bill told her. 'At least we can try.'

The scholarship examination took place towards the end of the month. Judy went with the girls to school that morning. Charlie was pale and quiet as they walked. At breakfast that morning Maggie had given her her lucky ha'penny.

'Look,' she said. 'It's got a hole in the middle. I found it once when I was weeding the garden and I've kept it ever since, for luck.' She tied it firmly in the corner of Charlie's handkerchief. 'There,' she said with a smile. 'It'll bring you luck too. Not that you need it, clever girl like you.'

Charlie didn't speak as they walked. Suzie ran off to join her friends in the playground as soon as they arrived and Judy bent to give her daughter a hug. As she held her she could feel her trembling.

'Don't worry, love,' she whispered. 'Just go in and do your best.'

Charlie turned a pale face up to her mother. 'What if I don't pass, Mum?'

'You will. But even if you don't it doesn't matter, we'll still be proud of you,' Judy assured her. 'We all love you very much.'

'I love you too, Mum,' Charlie whispered, glancing round in case someone else might hear.

Judy gave her daughter's bottom a gentle pat. 'Off you go then. See you at dinner time, and good luck!'

All morning at the office Judy thought about Charlie, wondering how she was getting on. The scholarship group had the afternoon off and Judy had promised to take both girls out to tea when she finished work. Bob Gresham had kindly suggested she might leave an hour earlier. At dinner time she was at the school gates waiting for the girls, her heart beating fast as she wondered how Charlie had fared. She needn't have worried. As soon as she saw Charlie running towards her she knew it wasn't just relief that was making her face glow like that.

'It was easy, Mum! I answered all the questions and did all the sums.'

Judy hugged her. 'That's good. Now just try to forget all about it. We might have to wait a long time before we hear the results.'

She took the girls to the Tudor Tearooms for their tea and they had toasted teacakes and chocolate Swiss roll to follow.

'When will we be able to get ice cream again, Mum?' Suzie asked. 'I can hardly remember what it tastes like.'

'Maybe it won't be long,' Judy said. 'Uncle Bill says the war will soon be over now.'

'Can we go and see Auntie Mary and Uncle Steve?' Charlie asked as they left the tearooms. 'I want to tell them about the exam.'

Judy laughed. 'Of course, if you want. We'll go on the way home.'

But when they arrived at the Greshams' house Judy sensed that it wasn't a good time. Steve opened the door to them and greeted them warmly enough, but when he led them through into the living room Mary looked pale and upset. Both she and Steve listened kindly and patiently to Charlie's account of the scholarship exam and wished her luck, but Judy could feel the underlying atmosphere and knew that there was something wrong. Her stomach began to churn with apprehension.

'Is this a bad time?' she whispered. 'Have you had news? Is it Peter?'

Steve turned to the girls. 'Why don't you young ladies run out and play in the garden?' he suggested. 'There's a ball in the shed, or you can take turns on the swing.'

When the girls had gone Judy looked at Steve. 'What's happened?'

Steve glanced at his wife. 'We heard this morning that Peter was in a large group of RAF prisoners who had escaped from their POW camp.'

Judy's heart leapt. 'He's escaped?'

Steve shook his head. 'The word is that the Gestapo shot over twenty of them. The rest are still at large. At the moment we don't know whether Peter is alive or dead.'

The silence hung heavily between them as Judy tried to take in what Steve had told her. It was broken by a stifled sob from Mary. Judy crossed the room to put her arms around shaking shoulders.

'Oh, Mary, I know it's hard to bear, not knowing, but there's always hope, isn't there? Until we hear otherwise.' She heard the words coming out of her mouth belying the fear and despair she felt inside.

'As soon as we hear anything we'll let you know,' Steve said. 'Thank you for coming to see us.'

Judy shook her head. 'I'm sorry we disturbed you at a time like this. If I'd known…'

'I would have called round to tell you anyway,' Steve said.

On the way home Charlie wanted to know why they'd been sent outside to play.

'Was Auntie Mary all right?' she asked. 'Her eyes were all red as though she'd been crying.'

Judy looked down at her perceptive daughter. How did you explain the brutalities of war to an innocent ten-year-old? 'I think she's coming down with a cold,' she said. She took both their hands. 'Come on now, let's hurry. Auntie Maggie and Uncle Bill will be dying to hear about the exam.'

Strangely enough there was a letter waiting for her back at Sea View. It was from Peter, and according to the date, had been written several weeks before. During the time he had been a prisoner she had received several letters; mostly so severely censored that they hardly made any sense and none of them containing any real information. This one was no different. In it he said that he was bored; that he wished he was still flying, and that he thought of her all the time and longed to be home. She read it quickly and tucked it into her pocket, the thought crossing her mind that it might be the last she ever heard from him. Although her throat was tight with unshed tears, she said nothing to Maggie and Bill, letting Charlie have her moment of glory, but after the girls were safely in bed and asleep she told them what she had learned from Steve and Mary that afternoon. Maggie shed a few tears and Bill looked grave.

'All we can do is hope and pray,' he said.

Six weeks later Bill came home bristling with news. He had been into town for some shopping and arrived home in a state of high excitement.

'Guess what?' he challenged Maggie who was busy in the kitchen preparing lunch. She flapped her hands at him exasperatedly.

'Get out of my way, you and your questions,' she said. 'I've got no time for your silly guessing games.'

'I met John Browning the ARP warden in the High Street,' he said, undeterred by her impatience. 'He was telling me that he and his missis had just come from a funeral. An old aunt of his has died and left them a bit of money.'

'Oh, well, good for them,' Maggie said, straining the potatoes.

'Yes, but that's not all,' Bill went on. 'Some of the money is tied up in the old lady's cottage. It's in Bradley Green, three miles out of town. And – wait for it – they're keen to sell it.'

She turned to look at him. 'You're not suggesting it might do for us, are you?' she asked. 'Some old shack out in the wilds? Falling to bits, I shouldn't wonder!'

'No! That's just it,' Bill insisted. 'John says this aunt was very particular and spotlessly clean.'

Maggie snorted disbelievingly. 'Well, he would say that, wouldn't he, seeing he wants to sell it? I can just imagine it, no running water or proper drainage, let alone a bathroom. And most likely a horrible earth closet out in the yard! Imagine that of a cold winter's night, you and your rheumatism!'

'No, you've got it all wrong.' Bill said, shaking his head. 'John told me that his aunt was a retired headmistress and not short of a bob or two. She bought the place when she retired before the war and she had a lot done to it when she moved in. He says it's a real little gem.'

'So *he* says,' Maggie said sceptically.

'Well…' Bill cleared his throat. 'I told him we'd take the bus out there and have a look tomorrow.'

'You did *what*? You might have discussed it with me first.'

'It's only to have a look,' Bill said. 'We don't have to commit ourselves. John says he'd lower the price if he could do a deal without involving an agent.'

'Well, all right, as long as you're prepared for a disappointment.' Maggie sighed. 'As you've let us in for it I suppose we'd better go. I can see there'll be no peace till we do.'

As it was a Saturday Maggie suggested that Judy and the girls might accompany Bill and her to Bradley Green. 'We can make an outing of it,' she said. 'I'm not expecting anything wonderful but at least we can make it an outing, and if it's a nice day we can take a picnic. The girls would love that.'

She'd been worried about Judy since the news came about Peter's escape. There was still no news of him, either good or bad. As long as he was in the POW camp he was comparatively safe, but now he was missing all over again. There had been no news of Sid either, and the uncertainty was taking its toll of Judy. She'd lost her appetite, and as a result, was losing weight. Several times when Maggie herself had wakened in the night and gone down-stairs she'd found Judy in the kitchen, drinking tea and rereading Peter's precious last letter.

How much longer could this war go on? She asked herself. Just how much more suffering could the human race be expected to take?

Charlie and Suzie were excited at the thought of a ride out in the bus and a picnic in the country. It was a fine day with more than a hint of summer in the air when they all set off to catch the bus. Bill was carrying the picnic basket and Maggie had a tartan rug rolled up under her arm.

Bradley Green was a pretty village with two pubs, a post office that doubled as a general store and a little church with a square tower. There was even a village green with a pond and ducks. The girls were enchanted. Bill had picked up the keys to the cottage from his friend that morning, along with instructions on how to find it.

They found Jasmine Cottage tucked away behind the church. When Judy saw it she caught her breath with delight.

'Oh, Maggie! It's everyone's idea of a dream cottage,' she said, looking at the rosy pantiled roof and split-flint walls. The front garden was still ablaze with spring flowers and a herringbone brick path led up to the front door.

Maggie pulled down the corners of her mouth. 'Mmm,' she said. 'I can almost smell the damp from here!'

Bill gave her a nudge. 'Look on the bright side, can't you? Let's at least see inside before you condemn it!'

Inside the smell was not of damp but of lavender and furniture polish. Bill gave his wife a triumphant look. 'There you are!' he told her. 'John said that a woman from the village has been coming in to keep the place aired and clean.'

The whole of the ground floor had been opened up, which gave it a spacious feel. The ceiling had oak beams and the walls were whitewashed, apart from the large brick fireplace, which retained its original cast-iron fire-basket. The room was furnished with a Welsh dresser and a comfortable-looking settee and chairs, covered in floral chintz. To one side a dogleg staircase led to the upper floor. Maggie's expression began to soften as she looked around her, but she made no comment.

A kitchen extension had been built on at the back and, contrary to Maggie's gloomy forecast, boasted running water and a modern cooker and sink as well as a range of cupboards.

'Look, there's gas too!' Bill proclaimed, turning on one of the cooker's burners. 'All mod cons, you could say.' He grinned at his wife. 'What did I tell you?'

'Mmm, we haven't seen upstairs yet,' she said guardedly.

When the girls began to follow Bill, Maggie and their mother up the stairs, Judy shook her head. 'You stay here,' she told them. 'Go out and have a look at the garden if you like. Five of us is too many.'

Upstairs were two bedrooms with dormer windows, one looking out to the front, the other to the back. Both had pretty views. Maggie tested the beds and found that they had spring mattresses, but Judy was looking at the hand-sewn patchwork quilts.

'Oh look, Maggie, aren't they pretty?'

Maggie sniffed, fingering the matching curtains. 'Mmm. Everything would have to be washed, of course.'

Bill called from the landing, 'Come and have a look at this then!'

They followed him into a tiny bathroom that was clearly part of the extension. The walls were tiled with pale-blue tiles and the white porcelain wash basin and bath gleamed with cleanliness. Bill grinned as he pointed to the lavatory.

'Not much like an outside earth closet, eh, girl?' he said to Maggie. 'It wouldn't bother me spending a pleasant half-hour in here of a winter's night,' he joked. 'Might even bring the *Daily Mirror* with me.'

Maggie's lips twitched in spite of herself. '*Bill Hurst!*' She gave him a nudge. 'Don't be so crude! In front of Judy too!' She glanced out of the window and saw Charlie and Suzie chasing each other round an ancient apple tree in the garden below. In that instant she knew that they had found their dream retirement home, though she didn't intend to admit she'd been wrong that easily.

They sat down to eat their picnic under an oak tree on the green. Maggie had made egg-and-cress sandwiches and some buns and the girls tucked in enthusiastically. To wash it all down there was a large flask of tea and lemonade for the girls.

As they waited for the bus back to Summerton Bill chattered excitedly. 'What about that vegetable plot? I'd be able to grow all the veg we'd need out there.' He smiled down at Charlie and Suzie. 'Tell you what, I'll rig up a swing for you girls on one of the branches of that old apple tree, ready for when you come to visit.'

'Don't go making silly promises,' Maggie warned. 'We haven't bought the place yet, and anyway, that old tree looks rotten to me. Want them to fall and break their necks, do you?'

Judy surreptitiously squeezed her arm. 'Don't spoil it for him,' she whispered. 'He's so excited.'

Maggie shook her head. 'He's always been the same,' she complained. 'Never thinks of the practicalities. That's always left to me.'

'Practicalities – like what?'

Maggie sniffed. 'Dry rot for one,' she said. 'It's sure to have that, a place that age. Then there's woodworm, deathwatch beetle, you name it. A place like that is a minefield of snags.'

But Bill got in touch with a friend who was a retired surveyor. He went out with Bill a few days later and gave the cottage a clean bill of health. In fact, in Bill's friend's opinion, the cottage was sounder than most of the modern buildings he'd looked at during his career. Maggie had to concede that there was no reason why they shouldn't make an offer for the place.

Suspecting that she knew the reason for Maggie's reluctance to commit herself Judy put it to her one evening as they were making a bedtime drink together in the kitchen.

'Is it that you hate the idea of leaving Sea View?' she asked gently.

Maggie sighed. 'I suppose that's part of it,' she confessed. 'Bill and I have been here for thirty-five years. It's been our life and it's given us a good living.' She looked at Judy apologetically. 'That sounds as though I want to go back on our arrangement. I don't. Believe me I feel more than ready to take things easy now. It's just that I wonder what we'll do with ourselves out there where we don't know anyone.'

'Bill can't wait to get his hands on that garden,' Judy reminded her. 'And there's bound to be a Women's Institute in the village. You'd love that and soon make lots of friends.'

Maggie smiled. 'I suppose you're right.'

'And Sea View would still belong to you. You could come and stay whenever you wanted and you'll still have control over everything.'

'That's true, and you'd visit us too in the off season?'

'Of course we would.'

Maggie smiled. 'I'm just being a silly old stick-in-the-mud, aren't I?'

'You do like the cottage, don't you?' Judy asked.

'I love it,' Maggie admitted. 'I just didn't want Bill to get carried away, so I played it down.'

'Then why don't you tell him that – and that you want to go ahead with the move? Put him out of his misery.'

Jasmine Cottage was priced very reasonably and the sale went through without a hitch. Although the cottage was fully furnished Maggie wanted to get rid of some things and replace them with a few treasured items from Sea View, so a removal date was arranged for mid June.

'Bill and I have decided to put an advert in the Railway Guide,' Maggie told her. 'That's the magazine we've always advertised in. We'll announce our retirement and tell all our old customers that Sea View is officially open for business again under the management of Mrs Judy Truman, our new young manageress.'

Judy blushed with pleasure. Her heart raced with nervousness at the thought of being in sole charge but she couldn't help feeling excited when, a week later Bill showed her the advert that he and Maggie had inserted.

'There you are, girl,' Bill said with a grin. 'You're a proper business woman now. How does that feel?'

Judy had to admit that it felt good. But before Sea View could start taking bookings under her management the war took an unexpected and frightening twist.

She was working away in the office on the morning of 6 June when Bob Gresham burst in, his face red and his eyes shining with excitement.

'It's happened at last!' he said.

Judy's heart leapt as she looked up from her typewriter. 'What has?'

'They've landed,' he said. 'The Allies. It's the second front we've all been waiting for. They've just announced it on the wireless and it sounds the business. I reckon Hitler's had his chips!'

Back at Sea View Bill was as excited as Bob had been. He'd only just got over the euphoria of Rome being liberated and now this.

'Listen to *this*!' he shouted, one ear on the latest BBC bulletin. 'It won't be long now!'

But Judy could only think of Peter. Her first reaction to Bob's excitement had been that there must have been word from Peter; and the news of the Allied invasion came as something of an anti-climax. It was wonderful, of course. Just what everyone had been waiting for but her only thought was of Peter and whether he was alive or not. Lying awake at night she tried to make sense of it. Why hadn't he stayed where he was now that the war was swinging the Allies' way? If only he hadn't tried to escape. As the weeks went by with no news of him hopes were fading fast, although none of them dared to admit it.

But close on the euphoria of the news of the Normandy invasion came the devastating realization that, contrary to Bill's prophecy, Hitler was far from finished. When the first of the shocking V1 raids on London came hopes of a quick ending to the war were smashed. Plans for Judy's first summer season in charge of Sea View were shattered as Summerton once again prepared to find room for more evacuees.

CHAPTER EIGHTEEN

When the shocking news of the first V1 raid was announced Maggie's first thought was to put off the move to the cottage. Judy wouldn't hear of it.

'You've got everything arranged now,' she argued. 'If there is another evacuation we'll have more room for them here if it's just me and the girls.'

'But Sea View is a business,' Maggie pointed out. 'You could take a couple but you can't fill the whole house up with evacuees. Anyway, what if it's not just London this time?' she asked fearfully. 'They say these things have no pilots. They could land anywhere. We might even get them here!'

Bill shook his head. 'They're steered by something called a gyroscope and they have just enough fuel to get them to where they want them,' he said patiently. 'This is the secret weapon Hitler's been on about for ages.'

'Gyroscope? I thought they were called doodlebugs,' Maggie said. 'I've heard that when the engine stops you've only got a few seconds and then, *bang*. No air-raid warnings or anything, just the noise and this flame in the sky.' She shuddered. 'No one flying them! It's frightening. We could all be smashed to smithereens in our beds.'

''Course we won't,' Bill said, frowning. 'They'll be set to drop on cities where there are factories and docks. What good would it do to bomb little towns like Summerton?'

'You don't know. Maybe it's meant to break our spirit,' Maggie insisted. 'To make us give in.'

'*Give in!*' Bill thrust out his chest. 'If he thinks he's going to do that to us British after all we've been through he's got another think coming,' he said stoutly. 'The Normandy landing has put the wind up Herr Hitler good and proper and they're gaining ground every day. This is just Adolph's dying kick. You mark my words. Anyway, it says in the paper that our RAF boys are already bombing the launching sites in Calais.'

Maggie and Bill moved to Jasmine Cottage on 20 June and on the same day Jack Mason, the billeting officer came around to ask if Sea View could take in a young woman and her baby son.

'This is a business and our livelihood,' Judy reminded him. 'I can't take many.'

Jack looked at her sceptically, his head on one side. 'Fully booked, are you?'

Judy had to admit that Sea View wasn't fully booked for the whole season.

'But we do have some bookings,' she said. 'So I have to keep the rooms free for them.'

'They'll probably cancel,' he said pessimistically. 'I doubt if many people are going to feel like a seaside holiday this summer. You might as well take this young woman and her little kid. They'll only take up one room.'

Judy sighed, torn between compassion and anxiety. She'd already given in her notice at the theatre, but now she wondered if there would be enough money coming in to support them all if Jack's gloomy forecast was right and she did have most of her bookings cancelled. 'All right,' she said at last. 'Just the one then.'

He smiled and made a note on his clipboard. 'Right, I'll bring them round later.'

True to his word he was back an hour later. 'I've brought your new guests,' he announced. 'This is Mrs Thomas and her little boy.' He handed Judy a suitcase and stood aside to reveal a weary looking young woman of about Judy's age. In one arm she carried a small, sleeping child, his head on her shoulder. The other hand was dragging a folded pushchair. The sight tugged at Judy's heart-strings as she remembered the night that she and the girls had arrived. They'd been so grateful for the warm welcome they'd received from Maggie and Bill. Now it was her turn to repay the kindness. She smiled and held out her hand.

'Come in. I'm all ready for you. You must be so tired.' As she closed the door she said, 'I'm Judy. I've got two little girls, who you'll meet later.' She held out her arms. 'Shall I take the baby? Your arms must be aching. Come upstairs and I'll show you your room.'

The girl handed the sleeping baby over gratefully. 'His name's David,' she said. 'And I'm Sally.'

Later, after baby David had been fed, bathed and put to bed, Sally Thomas joined Judy and the girls for tea in the kitchen. Charlie and Suzie were shy of this newcomer and ate their tea in silence, their eyes on their plates. When they had been excused from the table and had gone outside to play Sally remarked on how well behaved they were. Judy laughed.

'They have their moments, as you'll soon learn when they're used to you. They're going to love little David, though. Just wait till they see him awake and running round tomorrow. They love babies.'

Sally looked around her. 'You're not local, are you?'

Judy shook her head. 'No. We're from London.'

'Did you come down with the first lot?' Sally asked.

'Yes, as soon as war broke out.' Judy poured them both another cup of tea. 'It was chaos. There were hundreds of us, from the East End – Hackney. Where are you from?'

'Bromley,' Sally said. 'They're evacuating Kent and Sussex, where most of the doodlebugs seem to be falling at the moment. Bomb Alley, they're calling it.' She sighed. 'Makes you wonder what's next, doesn't it?'

'Bill says the war won't last much longer now.' Seeing Sally's puzzled look she went on to explain. 'Maggie and Bill Hurst own this guest house. They took us in when we first came here and they've been so kind to us. I used to work as a secretary at the theatre but now that Maggie and Bill have retired they've given me the job of managing Sea View.'

Sally looked surprised. 'Really? You landed on your feet all right then, didn't you?' For a moment she looked at Judy speculatively. 'Your hubby in the forces, is he?'

Judy hesitated. Her life was so complicated. Strictly speaking she didn't even have a 'hubby'. She didn't even know this young woman, who might only be here for a short time anyway. She decided to go for the easy option. 'Yes,' she said. 'He's abroad.'

'My Ken is in a Jap prisoner of war camp,' Sally said. 'He was captured out in Burma – not long after they were shipped out there. I thought at first he'd been killed and it was a relief to hear he'd been taken prisoner.' Her eyes clouded. 'Mind you, if everything you hear about those camps is right God only knows what he's going through, or what state he'll be in when he gets out.'

Thinking of Peter, Judy reached across the table to touch her hand. 'The war surely can't last much longer,' she said. 'All we can do in the meantime is keep on hoping.'

As they got to know one another Judy and Sally found they had quite a lot in common and they got along well. Charlie and Suzie soon got used to having her around and, as Judy had predicted, they fell in love with eighteen-month-old David on sight. They were always begging to take him for walks in his pushchair and played with him at every opportunity. Sally was a willing worker and a great help to Judy once the visitors began to come. Contrary to Jack's glum prophecy the cancellations were very few. Most people were only too glad to get away from the cities for a breath of sea air.

Just before school broke up for the summer holidays Charlie came home with the long-awaited brown envelope clutched in her hand. She ran in breathlessly through the back door, her face scarlet as she handed Judy the envelope.

'It's *it*, isn't it?' she gasped. 'The result.'

Although Judy's heart gave a leap she managed to keep calm in front of Charlie as she slid her thumb under the envelope's flap and drew out the contents. With Charlie watching breathlessly, her eyes like saucers, she scanned the letter then looked up.

'You've passed!' she said with a smile. 'You start at St Hilary's High School for girls in Mellingford on September the eleventh.'

Charlie let out a whoop of joy and grabbed Suzie, who had just followed her through the door. 'I've passed! I've *passed!*' she shouted, whirling her sister around. 'I'm going to go to school all by myself on the bus and wear a posh uniform like the schoolgirls in the story books.'

For a second Judy's heart sank. *Uniform.* That was something she hadn't given a thought to. How would she afford all the necessary clothes and equipment? And anyway, weren't these things almost impossible to get in these days of clothes' rationing and shortages? Then there were the bus fares. Mellingford was five miles away. But one look at Charlie's ecstatic face told her that she'd walk over hot coals to get her what was necessary. Somehow she'd just have to work it out.

Later that evening, after all the children were in bed, Judy studied the list of requirements attached to the letter Charlie had brought home. Jumpers and gymslips for winter: striped cotton dresses for summer; gabardine coat; blazer; felt hat; panama hat; gym and games kit; shoes; sandals; plimsolls. Tennis and badminton rackets; hockey stick, not to mention badges, (hard and soft); hatbands and name tapes (to be sewn into every item). The list seemed endless. Judy's head ached with despair until she spotted a note at the bottom of the page.

Owing to current austerity, clothing rationing and wartime budgets, a sale of second-hand uniform and equipment will take place on Friday 1 September, to coincide with the school's open evening for new pupils and parents.

Judy and Charlie travelled into Mellingford on the bus on the evening of 1 September. Charlie was in a great state of excitement, totally oblivious of her mother's fear that she might have to present herself at the school on the great day improperly dressed and equipped, or of the sleepless nights Judy had spent worrying about it.

Charlie's best friend, Dinah Jones, had also achieved a place at St Hilary's and she and her mother joined Judy and Charlie on the bus. The girls sat chattering like excited little monkeys in front, while Judy and Kath, Dinah's mother sat behind. Judy soon discovered that Kath Jones also wanted to take advantage of the school's second-hand sale, and she guessed that they weren't the only ones. She hoped fervently that there would be enough uniforms to go round.

'I thought I'd get the winter outfit and sports stuff to start with,' Kath confided. 'By next spring the kids will have grown anyway.'

Judy agreed that this was a good plan, and as Dinah was quite a bit smaller than Charlie she was relieved that there would be no contest between them for sizes.

The two little girls enjoyed the conducted tour of the school and fidgeted only slightly during the headmistress's speech. After that there was coffee and biscuits and then, at last, the much awaited sale. Judy and Kath were quick off the mark and were first through the door.

On the bus home with bulging carrier bags the two mothers were well pleased with what they had managed to get. To their great relief their daughters would arrive at school on the first day of term correctly turned out and at very small cost, thanks to the headmistress's forethought. Judy had to concede to herself that even war had its upside. Maggie and Bill had come up trumps with clothing coupons for all the underwear and Maggie had promised to help with the sewing-in of name tapes. As for Charlie, there was no prouder little girl in Summerton-on-Sea as she eagerly awaited 11 September.

CHAPTER NINETEEN

As Charlie was eager to tell Auntie Maggie and Uncle Bill all about her new school and show them her uniform Judy took both girls to see them one Saturday afternoon, soon after the open evening at St Hilary's.

Jasmine Cottage looked delightful in the afternoon sunshine and the girls ran eagerly up the path, Charlie clutching a carrier bag containing her precious uniform. Inside Maggie had the place looking pristine. The whole cottage smelled clean and fresh and there were flowers from the garden on the mantelpiece. She opened the front door and hugged them all, inviting them in and bustling through to the kitchen to put the kettle on.

'Uncle Bill's in the garden,' she told the girls. 'Go and say hello and tell him the kettle's on. That always shifts him.' She smiled at Judy as they ran out through the back door. 'How are things then, love?'

'Fine.' Judy sat down at the table. 'Sally fits in well with us all and she helped a lot with the visitors. The girls love little baby David.'

'Well, that's good.' Maggie eyed her visitor warily. 'No news then – about...'

'Peter? No.' Judy shook her head. 'I pop into the theatre now and again to see Bob, but there's been no word.' She swallowed hard and smiled at Maggie. 'Carol's back working in the office now, did I tell you?'

'No. That's good. How is she?'

'Fine.'

'And her little boy?'

'He's fine too. Carol has met someone new,' she said. 'His name is Derek and he's in the RAF.'

'That's good. She's only young.' Maggie was looking at Judy. 'Nothing about Sid, then?'

Judy shrugged. 'No, and I doubt whether I'll ever see him again. At least I know I don't have to divorce him now.'

Maggie looked thoughtful. 'Are you happy, love?' she asked.

Judy smiled ruefully. 'I can't complain. I've got so much, Maggie: a wonderful job, thanks to you and Bill; two lovely healthy children. Charlie would never have had this opportunity of a good education if we'd stayed in London.' She paused to swallow the lump in her throat. 'If only I could know somehow that Peter was alive and coming home. I try not to think about it but it's on my mind day and night.'

'I know, love. I know.'

The back door burst open and the girls ran in. 'Uncle Bill has made us a swing,' Suzie said excitedly. 'We've both had a go on it. It's lovely.'

'And he's going to grow carrots and cabbages and peas,' Charlie said. 'I love peas.'

Maggie laughed. 'Did he tell you how long we'll have to wait before we get all this veg he's promising?' she asked. 'He won't even be able to sow the seeds till next spring.'

'You can't rush nature,' Bill said as he followed the girls through the door. 'Got to be patient, Maggie, old girl.'

'Not so much of your "old girl." Maggie lifted the teapot and added it to the tea tray she'd already prepared. 'Off you go and wash some of that muck off your hands before you sit down to tea.' She smiled at Charlie. 'Then this young lady can do her fashion parade for us.'

After tea Charlie put on her new uniform and walked up and down the living room, hand on hip in true model fashion for Maggie and Bill's approval. When she'd gone upstairs to take it off again Judy told them how she'd managed to buy all of it second hand at the school's open evening. Charlie returned and handed the carrier bag to her mother.

'I folded it all up carefully,' she said. 'So it wouldn't get creased.' She looked at Maggie and Bill. 'There's a gymnasium at St Hilary's *and* a swimming pool. I'm glad I already know how to swim – and I'm going to learn how to speak French and Latin and do geometry and something else called algy – algib....'

'And what about you, Suzie?' Maggie asked.

Suzie looked up. 'I'm going to take my first ballet exam in December,' she said shyly.

Judy turned to her in surprise. '*Suzie!* You never said.'

Suzie blushed. 'Well – you've been so busy with Charlie's new school and everything.'

Judy reached out an arm and hugged her younger daughter close. 'But what you're doing is exciting too. You should have told us.'

''Course you should,' Charlie put in, slightly shamefaced. 'Why didn't you tell anyone, you silly sausage? You're making me sound like a great big show-off!'

Judy laughed. 'Haven't I got two clever daughters?' she said. 'Aren't I a lucky mum?'

The girls went off with Maggie to help with the washing-up while Bill sat back in his chair and lit his pipe. 'Good about Paris being liberated, wasn't it?' he remarked as he applied a match. 'I don't like these bloomin' V1 flying bomb things, though. I don't say anything to Maggie but at the moment it looks like swings and roundabouts. The Allies aren't getting it all their own way in spite of the Normandy landing.' He shook his head. 'Pity that attempt on Hitler's life failed. Pity the poor devils who planned it. I wouldn't like to be in *their* shoes.' He looked up with a smile. 'The one bright spot is that we're going to be able to take the blackout curtains down soon. That'll be a treat and a half, won't it? If the V1s haven't got pilots they can't see us, can they?'

On Charlie's first day at her new school Judy went to the bus stop with her. Dinah was waiting with her mother. Both girls looked pale and apprehensive but they waved bravely as Judy and Kath saw them onto the bus.

'I hope they like it,' Kath Jones said as they began to walk away. 'I remember when I went. The headmistress was a proper old battle-axe in those days and my form mistress wasn't much better. I always seemed to be getting detentions.'

'You went to St Hilary's too?' Judy said in surprise.

Kath smiled. 'Yes; much good it did me though. I never stayed on for school cert, or anything. Left at fourteen, dead keen on getting a job and earning my own money.' She sighed. 'Married at eighteen and had Dinah soon after. I wish I could have those years back.'

Judy nodded. 'Don't we all?' She was thinking about the way Sid had sweet-talked her, swept her off her feet and made her pregnant, and of the catalogue of disasters that had followed. 'That's the trouble with being young,' she said regretfully. 'You think you know it all. You never listen to good advice.' She smiled. 'Still, I wouldn't have missed having my girls.'

She needn't have worried about Charlie being disappointed with school. She came home full of it. Her form teacher was *wonderful*; her lessons were *wonderful*, in fact everything was *wonderful*. Each morning she was up and ready long before it was time to leave and couldn't wait to get down to the bus stop.

Sally was amused. 'Long may it last,' she said with a shake of her head. 'I hated school myself. Couldn't wait to leave.'

Twice a week Judy accompanied Suzie to dancing school in the evenings. As the date of the ballet exam drew closer she was growing more and more nervous. Judy went to see Miss Paige, worried in case Suzie was being pushed to take the exam too soon. Miss Paige waved her fears away.

'She's one of the most talented students I've ever had,' she said. 'I've been thinking along the lines of getting her through these exams with a view to training to be a professional. I know your own mother is a dancer, so it's a career you're familiar with.'

Judy was only partly reassured. 'But she's so nervous.'

'I know, but it's only confidence she needs and passing the exam will give her that.' The dance teacher patted Judy's arm. 'Don't worry about her, Mrs Truman. I have no doubt that she'll pass with flying colours. The ability is there in spades. Once the music begins and she begins to dance she'll forget her nerves.'

*

As the weeks went by the evenings drew in and it was often dusk when Judy walked home from taking Suzie to her dancing class. One evening in mid-November it was darker than usual and beginning to rain. As she turned the corner she saw a figure near the gate of Sea View – a man's figure. He wore civilian clothes; he was huddled into an overcoat that looked too large for him; the brim of his hat pulled down over his eyes. Her heart missed a beat. Was it Sid? Had he come to demand her help – money? She hung back a little but he turned and, seeing her, began to walk in her direction. His speed increased until he was almost running and she stopped dead, her heart in her mouth. Her first panicking instinct was to turn and run, then he called her name and her mouth dropped open in astonishment as she recognized the voice.

'*Peter!*' She ran towards him and as he held out his arms to her she ran into them. 'Peter! Oh Peter, I can't believe it. You're here. You're *alive!*' With her arms around him she could feel how much weight he'd lost, even through the heavy overcoat. Drawing her head back she looked at him. Although his face was in shadow she could see the hollows under his eyes and his prominent cheekbones. Reaching up she touched his cheek. 'Oh my darling, what have they done to you? I thought I'd never see you again. I've missed you so much.'

'I've missed you too. The thought of you was all that kept me going.' He kissed her, his lips desperately hungry on hers as though he couldn't get enough of her. Through the cloth of his overcoat she could feel him trembling.

'Come inside,' she said. 'Come in and let me make you a hot drink. It's cold out here. It's raining. You're getting wet.'

Charlie was staying overnight at Dinah's so that they could do their homework together, and as little David had a cold Sally had been going to bed early in case he was restless, so Judy knew that the kitchen would be empty.. She switched on the light and turned to look at Peter as he shrugged off his overcoat. He was a shadow of his former self, painfully thin, his cheeks hollow and his skin pallid and stretched over his jaw and cheekbones. But his eyes were the same. In them shone the Peter she knew: young and vital, shining with love for her. She held out her arms, gathering him close. 'I can't believe I'm not dreaming,' she said, tears tightening her throat. 'I want to hear all about it. Just let me put the kettle on. Let me hang that damp coat up. Sit down, you look exhausted.'

He smiled the old familiar smile. 'You sound just like Mum,' he said.

She made a pot of tea and they sat side by side at the kitchen table as Peter unfolded the story of his escape.

'I lost a lot of good chums that night,' he said. 'How I didn't get caught in the crossfire I'll never know. The rest of us split up and I still don't know who else got away. The camp was quite close to the Czech border and I spent quite a lot of nights sleeping rough and hiding in bombed-out buildings and under hedges, eating whatever I could scavenge. One night I was so tired I risked crashing out in a shed in someone's back yard. I meant to be gone at first light but I overslept and when a man came in and found me I thought my number was up. But it turned out to be my lucky day. He and his family were sympathizers. They took me in and hid me.' He grinned. 'But the best part was how they did it. You'll never guess what they did for a living.'

Judy shook her head. 'No, tell me.'

'They ran a puppet theatre! The Germans had allowed them to carry on with it because they liked their shows. In fact they were often summoned to go to the camp I'd escaped from to perform. Everyone connected to the theatre was related and the way they hid me was pretending I was just another relative. Luckily I knew how to manipulate the puppets, so I was able to work backstage out of sight with them.'

'And no one ever questioned your being there?'

'No. Why would they? I was just another family member. Once we even went to the camp.'

'Oh my God!' Judy gasped. 'You must have been terrified.'

Peter smiled ruefully. 'I can't say it was my most comfortable evening.'

'Why did they risk taking you? Why not leave you behind?'

He shook his head. 'The troupe was always counted; one less

really *would* have looked suspicious. Besides, they needed me. They were short of puppeteers.'

'So what happened in the end?'

'They had contacts. They'd helped escaped prisoners before. It was horribly risky for them. If they'd been found out it would have been instant arrest and most probably execution. I owe them my life and one day I'll go back and find them again – say thankyou.'

'So how did they get you away?'

'They smuggled me to a remote field, late one night. A light aircraft was waiting. It got me to Switzerland – and then the Swiss authorities got me home.'

'When was this?'

'A month ago.'

Judy frowned. 'A *month*? So why didn't you get in touch? Where have you been since?'

'In hospital. On the plane on the way home to England I suddenly went down with some sort of fever and by the time we landed I was rambling – not making any sense. I'd discarded my dog-tags long since in case I got caught, and no one knew my name or number. They put me into hospital in London and treated me with some new wonder drug that they've been using on the troops. It's called penicillin and it worked a treat. When I came out of hospital I had to report back to the RAF for the usual debriefing and...' He spread his hands. 'Here I am. I got home this morning.'

Judy took his hand. 'Your mum and dad must have been over-joyed.'

He grinned. 'They were quite pleased to see me. I think they thought they'd got rid of me for good.'

'I've prayed and prayed for your safe return,' she whispered.

His fingers tightened round hers. 'And all I ever dreamed of was coming home to you. I lived and relived our beautiful night together.' He raised her hand to his lips. 'And now you look even lovelier than you did in my dreams.'

'Peter,' she whispered. 'I have so much to tell you. I went to a solicitor to try to divorce Sid, but he made enquiries and found out that Sid had deserted from the Army. Obviously I couldn't file for divorce until he was found, so I went down to Kent to see if his mother had heard from him. She sent me away with a flea in my ear, but one of his sisters-in-law came after me and she told me that she was pretty sure that Sid already had a wife when he married me.'

Peter's eyes were wide as he looked at her. 'Is it true?'

'Yes. I managed to find out where she lived and I went to see her. She told me everything. Sid has two grown-up sons by his legal marriage. He lied to her as well. It seems he was as devious and vicious to her as he was to me.'

'So you've never been legally married?'

'No.'

'That's great! Aren't you pleased?'

She frowned. 'Not altogether. Can you imagine how it makes me feel, Peter – knowing I've been living with a man I wasn't married to all those years? And some day I'll have to tell the girls that they are illegitimate. All these years I've been living a lie. I feel such a failure.'

'A *failure*?' He stood up and pulled her to her feet, holding her close. 'Don't ever let me hear you say that again. A young woman who's brought up two lovely children on her own? Who's struggled to better herself and be a good breadwinner; who's been loyal enough to put up with a thug like Sid Truman when all the time he's nothing but a liar and a cheat? No one could *ever* call you a failure.' He looked down at her. 'Don't you see what's important in all of this, darling? We can get married now; as soon as you like!'

She shook her head. 'But it's not as simple as that. Sid's still missing – on the run, I suppose. He still doesn't know I've found out that his marriage to me was bigamous and until I talk to him I can't draw a line under it. I need him to come back and face up to the truth. I have to make him own up to everything somehow. But he's still the father of my children so he has the right to see them if he insists. All that has to be worked through, and yet the thought of even *seeing* him again terrifies me.'

'When they do catch up with him he'll go to prison,' Peter told her. 'There'll be a court martial as well as a civil case for the bigamy. He'll go down for a very long time, so I don't think you need worry about him having access to the girls. You don't have to be frightened of anything ever again, Judy,' he told her. 'Not now that I'm here. Everything's going to be all right. We love each other and that's all that matters.'

'But what about Mary and Steve, Peter? What will your parents think of you marrying a woman like me with two children and a criminal, bigamous husband?'

'Mum and Dad love you and the girls,' he told her gently. 'I'm pretty sure they guessed long ago how I feel about you. And when I tell them what you've told me tonight they'll feel nothing but happiness for us.'

He held her close and kissed her so deeply that she thought her heart would stop beating. It still felt like a dream; the dream she'd had so many times; the one she had begun to think might never come true. Any minute she might wake and find it was all fantasy … Suddenly the kitchen door flew open, shattering their moment of rapture.

'He's dropped off now, Judy. Shall we...?' Sally stopped short in the doorway. '*Oh!* I'm sorry. I didn't realize…'

They sprang apart, shocked by the sudden intrusion. Judy quickly composed herself. 'Sally, this is Peter Gresham – my – a friend.'

'Yes, I can *see* that!' Sally looked Peter up and down speculatively. 'A *good* friend by the look of it! Do you want me to go out and come in again?'

Judy glanced at the kitchen clock. 'No. I'll have to go and pick Suzie up now. I hadn't noticed the time.'

'I'll have to go too,' Peter said, reaching for his coat.

Sally's back was stiff with disapproval as she turned to fill the kettle at the sink. Judy went into the lobby and fetched her own coat. 'I'll see you later,' she said to Sally's back. 'I won't be long.'

'Please don't hurry on *my* account,' came the reply.

'Who is she?' Peter asked as they walked down the path.

'She's Sally Thomas. She and her little boy are evacuees from Kent,' Judy explained. 'You know about the V1s?'

He nodded. 'I encountered a few of those little treats while I was in London. It's V2s now, even nastier, so it looks as though you've got her for a while yet.' He took her hand. 'She's got a bit of a nerve, hasn't she, talking to you like that?' He frowned. 'Where are the Hursts, by the way?'

Judy realized that there was still so much more news to tell him. 'They've retired, bought a cottage out at Bradley Green.' She smiled. 'Believe it or not, I am now manageress of Sea View. But it's a long story.' He let go of her hand and wrapped an arm around her shoulders, hugging her close to his side. 'I'll walk with you to the dancing school,' he said. 'I can't wait to hear all about it.'

Suzie was delighted to see Peter, although she was a little shy. It was so long since she had seen him and to her he looked 'different'. For his part Peter couldn't believe how much she had grown.

'Last time I saw you, you were only knee high to a grasshopper,' he said, making her laugh.

'I'm going to take my ballet exam in two weeks' time,' she told him proudly. 'And Charlie goes to St Hilary's High School now.'

'Good heavens!' Peter said. 'I'd better not go away again or you'll be Queen Suzie and Charlie will have taken over from Mr Churchill!'

Peter said goodnight to them at the gate, kissing Judy briefly and whispering that he would be having a long talk to his parents when he got home. Suzie was so tired after her ballet class that she was quite happy to drink up her cocoa and go straight up to bed. Judy came downstairs to find Sally waiting for her at the kitchen table, her eyes glinting and her lips pursed as she waited to have her say. As soon as Judy closed the door she began her tirade.

'Women like you should be ashamed of yourselves,' she began, her voice quivering with emotion. 'There is your poor husband, fighting for freedom for you and his children in some hell-hole abroad – risking his life. And here you are, having wangled your way into this nice cushy little number, carrying on with some bloke and trying to pass him off pathetically as your *friend*. I might as well tell you straight, Judy. I think it's downright disgusting!' She took out her handkerchief and sniffled into it. 'And anyway, why isn't *he* in the services? A conchie, is he?'

Judy surprised herself by remaining perfectly calm. 'You don't know the facts, Sally,' she said quietly. 'It's actually none of your business but I'm going to put you straight anyway. So put the kettle on, sit down and listen.'

CHAPTER TWENTY

As Judy slowly unfolded the story of her life as Mrs Sid Truman Sally's expression gradually changed from one of righteous indignation to shame and embarrassment.

'I'm so sorry, Judy. I just assumed...'

'I know you did. And anyone might have done the same,' Judy said. 'But maybe you should learn the facts before you judge people. Peter is the only man I've ever truly loved. He's been through hell in a prisoner of war camp and risked his life escaping. After the escape, when so many of them were shot, we all thought he must be dead. We'd heard nothing of him for months until tonight, so maybe I can be forgiven for being happy to see him.'

'Of course.' Sally reached out a hand. 'I feel awful. Please forget the things I said. It's just with Ken being banged up in that awful Jap place...'

Judy shook her head. 'Let's say no more about it, Sally.'

'I'll try and make it up to you. I'll do anything you say. I'll leave if you want me to.'

'Of course I don't want you to leave,' Judy said, shaking her head. 'Things aren't always what they seem. Let's leave it at that.'

They drank the cocoa Judy had made in silence, then Sally looked up. 'He looks really nice, your Peter; a bit poorly, though.'

'He was ill with some sort of fever when he first got back to England,' Judy told her. 'Understandable after all he'd been through. But his mum will soon have him fit and well again if I know anything about her.'

'So – now that you know you're free will you and he...?'

'There's a lot to be thought out before that can happen,' Judy told her. 'As I told you, Sid, my husband, has deserted from the Army but I have a strong feeling he'll come here sooner or later, either for money or for my help and support, maybe both. I'm dreading it, but when it happens I'm going to have to turn him in.'

'Oh God!' Sally gasped. 'Could you really do that?'

Judy nodded. 'I don't have a choice. I've lain awake night after night thinking about what I should do. I can't become involved, for the children's sake, and as he married me bigamously I don't feel I owe him any loyalty.'

'After all he's put you through, I can't say I blame you.' Sally said.

'The only thing is, he's still Suzie and Charlie's father. How do I justify my action to them?'

'From what you say he hasn't been a very good father,' Sally pointed out. 'He's an out-and-out crook, isn't he – a bully, too? They're old enough to know that.' She looked again at Judy, her eyes full of contrition. 'I'm so sorry for all those things I said – about Peter too, especially now I know how brave he is. Can you ever forgive me?'

'I told you – we'll forget it.'

'I'm going to have to bite my tongue in future before I open my stupid mouth.'

Judy laughed in spite of herself. 'Sounds uncomfortable.' She gathered up the cocoa mugs and carried them to the sink. 'Let's go to bed now. Tomorrow is another day.'

December came in with a flurry of snow and Judy could hardly believe that Charlie's first term at St Hilary's was almost finished. There was a lot to do. Judy had invited Bill and Maggie to join them for Christmas. She knew they would be missing Sea View and for their part she and the girls missed them too. As well as the Christmas shopping there was to be a party at St Hilary's. Mothers were asked to contribute something tasty for the tea, which wasn't easy on the rations. Then there was Suzie's ballet exam. The exams were to take place at Miss Paige's school where a professional dancer would come to adjudicate. As the day grew closer Suzie became more and more nervous.

Charlie was supportive. 'You'll be OK,' she assured her sister with a nudge. 'I felt just the same when I took my scholarship exam, but I knew inside me that I could do it and so do you.' She poked Suzie in the ribs. '*Don't* you?'

'Yes, I can when it's only Miss Paige watching,' Suzie said. 'But what if I do something silly on the day – fall over and make a mess of it?'

Charlie laughed. 'As if *that* will happen! You're not a bad dancer and you're not clumsy, are you? Well, not *very*.'

Suzie laughed in spite of her apprehension and seemed reassured by her sister's back-handed compliments.

On the day before the exam Judy had a cable from her parents. They were on their way home and hoped to be able to spend Christmas with Judy and the girls at Sea View. Judy was delighted at the thought of seeing her mum and dad again. There would be so much to tell them. In her letters she hadn't mentioned Sid's desertion or the fact that they had never been legally married. No one really knew who censored the letters that travelled to and fro, and she thought it better not to risk revealing anything too contentious.

On the evening of Suzie's ballet exam Judy took her along in plenty of time. Peter went along with them, having insisted on picking them up in his father's old car. Suzie was pale and quiet as she sat beside her mother on the back seat, and Judy took her hand and gave it a reassuring squeeze.

Peter had been a regular visitor at Sea View since his return and Judy was pleased to see him slowly returning to his former self. He had put on weight and the hollows in his face were smoothing out. After they'd dropped Suzie off he suggested taking Judy for a drink while they waited for the exam to be over.

'To stop you from agonizing,' he said. But Judy knew that although there was no one she would rather be with at the moment than Peter, no drink in the world would stop her worrying about Suzie until the exam was over.

Sitting by the fire in the lounge bar of the Prince Albert he bought them each a glass of rather inferior sherry, which was all that the pub had to offer in the way of 'shorts'. Peter took one sip and pulled a face.

'Tastes like furniture polish,' he said. He looked at Judy's face and reached out to take her hand.

'Oh, come on, relax. She's going to pass with flying colours,' he said. 'But even if she didn't it wouldn't be the end of the world, would it, sweetheart? She's only nine.'

Judy shook her head. 'Sorry. I just want it for her so much. She doesn't say much but I know how much it means to her.'

'I know.' He squeezed her hand. 'Why don't you bring the girls round to see Mum and Dad at the weekend?' he said. 'They were saying only the other day that they haven't seen you for ages.'

'I've been so ashamed since I heard that I've never been legally married. An unmarried mother of two children – how does that make me look?'

'It's not your fault,' he told her. 'You're the victim in all this. Look, I've had a talk to them both. I've put them straight on the situation. They know how I feel about you and now they know that once everything gets straightened out we're going to be married. They're fine with it, so there's no need for you to worry.'

She looked at him. 'Are you sure? You're not just saying that?'

'Of course I'm not.'

She looked doubtful. 'It can't be what they want for you.'

He slipped an arm round her shoulders. 'After what we've all been through what they want for me is to be alive and back home again. Seeing me happily married to the girl I love will only be a bonus.' He bent and kissed her. 'So – will you come?'

Judy smiled. 'Of course we will.' She glanced at the clock over the bar. 'Maybe we'd better get back now. The exam will be over soon.'

The little dancers all had cards to be marked by the adjudicator at the time of their exam, so there was to be no waiting for results. As they drew up outside the hall where the classes were held, Judy hung back. Peter took her hand.

'Come on. Bite the bullet. This is it. You go in. I'll wait in the car for you.'

Inside the hall all the little girls were chattering as they changed into their outdoor clothes. Miss Paige spotted Judy right away and came across with a tall, elegant lady, obviously the professional dancer who had adjudicated.

'Mrs Truman, this is Miss Angelica Kowalski from the Kowalski School of Ballet. I'm delighted to tell you that she has passed Suzanne with distinction.'

Miss Kowalski held out a long white hand to Judy. 'Your daughter shows great promise as a dancer,' she said. 'I hope you will allow her to pursue her dancing with a view to taking it up as a career later.'

Judy felt her cheeks flood with colour. 'Thank you,' she said, shaking the delicate hand. 'But of course, it will be up to Suzie. If it's what she wants then of course she'll get all my support.'

Suzie joined them, her eyes as big as saucers as she looked up at her mother. 'I passed,' she whispered.

Judy bent to give her a hug. 'Of course you passed. No one ever thought you wouldn't!'

As Peter had suggested, Judy took the girls along to visit Mary and Steve Gresham the following Saturday afternoon. She hadn't seen them since Peter got home and though he had assured her that they were happy about the situation, Judy still felt apprehensive as she knocked on their door. Steve answered it to them, the usual warm smile on his face when he saw them.

'Come on in all of you,' he said. 'Lovely to see you. Peter's upstairs. I'll give him a shout.'

'We've brought your Christmas cards in case we don't see you again before the big day,' Judy told him. 'And to tell you Suzie's news.'

'Well, we've heard that,' Steve said with a smile for Suzie. 'Peter couldn't resist telling us. Come on through,' he invited. 'Mary's in the living room doing some running repairs on the puppets' costumes.'

Mary sat at a little table in the window of the living room, working away at her sewing machine. She looked up when they came in, taking off her glasses.

'Judy! How lovely to see you, and the girls. What's all this I hear about our little ballerina?'

'I passed,' Suzie told her proudly. 'When I grow up I'm going to be a proper dancer. The lady said I could.'

'And I'm sure you will,' Mary said. 'We shall all come and see you at Covent Garden and we'll be so proud.' She looked at Steve. 'Are you going to make us some tea, dear? I'm sure we're all gasping for a cup.' As he turned towards the door she called out. 'There's some Tizer in the pantry for the girls. You can give them a glass now if you like.' She smiled at Charlie and Suzie. 'Go with Uncle Steve. He might find you some biscuits too.'

Judy was all too aware that she was about to have a one-to-one talk with Peter's mother and something inside her shrivelled. Was she about to be advised to back down?

Mary got up and closed the door, indicating an armchair by the fire. 'Do sit down, dear.' She took the chair opposite. 'Peter has told us all about the trouble with your husband. We're so sorry.'

Judy swallowed hard. 'Thank you.'

'He also told us that the two of you have been in love for some time; since before he was taken prisoner.'

'That's right. I was very young when I married Sid. I didn't know anything about life at all. It was all a terrible mistake. Until I met Peter I didn't know what it was to be loved.'

Mary looked at the floor. 'Nevertheless, you were a married woman.' She said. 'Or at least to all intents and purposes you were.' She paused. 'Peter is a very special young man. Obviously I'm prejudiced because I'm his mother.'

'Yes, he is special,' Judy said quietly. 'Very special.'

Mary cleared her throat. 'My dear, you're both still very young in spite of the amount of living you've both been through. In wartime emotions seem heightened – exaggerated if you like.'

'Not ours,' Judy said quietly. 'Since Peter was taken prisoner, all the time he was missing after the escape, my love for him has grown deeper. He says he feels the same.'

'And I'm sure you both believe that now.' Mary bit her lip. 'But at the moment it's all very romantic – dramatic and emotional; his miraculous survival after the escape, his homecoming.' She shook her head. 'I don't want him – or *you* – to make another mistake.'

She twisted her hands together in her lap and Judy could see her searching painfully for the right words – ones that wouldn't wound. 'For instance,' she said at last. 'I don't think he has any idea what it means to take on another man's children. I know at the moment they're fond of him and he of them, but the time would inevitably come when he'd need to discipline them and they might resent that. He isn't, and never could be their father.'

'They know that,' Judy said. 'They're not babies, they're good girls and whatever Peter said or did, he could never hurt them as much as their real father has.' She paused, looking at Mary's bland expression. Was she fighting a losing battle? Would Mary believe her if she told her about the way Sid had cancelled Suzie's dancing classes and pocketed the money paid in advance for them? Would she believe her if she told her of his unfounded accusations and subsequent punishments? How would she react if she knew about eight-year-old Charlie's brave attempts to protect her from Sid's vicious blows? Could she comprehend what it was like to be constantly abused and lied to? Looking at Mary she doubted if she'd ever encountered such behaviour in her comfortable middle-class life. It was probably totally outside her understanding. Her heart sank as she realized just how squalid her life must sound to Mary Gresham and she understood why she would never be happy to accept her as a daughter-in-law.

'Their father was a cruel bully,' she said softly. 'My girls have had to witness things that no child should ever have to see. And now that he has become a deserter and a known bigamist he's a criminal too.' She smiled wryly. 'So, as the wife of a man like that I'm not much of a prospect, am I, Mary? I understand that.' She took a deep breath. 'And what makes it worse is that now I'm faced with the prospect of breaking it to my girls that they are illegitimate.'

'Not when we're married, because I intend to adopt them and give them my name.'

Both women looked up to see Peter standing in the doorway. 'It doesn't matter what you say, Mother,' he said. 'Judy and I will be married just as soon as we can. We'll be a proper family.' He moved across the room to put a hand on Judy's shoulder. 'And

198

maybe we'll even have kids of our own one day – your grandchildren.'

'No!' Judy stood up and turned to Peter. There was a huge lump
in her throat and she knew that she had to get what she had to say
over with quickly before the tears began.

'No,' she said again. 'We have to face the facts and be practical,
Peter. Your mother's right. It can't happen. I should have seen
that a long time ago. You deserve a wife who's your equal; a girl
without the kind of messed-up background that I have. It's all
been a dream but now it's time to wake up. It has to end, Peter. It
has to end – *now*.'

CHAPTER TWENTY-ONE

All the way back to Sea View Judy put up a pretence that everything was normal for the girls' benefit. They were puzzled about their sudden departure from the Greshams' house and Charlie kept casting sidelong glances up at her mother's face, her eyes troubled.

'You all right, Mum?' she asked as they let themselves into the house. Judy forced a smile.

'Of course I am. Why don't you go upstairs and write the rest of your Christmas cards. You'll be breaking up from school next week and you want to have them all ready, don't you?'

Suzie started up the stairs but Charlie hung back. 'Mum, you're not all right, are you? You look all funny.'

'Funny?'

'No, not *that* kind of funny; all sort of *squished* – as if you're trying not to be sad.'

'Of course I'm not sad. Off you go and do your cards.'

Charlie went reluctantly upstairs to join her sister, glancing back at her mother as she went. Judy went into the kitchen and shut the door. Once alone, she gave in to the overpowering urge to cry that she had fought so hard to resist since leaving the Gresham's house. Sitting at the table she laid her head down on her folded arms and allowed the tears to flow. How could she ever have kidded herself that she could marry Peter? It was all a dream; a fantasy she had held on to for so long. Now that she thought about it, it had never *ever* been a possibility. Peter had been well educated. His parents had gone without to see that he and his brother went to the best schools. He would soon have found her limited intellect tiresome and frustrating. And then there was the scandal of her bigamous marriage. Mary had been right. She had said nothing nasty: nothing that wasn't true. She had only spoken as she did out of consideration for them both.

She didn't hear the door open and when Sally's voice spoke she jumped.

'Judy! Whatever's the matter, love?'

Judy sat up and fumbled for a handkerchief in her pocket, shaking her head, still unable to trust her voice not to tremble.

Sally sat down opposite her at the table, looking at her with concern. 'Come on, tell me,' she said, reaching out a hand. 'A trouble shared, as they say. Is it your hubby? Has he shown up?'

'No.' Judy swallowed hard. 'It's Peter and me. We've split up.'

'You've *what?*' Sally's eyebrows shot up. 'You and Peter – after all you've both been through – but *why?*'

'It's for the best.' Very slowly Judy told Sally about the conversation she and Mary had had that afternoon, being careful not to paint Mary and a bad light. Nevertheless Sally was indignant.

'Old cow!' she said. 'Doesn't she want her son to be happy? Can't she see any further than her own toffeenose?'

'She's not a snob,' Judy said. 'She and Steve are hard-working people and they've been really kind to the girls and me. But she wants the best for her son, especially after all he's been through.'

'What – and you're not *it?*' Sally shook her head.

'I daresay that if it was my son I'd feel the same,' Judy told her. 'Can't you remember what you thought of me to begin with?'

'That was before I knew the facts,' Sally protested. 'Presumably *they* knew all about you from the start.'

'That's just it,' Judy said. 'Obviously they never even considered me as a future daughter-in-law. It must have come as a shock when Peter told them. All the stuff about Sid already having a wife before he married me – it's a big disgrace, isn't it? It might even make the papers when they catch up with Sid and it eventually comes out. They'd rather die than be involved in that. I daresay I might too if the boot was on the other foot.'

'No, you wouldn't,' Sally said stoutly. 'You're a better person than that.' She stood up. 'Let me make you a cuppa. You look done in.'

'Where's David?' Judy asked.

'In the hall, fast asleep in his pushchair.' Sally grinned. 'Let sleeping kids lie, I say. He'll soon let me know when he wants his tea.'

But the kettle had barely boiled when the front doorbell rang. Sally went and came back a few minutes later. *It's him*, she mimed at Judy as Peter appeared at her shoulder. 'I'll get David bathed now,' she said with a wink. 'Don't forget to make the tea.'

Peter came in and closed the door. 'I'm sorry about Mum,' he said. 'I don't know what she was thinking about. You didn't take her seriously, did you?'

Judy turned from his outstretched arms. 'She was only talking common sense,' she said. 'She didn't mean to hurt me.'

'So if you think that why did you say what you did to me?' he asked. 'Why did you walk out?'

'Because all that she said was true, Peter. Everyone says the same. The war makes people feel things more deeply. It makes folks go a little mad. But soon the war will be over and we'll all have to settle down and face up to cold reality.'

'I don't know what you mean about *cold reality*. There's nothing mad about what I feel for you. I thought you felt the same and yet you can give up all we feel for each other as easily as this?' His face was red with rising anger.

'I'm giving up for your sake, Peter – because I love you too much for it all to go wrong. You'll thank me for it one day.'

'What a load of rubbish!' He raked a hand through his hair. 'You're talking like a cheap novelette!'

She turned away. 'Perhaps that's the only way I'm capable of talking,' she told him. 'You're proving your mother's point.'

'So – because of what Mum said – a few bigoted remarks, you decide that you don't want me any more. Is that what you're saying?'

'You know that's not what I'm saying.' She turned to him, tears in her eyes. 'You're making this so much harder, Peter.'

'Oh! I'm *so sorry* I'm making it hard for *you!*' She could see the tears glinting in his eyes now and she knew he was hurting as much as she was. She longed to put her arms around him but she made herself stay where she was, the table between them, her hands clenching and unclenching at her sides.

He went on, his voice rough with emotion, 'If it had been the other way round I'd have fought for you like a tiger,' he said. 'If you can give up this easily perhaps it's just as well that we do part now.'

It took every ounce of her control not to go to him. Every nerve in her body screamed at her to put her arms around him and hold him fast – never let him go. 'Perhaps it is,' she made herself say.

For a long moment he stared disbelievingly at her then he turned and strode out of the house, slamming the front door behind him.

During the week that followed Judy made sure that she filled every waking hour. It wasn't difficult. There was so much to do; baking for St Hilary's Christmas party and planning the food for their own festivities. She decorated the house with the help of Charlie and Suzie, who sat at the kitchen table for hours making coloured paper-chains. Last but not least she prepared a room for her parents' visit, washing the curtains and bedspread and vacuuming the carpet until her arms ached. She fell into bed exhausted at night but, although she was dog-tired, refreshing sleep refused to come. She tossed and turned, dreaming chaotic dreams of Peter. He was back in the POW camp; he was escaping – running – being caught in a hail of bullets – falling, fatally wounded, too far away for her to reach him.

She looked forward so much to the day of her parents' arrival. She longed to see them and to be caught up in their stories and news and their cheerful presence, maybe to forget just for a few days the future she had hoped to share with Peter, now shattered.

Christine and Harry sent a telegram when they arrived back in England on 23 December. They would have to attend their debriefing at Drury Lane but they hoped to catch a train for Summerton-on-Sea, arriving at six o'clock in the evening.

Judy read the telegram out to the girls, who jumped up and down, squealing with excitement.

'Can we all go to the station to meet them?' Suzie begged.

'Of course we can.'

'I'll stay here and have the table set,' Sally said. 'I can't wait to meet two professional entertainers. Do you think they'll perform for us over Christmas?'

Judy smiled. 'Just try and stop them,' she said. 'I know Bill and Maggie will be looking forward to a good old sing-song with them.'

On the twenty-third the girls were fizzing with excitement. They could hardly wait for it to be time to leave for the station. They hardy ate any lunch and in spite of Judy's suggestions for things to occupy them they found concentration impossible as they waited impatiently for darkness to fall.

At last it was time to put on their coats and shoes. Judy took a last peep into the oven at the casserole she'd made and Sally promised to lay the table and put the potatoes on ready for their return. They were just walking down the front path when Judy saw Mary Gresham coming towards her. She paused at the gate.

'Oh, Judy, you're going out.'

'We're on the way to the station to meet my parents,' Judy told her, her heart beating faster with apprehension. Why was Mary here? Was something wrong – was it Peter?

'In that case I mustn't keep you,' Mary said. 'But I do really need to speak to you.'

Judy glanced at the girls. They looked at her with a mute appeal to hurry up. 'You start walking,' she told them. 'I'll catch you up in a minute.'

Reluctantly they began to walk on ahead and Judy turned back to Mary. 'I don't have much time,' she said. 'I'm sorry.'

'Please, Judy, I want to apologize for everything I said to you the other day,' Mary said hurriedly. 'Peter is making himself ill. He won't speak to me – he says I've ruined his life and yours as well. He's not sleeping or eating properly. I can see now how very much you mean to him.' She laid a hand on Judy's arm. 'Please, dear, will you come and see him – talk to him? He won't speak to me or his father.'

Judy felt as though she was being pulled inside out. 'What do you want me to say?' she asked. 'I've already had to pretend I don't want to marry him. It's painful for me too, Mary. I love Peter very much and ...'

'I know that and all I want…'

A sudden cry made them both look up. A car was driving down the road. Charlie was running back. '*Mum!*' she called. 'Is this Granny and Granddad?'

'They must have got in early and found a taxi,' Judy muttered. She looked at Mary. 'I can't talk about this now, Mary, but I …' the rest of the sentence hung in the air as the car stopped and a figure got out from behind the wheel.

'Oh my God - *Sid!*' Her hand flew to her mouth. Suddenly both girls were at her side, their hands finding hers and holding tight, their faces taut with apprehension as they looked up at her.

As he walked towards them his lip curled in a sneer. 'Inside,' he said abruptly.

'*No!*' Judy stood firm, squeezing the two small hands clutching hers. 'You're not coming in.'

'Oh yes I am! I'm your husband and you'll do as I say,' he hissed, thrusting his face close to hers. 'I know you're on your own. I've seen that advertisement about Sea View and Mrs Truman, the *vibrant new manageress*,' he mocked. 'The old codgers snuffed it, have they – left you the lot? Well, don't you forget that what's yours is mine. I'm coming in all right and you can't stop me.'

'Yes, I can,' Judy told him, her heart thudding in her chest. 'You're not my husband and you never have been!'

Just for a moment he stopped short, taken aback, but he quickly recovered. 'Don't talk crap. I married you, didn't I? Your flamin' dad saw to that.'

'But you were already married – to Joan down in Tilbury? You're a bigamist, Sid. You're a deserter and a fugitive. I haven't seen or heard from you for months and I won't have the girls involved in your crimes.'

His hand shot out and grasped her jaw, squeezing painfully. His face was so close to hers that she could feel his breath on her cheek.

'Whatever you say don't alter the fact that these kids are mine,' he hissed, spraying spittle into her face. 'If I wanted to I could…' but at that moment the front door opened and Sally stepped out onto the porch.

'*Judy!* Where are you?' She pressed the button on the torch she was carrying, swinging the beam around to find them in the darkness. 'Your mum and dad have just telephoned. They've arrived and they said not to go to the station, they're on their way.' The beam found the little group by the gate, Sid standing menacingly over Judy and the girls. Sally shouted, 'Hey! Who are you and what do you think you're doing?'

For a split second it was as if they were all cast in stone, then suddenly Sid let Judy go and made a feverish dash for the car. As they watched he leapt in and pulled the starter. The engine coughed once and stopped. He tried twice more and when the car sprang to life he revved the engine madly as he swung the wheel in an attempt to turn. Judy looked on in horror as the car shot wildly across the road and then reversed with a scream of tyres. Both girls turned their faces into her side and began to cry.

Now, in a panic-stricken rush to be gone, Sid released the brake and let in the clutch all at once. The car sprang forward, and Judy saw at once that it was out of control. Seeing what was about to happen she reached frantically for the girls. She managed to grab a shocked Charlie and pull her into the gateway out of harm's way but Suzie stood directly in the car's path, motionless as though mesmerized. It happened in a split second right in front of Judy's horrified eyes. The roaring car mounted the pavement and pinned Suzie against the wall. Her scream of pain froze Judy's blood.

The next minute Sid ground the gear lever into reverse and backed off, leaving his child lying still and silent on the pavement. Before anyone could try to stop him he had roared away, the car weaving and swaying erratically and the engine screaming in protest. With a sob Judy threw herself onto her knees beside Suzie as Sid and the car disappeared into the darkness.

CHAPTER TWENTY-TWO

The little group sitting in the hospital waiting room was silent, still too numb with shock to speak. Suzie had been taken straight into surgery when she was admitted and now they waited with bated breath for someone to come and speak to them.

When Judy had bent over Suzie's unconscious little body she had seen at once that her legs had been badly injured. There was an alarming amount of blood on the pavement and it was all she could do not to faint herself, with shock and fear.

Inside the house Sally had telephoned for an ambulance. Harry and Christine, who arrived moments after the accident, insisted on following the ambulance. Now they all three sat in shocked silence, each of them distraught and praying desperately that the outcome wouldn't be as bad as they feared.

After a while Harry got up. He returned a few minutes later with three cups of tea. Judy sipped hers and looked up, suddenly aware that her parents had travelled a long way.

'You must be starving,' she said. 'I'd made you a casserole. It was all ready when...'

Christine shook her head. 'Bless you, I couldn't eat a thing. Food is the last thing on my mind.'

'Anyway, it'll still be OK tomorrow,' Harry said cheerily. 'That's the best of a casserole.' He drank his tea down quickly, one eye on his daughter. 'I blame myself,' he said suddenly. 'All this is my fault. If I hadn't insisted on that bastard marrying you none of this would have happened.'

'He wasn't free to marry me anyway,' Judy said. 'I found that out when I tried to divorce him.'

Harry and Christine looked at each other, aghast. 'You mean

that all these years – after all he's put you through...'

Judy shook her head. 'It's no good going back over the past now and it's pointless to blame anyone,' she said. 'All we can hope for is that Suzie will – be all right.' She looked at her mother. 'She was dying to tell you that she'd passed her first ballet exam a couple of weeks ago.'

Christine's mouth dropped open. '*Ballet*? Oh, bless her little heart!' Tears welled up in her eyes. 'He always said he'd stop her dancing, didn't he?' she said bitterly. 'Well, he's got his wish now so I hope he's happy!'

'*Chris*!' Harry frowned at his wife. 'Don't talk like that.' He cast a quick look in Judy's direction. 'She'll dance again – 'course she will. She's a plucky little thing, our Suzie. She might not make much noise but she's always been determined in her own way.'

Suddenly the door opened and Peter walked in. His face was grey with anxiety. Without a word he held out his arms and Judy stood up and went into them.

'How is she?' he asked.

She looked up at him. 'Still in the operating theatre. They said someone will come and talk to us when she's – when they've – finished.' She clung to him, so grateful for the warmth and reassurance of his arms. 'Oh, Peter, thank you so much for coming.'

'How could you think I'd leave you to face this alone?' Over Judy's head he nodded at Harry and Christine. 'It's so good that you're here,' he said.

Judy sat down again and drew Peter down beside her. 'Did your mother tell you what happened? She arrived just as we were leaving. I was in the middle of speaking to her when Sid turned up and suddenly everything was chaos.'

'She rang me from Sea View,' he said. 'She stayed on with Sally for a while. The poor girl was in a state of shock.' He took her hand and squeezed it. 'But it's thanks to her quick thinking that the police have arrested Truman.'

'They've got him?'

'Yes. It was lucky that Sally had a torch. She had the presence of mind to pick up and memorize the car's registration number and she gave it to the police. The car was stolen, as you'd expect, but they got a bonus when they found a much wanted Army deserter at the wheel.'

'Good for Sally,' Harry said. 'I hope they lock him up and throw the key away.' He looked at Judy. 'It's over now, love. You don't have to see him again, *ever*, thank God.'

'I know, Dad. Trouble is, it's the end of one nightmare and the beginning of another.' She looked at her father. His face was drawn and lined with exhaustion. Her mother looked weary too. She realized suddenly how much they'd aged since last she saw them. 'Why don't you both go home?' she suggested. 'It could be ages before we know anything and you've had a long journey. There's hot food back at Sea View and you could freshen up and get some sleep. I'll ring as soon as we have any news.'

They both protested but Judy managed to persuade them in the end. Mainly because Peter insisted that he wasn't going anywhere until they knew that Suzie was out of danger.

When they'd gone Judy looked at him. 'You'll never know how good it is to have you here,' she said.

He slipped an arm round her and drew her close. 'And this time it's for good, no matter what anyone says,' he told her. 'Mum saw everything. She was appalled at what happened tonight. I don't think she had any idea that a man could be so vile. His own daughter! She couldn't believe that he didn't even stop to see if she was all right.'

Judy shook her head. 'I don't want to think about it. The sight of her lying there will haunt me for ever.'

He looked down at her with concern. 'You look all in. Try to have a nap.' He cupped the side of her head and drew it down onto his shoulder.

'I feel as though I'll never sleep again,' she said. 'Not until I know she's all right.' But a few minutes later he heard her breathing change and, glancing down, saw that her eyes had closed with sheer exhaustion.

When the door opened half an hour later Judy was instantly awake, sitting up and looking fearfully at the two people who had entered the room. The sister of the children's ward came in, accompanied by a tall elderly man in a dark suit. The sister introduced him.

'Mrs Truman, this is Mr Faulkner, who has operated on your daughter.'

Judy and Peter both stood up but the man indicated that they remain seated and sat down opposite them. 'Suzanne has come through surgery well,' he told Judy. 'Both her legs were broken and she also suffered some crush injuries. There was some internal bleeding which turned out to be a ruptured spleen, which we have removed.'

Judy gasped and the surgeon reached across to touch her hand. 'Please don't be alarmed, Mrs Truman. It could have been much worse. We can all of us manage very easily without a spleen.'

Judy swallowed hard. 'Her legs?' she whispered. 'Will she – walk again?'

Mr Faulkner smiled. 'Oh yes. Children's bones are very resilient. She should heal well. It will take time, of course, and quite a lot of physiotherapy and perseverance but I'm sure she'll get all the care and encouragement she needs.'

'Can I see her?'

He nodded. 'Of course you can. She's still sleeping off the effects of the anaesthetic but you can rest assured that she's going to be all right.'

Judy looked at Peter and he smiled. 'You go,' he said. 'I'll be waiting here for you.'

In a dimly lit side ward Suzie lay tucked neatly into bed, a cradle under the covers to keep them away from her legs. Her closed eyelids were violet and luminous in her pale face and she looked so tiny and vulnerable that Judy's throat tightened. She bent and gently kissed the cool little forehead. Feeling under the covers she found one small hand and held it warmly in both of hers, as though she could infuse some of her own strength into her little girl.

'I'm here, sweetheart,' she whispered. 'Mum's here and you're safe. I'll never let anything hurt you like that again, I promise. Charlie and I love you so much. We all do.' Her heart leapt as she thought she saw Suzie's eyelids flutter and felt a slight movement of the little hand in hers. She looked up as the sister appeared in the doorway. 'I think she can hear me,' she said. 'I think she knows

I'm here.'

'Better let her rest now, Mrs Truman,' Sister said kindly.

Judy tucked the little hand back under the covers and bent to kiss Suzie's forehead. She thanked the sister and with one last backward glance she left the ward.

Peter was waiting. He held her as she let the tension go and gave in to the tears she had held back since the accident. Out in the car park she climbed wearily into the car, and as soon as he was in his seat Peter turned to her.

'I'm never letting you or the girls out of my sight from now on,' he said, drawing her close. 'I'll never let anything like this happen to you again. I love you so very much, Judy, and as soon as Suzie is better we're getting married.' He looked down at her with a wry grin. 'If you'll have me, that is.'

Judy let her head fall onto his shoulder. 'There's nothing I want more.'

Christmas was taken out of Judy's hands. Maggie took over in her old kitchen as though she had never been away, with Christine and Sally as willing helpers. Judy wasn't allowed to do a thing.

'You've done all the shopping and preparations,' Maggie told her firmly. 'Now you can just concentrate on Suzie.'

Charlie was lost without her sister. When she was allowed in to see her on Christmas Eve she was clearly shocked by the sight of both her legs in plaster casts and the fact that she had stitches in her tummy. All the way home she was silent and the moment they got in she ran straight upstairs to her room. Judy found her there weeping quietly. Without a word she gathered her close.

'Don't cry. She's going to be all right,' she told the sobbing child.

Charlie looked up at her. 'But how will she ever be able to dance again with her legs like that?' she asked. 'She won't even be able to walk.'

'Yes, she will.' Judy brushed the damp hair away from Charlie's forehead. 'The plaster casts will come off in a few weeks' time and then she'll have special exercises to learn to walk again.'

'But will she ever be able to *dance*, Mum? It'll break her heart if she can't.'

Charlie was voicing the question that Judy had refused to allow herself to think about so far. She took a deep breath.

'We'll just have to wait and see,' she said. 'For now we just have to be thankful that she'll be able to walk.'

'What about school, though?'

'She may have to miss some time but we'll make arrangements for her to have some lessons at home. I'll go and see Mrs Thompson.' Judy gave her daughter a quick hug. 'Now come down and eat the lovely tea that Auntie Maggie has made. Tomorrow is Christmas Day and we'll go to the hospital and take all Suzie's presents. That'll cheer her up.'

Charlie looked thoughtful for a moment, then she suddenly said, 'Mum - what about Dad?'

'What do you mean?'

'Did he hurt Suzie on purpose?'

'No. It was an accident.'

'So why did he just drive away? Why didn't he stop to see if she was all right?

Judy sat down again. 'Your dad was a very frightened man. He ran away from the Army. That's a crime and the police were after him.'

Charlie looked at the floor. 'Is he – will he be coming back to live with us again?'

'No. The police have caught him and he'll have to spend a long time in prison for what he did.' Judy put an arm round her elder daughter, deciding that it was time to tell her the truth. 'But there's something else, Charlie. I found out a few months ago that your dad and I were never properly married. When he married me he already had another wife and two sons.'

Charlie looked up at her with startled eyes. 'Does that mean he's not our real dad?'

'No. It only means that he's not really my husband. But after what he's done he's never going to be allowed near any of us again.'

'Promise?'

'I promise. And there's something else. Peter and I are going to be married soon, and Peter wants to adopt you both. Would that be all right with you?'

'Adopt?' Charlie's mouth dropped open. 'What would that mean?'

'It means that after we're married we'll all have his name and he'll be your stepfather.'

Charlie's face broke into an incredulous smile. '*Honest*?'

'Honest.'

Charlie paused, thinking the new situation through carefully. 'So, I'll be Charlotte Gresham and Suzie will be Suzanne Gresham?'

'That's right.'

She smiled. 'So can we call him Dad?'

'That's something you'll have to discuss with him.' Judy laughed. 'You're pleased, then?'

'Oh *yes*. Mum...'

'Yes?'

'When you and Peter get married can me and Suzie be brides-maids?'

Judy smiled. 'I hadn't even thought that far, but yes, I suppose so.'

'That'll be something to make her hurry up and learn to walk again, won't it?'

As Judy was leaving the room Charlie suddenly said, 'After tea I'm going to make Suzie a card with a rainbow on it.'

'Are you? That's nice.'

'Do you remember that night when we first got here and we saw a rainbow? You told me that it meant a promise.'

'I remember.'

'I've seen lots of rainbows since then and I always make a wish,' Charlie said solemnly. 'There isn't a rainbow now but I'll draw one and wish on that. Wishing to make Suzie dance again will be the biggest, most enormous wish I've ever made.'

Judy hugged her daughter. 'Come down and have your tea now,' she said. 'You can make your card later.'

*

Christmas Day on the children's ward was very festive. Suzie was looking better, sitting up and smiling when her visitors arrived. Maggie and Bill had been to see her in the morning but the afternoon was reserved for family. Peter had arrived with a present for Suzie from his parents and when Suzie opened it her eyes lit up when she found a beautiful doll with real blond hair, wearing a spangled pink tutu and ballet shoes.

'She's called Fiona,' Peter explained. 'But you can call her whatever you like.'

Suzie stared at the doll, entranced. 'I'll call her Princess Fiona,' she said. 'She's even prettier than the princess in the Cinderella puppet play.'

Judy was staring at the doll. 'Where on earth did Mary manage to find a doll like that?' she asked. 'She's absolutely gorgeous.'

'It was Mum's when she was a little girl,' Peter told her. 'But the clothes are new. She made them herself because she remembered how taken Suzie was with the princess in Cinderella.'

Judy was touched by Mary's kind gesture. Clearly she had changed her mind about accepting Judy as her daughter-in-law.

CHAPTER TWENTY-THREE

By the time Suzie came out of hospital Christine and Harry had returned to their duties and Peter had reported back to the RAF. Maggie and Bill suggested staying on to help Judy, but she insisted that she could manage. Sea View had several bookings early in the January, mainly service couples taking brief honeymoons, and she was grateful for the income it would bring. She was learning that winter could be a lean time in the seaside guesthouse trade.

To begin with Suzie had her bed downstairs and Charlie was her willing slave. Nothing was too much trouble as she waited hand and foot on her sister. Even after the new term began and she returned to school she would hurry home each afternoon to attend to Suzie's every need.

After six weeks the plaster casts came off and Judy was shocked and concerned to see how thin and wasted Suzie's legs had become. They were also still discoloured by bruising from her injuries. But the physiotherapist assured her that they would soon be back to normal with the help of daily exercises and a lot of resolve.

Eager to get back on her feet, Suzie persevered steadily with her daily exercise regime, in spite of the fact that it was often painful and exhausting. However, it was Charlie who grew frustrated.

'Why does it take so *long*?' she wailed after Suzie gave in, tired out halfway through an exercise session one afternoon. 'I thought her bones had mended now.'

'They have, but her muscles have to learn how to do things again,' Judy explained. 'It's the same as if you'd lost your memory. You'd have to learn all over again how to read and write and do arithmetic. Suzie's legs have forgotten how to walk and it's very hard and tiring making them remember what to do.' Judy gave her daughter a hug. 'Don't make her feel she's not trying,' she said. 'She's working really hard, but it's all going to take time. She needs lots of encouragement.'

'I know.' Charlie sighed. 'But I want to see her dancing again.'

'So do I, and I'm sure she does too. But it's no good trying to rush things.'

Judy received a visit from the police. They told her they had also been to visit Joan Truman. Each of them was questioned about Sid's bigamous marriage, the dates were verified and the marriage certificates examined. They questioned Judy and Sally about Suzie's accident too. But they explained that Sid was to undergo a military court martial first, and if he was found guilty of desertion the punishment could be severe.

'So severe,' the policeman told her gravely, 'that the other charges might never be brought.'

When Judy asked what that punishment might be the policeman just shook his head, refusing to be drawn.

'So he might get away with severely injuring his own daughter?' Judy asked, angrily.

The policeman shook his head. 'Believe me, he is not going to get away with anything.'

Judy was shocked to learn later from Peter that the maximum penalty for desertion was death, but when Sid's court martial was held he received a lengthy custodial sentence. He was also to be charged in a criminal court with a string of other offences: taking and driving an uninsured motor vehicle; reckless driving incurring a serious injury; failing to stop after an accident and, last but not least, bigamy. It seemed that Sid Truman would not be released for a very long time.

By the time Easter came around Suzie was able to walk short distances without her crutches. Sea View was fully booked for the holiday weekend. The war news was good and Bill proclaimed gleefully that it was only a matter of time before they would be celebrating victory.

In February Sally decided to return to London. There had been no raids for some time and she was keen to see her family again and check that her home was still intact. Before she and little David left Judy gave a party for them. Mary and Steve came and so did Maggie and Bill as well as other friends Sally had made during her stay at Sea View. On the morning of her departure she hugged Judy warmly.

'I'm so sorry for all those horrible things I said to you when Peter was here that night,' she said.

Judy shook her head. 'You weren't to know the true facts,' she said. 'And you more than made up for it with your prompt action on the night Suzie was hurt. You were responsible for Sid's recapture too. We can never thank you enough.'

Sally smiled, her eyes moist with tears. 'We'll keep in touch, yes?'

'Of course we will. Let me know when your husband comes home. And if you want to bring him down for a holiday, it's on the house.'

'Thanks. I might take you up on that.' Sally hugged her once again. 'Well – this is goodbye then. I love you, Judy. I'll never forget you and the girls.'

As spring arrived and the days lengthened Summerton-on-Sea began to prepare hopefully for its first peacetime summer. The Pier Theatre reopened and posters began to appear for a summer variety show. Mary and Steve Gresham opened up the puppet theatre and prepared to spring clean and do the annual repairs. Mary had been busy all winter mending old costumes and making new ones for the puppets. She suggested that Charlie and Suzie might like to help out during the summer holidays for pocket money; an idea that both girls accepted eagerly. A new owner bought the café and ice-cream parlour on the promenade. It was rumoured that he was a repatriated prisoner of war. And the shop that sold buckets and spades and postcards was being repainted and smartened up. It was all very heartening for Judy, who looked forward to a good season at Sea View.

Peter came home on leave just after Easter. He was now confined to ground-crew duties back at Bircham Newton which he found boring and frustrating, though Judy was secretly glad that he was now out of danger. She had listened to the accounts of the huge bombing raid on Cologne and thanked God that Peter hadn't been part of it.

He had been home for two days when the news broke of Hitler's dramatic suicide.

'That's the end, then,' he said. 'It can only be a matter of days before the surrender now.' He looked at her. 'I can't think of a better time for setting our wedding date, can you?'

Judy's heart leapt. 'When is your next leave?'

'I can get special leave for my wedding,' he told her. 'So – when shall we say?'

She held her breath. 'June the fifth,' she said. 'It's my birthday. Is that too soon?'

He kissed her. 'Can't be soon enough for me.' He looked at her thoughtfully. 'But there's something we need to talk about first.'

'What?'

He sighed. 'There's the question of what I'm to do after I'm demobbed. I went more or less straight into the RAF from the sixth form. I've no trade or profession. With a family to support I'm going to need a decent job.'

'We've got Sea View,' Judy pointed out.

He shook his head. 'Let's face it, darling. Sea View isn't going to be enough to support four of us. There's nothing much doing in the winter months and besides, frankly, I think I'd be bored. I need a proper career.'

Judy was crestfallen. 'I hadn't thought that far. So, what do you want to do?'

'Well…' He took a deep breath. 'Before I was called up I had an interview at Cambridge University. I was offered a place but that was put on hold when the war began. I've heard that I could apply again. It might mean another interview, of course, and I might not get in but it's worth a try. It would mean three years' study – away from home.' He looked at her. 'How would you feel about that?'

Judy felt slightly deflated. She had visualized them being together after the wedding, not apart. It would be the same as it was now, with Peter in the RAF and coming home on occasional leave. He saw her expression and read her thoughts.

'It wouldn't be all that far from here,' he said. 'I could probably come home every weekend. And there'd be the vacations too of course.'

'What would it cost?'

'There'd be a government grant,' he told her. 'I hear there'll be special concessions for ex-servicemen.'

'I see. And what would you study?'

'I'd like to do civil engineering,' he told her. 'Once I qualified I'd be able to get a good job and you wouldn't have to work so hard – or at all unless you wanted to.' He looked at her. 'So – what do you say?'

She looked at his eager face and knew she had no choice. 'I say – go ahead and try for it.'

He hugged her close. 'I knew you'd say that. I want to make a good life for us all. I'd quite like us to have a child of our own one day, if that's what you want too.'

'Of course I do.'

'But to make all that possible I really need to have a proper profession.'

'I know.' She looked up at him. 'I'm so lucky,' she whispered. 'So lucky to have you.'

As soon as the peace was declared the bookings rolled in at Sea View, but once the euphoria had died down Judy began to doubt the wisdom of the wedding date she had chosen. However, Maggie had already foreseen the problem and came to the rescue.

'Bill and I will move in and keep the place going and look after the girls till you get back from your honeymoon,' she announced. 'By the way, where are you going?'

Judy didn't need to think about that. She and Peter had already decided where they would spend their wedding night. 'It's just a little village pub,' she said. 'It's called the Queen of Hearts but it's got special memories for us.'

'I see,' said Maggie knowingly. 'Well, ask no questions, I always say.'

To Judy's surprise and delight Mary offered to make her wedding dress and two small dresses for Charlie and Suzie, the bridesmaids-to-be. Suzie was walking well now but she still insisted on doing her daily exercises. She had already persuaded Judy to book her in with Miss Paige for the autumn term's dancing classes and was working hard towards it.

On the morning of 5 June, Judy wakened to a sunny morning. As the realization that it was her wedding day slowly sank in she could hardly believe she wasn't dreaming. So much had happened since that September night when they had first arrived in Summerton-on-Sea. Their lives had changed so much that it was sometimes hard to remember the life they had left behind. But meeting Peter had been the best – the loveliest thing to have come out of it. Sometimes she had to pinch herself to believe that all this was really happening – to her, Judy Mitchell, soon to be Mrs Judy Gresham.

She opened her eyes and looked at the dress hanging on the outside of the wardrobe. She had asked for something simple and Mary had made her a dress of cream silk, using a roll of material she had had stored away since before the war. It had a slim skirt with a tiny flared peplum at the waistline and a heart-shaped neck. She was to wear a pink rose in her hair and carry a posy of pink and white rosebuds.

Charlie and Suzie were delighted with their dresses, both in pale pink with cream sashes. They were mid-calf length with two layers of net overlaying the skirts, making them look like two little ballerinas. Suzie especially was thrilled with the look. Everyone had been invited to the wedding. Sally was coming down from London and Judy had invited Carol and some of the girls from the theatre. It was going to be a day to remember, the happiest day of her life.

The bedroom door opened and Christine came in, bearing a breakfast tray.

'Breakfast for the bride,' she announced, setting the tray down on the bed. Judy shook her head.

'I couldn't eat a thing,' she said, sitting up. 'I'm far too excited.'

'Oh yes you could,' Christine insisted, pouring a strong cup of tea and buttering a piece of toast. 'Can't have you fainting at the church door. That wouldn't do at all.' She smiled at her daughter. 'Come on now, eat up and then I'll help you to dress.'

Peter was waiting at the altar with Paul, his brother and best man standing beside him. He looked tall and handsome in his RAF uniform. He turned his head slightly as the organ struck up and Judy began the walk down the aisle on her father's arm. His face when he saw her spoke volumes.

Just before they took their first steps Harry turned to his daughter and whispered, 'The best of luck, my lovely girl. You deserve the best of husbands and I reckon that's what you're getting.'

Judy smiled back at him. 'I am, Dad. I am.'

He raised an eyebrow at her. 'Forgive me – for Sid and everything?'

For answer Judy merely squeezed his arm and smiled. 'Let's go, Dad.'

At last it was over. The service was moving and beautiful and outside the church in the June sunshine they posed for photographs. The reception, which had been catered for by Maggie and Mary, was held at Sea View and the guests staying there were invited to join in. Harry made a speech which had the assembled guests chuckling and Paul made a good best man's speech with slightly embarrassing stories about his elder brother's exploits as a child. The cake was cut and the bride and groom toasted. Harry played the piano whilst guests circulated and chatted. Christine appeared at Judy's elbow.

'I think you could slip away now if you wanted to,' she said. She glanced at Peter. 'I'm sure you're dying to get her to yourself.'

He grinned and slipped an arm round Judy's waist. 'You bet. Do you think anyone will notice?'

'Not if you're quick.'

But Judy came downstairs after changing to find that they weren't going to be allowed to get away as easily as that. All the wedding guests were assembled in the hall waiting to cheer them off.

'The bouquet!' someone called. 'You have to throw your bouquet!'

Judy turned her back and tossed the posy over her shoulder to whoops of delight. When she turned she saw that a blushing Carol had caught it. They ran the gamut of showers of confetti onto the drive and climbed into Peter's father's car, especially lent for the occasion. Eventually, to good-natured shouts and whistles they were on their way.

Judy slipped her hand through Peter's arm and nestled her head on his shoulder. 'What a lovely day,' she sighed. 'I can't believe it's all over.'

'It's only just beginning, Mrs Gresham,' Peter said. 'We have our whole lives to look forward to now. I don't know about you, but I can't wait.'